Amenta by Kristy Rush

This book is dedicated to everyone who loves books.

ISBN: 979-8-218-23963-3

Cover design by: Art Painter
Library of Congress Control Number: 2018675309
Printed in the United States of America

Chapter 1

Some people would say I was born under a bad sign. I always wondered what that meant. At first I thought it was an excuse for having some bad luck, but my bad luck went well beyond a touch.

I was unlucky at everything I tried. I never won anything, not even a stuffed animal or one of those carnival fish that end up belly-up in the commode the next day. Just last month, my dad had to quit his job, and now we're running really low on money. A few weeks ago, I had to leave my friends and move across the country. Worst of all, my mom was pretty sick, and she just kept getting worse.

In my mind though, there really was a sign…a bright red neon sign that hung over my head. In a flowery script, it pulsed "unlucky" with an accusing blue arrow pointing right at me.

My dad let me sleep on the couch from time to time. He thought it was a good thing to let me sleep when I could. When I was younger, my mother and I used to have midnight tea parties to scare away my monsters and I could feel them lurking all around me. I untangled myself from the blanket that my father had draped over me and padded into the kitchen.

Spot, my cat, was wrapped like a black question mark on top of the heating duct, seeking any warmth he could find in the drafty apartment. Feeling sorry for him, I bent and scooped him up in my arms. I sat for a while at the kitchen table, stroking his rich fur, cooing into his ear. "Why am I not afraid of you, black cat? I should be. You should be at the top of my list, but you're just not that scary." Although I wanted some tea, it just reminded me of my mother. I felt alone, having tea without her, so I sat with my cat and rubbed the soft fur that grew between his ears.

Suddenly, Spot moaned and leapt from my lap. I once heard that dogs had the ability to see ghosts, and that was why they sometimes barked at nothing, like the ceiling or the empty corner of a room. Maybe cats could see monsters.

In fact, it did feel like something was studying me from the corners of the room. I felt this way a lot lately…ever since mom had to leave. Maybe it was loneliness, sadness, fear? I shook my head; I was overwhelmed.

After a few moments, the dark feeling began to fade but did not disappear completely. I shook away the feeling of being watched. Bed, I told myself. The only place I should be right now is bed, but with bed came sleep…and the nightmares. Mine were the big nightmares, the real ones, where your mom dies or your dad leaves…the ones where the monsters not only live under your bed, but they come out to get you.

We couldn't afford to leave the kitchen light on, so I flipped the switch, hoping the strange feelings would stay away. Spreading my arms, I groped my way along the rough stucco. My fingers found the waxy wood that framed the bathroom door. I slipped through the doorway, squinted, and flicked the light switch. Instead of buying a shaded fixture, the landlord had installed a frosted bulb in the socket above the sink. Dirt had collected in a round spot at the bottom, and it bulged like an eyeball.

I turned on the water to the sink, warm water could only be won by mixing what came out of separate hot and cold faucets in the sink bowl. Cold would suffice. Scooping up water in my cupped hands, I drew it to my face. My skin crawled. It felt as if the house was spying on me. Once again, I shook off my discomfort and attributed it to a lack of sleep. I glanced in the mirror and my reflection commanded attention. I stepped back quickly, water trickling onto the tile floor. Was that really me? I leaned in to look more closely. My skin looked pale and almost transparent like wax paper. Shadows ringed my eyes and only intensified their frigid blueness. My black hair was an eerie contrast to my faded skin tone, and when I combed my fingers through it, it swirled like smoke around my face. My lips were red and drawn in a firm, even line. I thought I looked like a vampire, like the victims in those old movies I watched with

Mom. I was Lucy, the girl that was always the bloodsucker's first victim, and I too saw myself wasting away. If only a vampire would show up and make me forget...I would succumb.

Late fall in Pittsburgh is a very dark time. The clouds sleep on the hilltops and the sun neglects to make an appearance. My Texas tan faded quickly when we came here and I think the clouds just added to my overwhelming feeling of sadness. Now you could call me pale, quite pale. I thought my eerie appearance might be a result of the light bulb, swollen and wart-like above the sink, but even in the yellow cast anyone could tell I was hurting.

Disheartened by my appearance, I turned off the water, hit the light switch with a curled fist, and entered the darkness of the hallway. Lightly running my fingers against the wall, I padded back to bed and crawled beneath the covers.

As I curled my body against the darkness, I became aware of a strange noise, a soft lament, unbearably tender. At first I thought it was coming from inside the walls, so I pressed my ear against the rough stucco and strained to recognize the sound. Initially, I thought it could have been a child, but as I listened I understood and my heart crumbled. It was Dad crying softly, so I wouldn't hear. He held my mom's sickness inside him. He hadn't laughed or even smiled for months. He was always at the hospital, hardly ever with me, and I missed him terribly. I was 17 though, and able to look out for myself. That was what I had done for most of the past year, and unfortunately, I was getting used to being alone.

We couldn't afford to rent a decent place, or even close to it, so we settled for this awful house. Mom had been sick, in and out of the hospital for about a year, and just over a month ago, Dad quit his job to take care of her. We moved to Pittsburgh for a new treatment program at a renowned medical center.

In Texas, I tended to fade in and out of school depending on how Mom felt, but at least I had friends who understood. Here, there was no one. This house didn't echo Dad's laughter like our old house. It was eerie and silent, as if it already housed the dead. I don't know if this house had a bad atmosphere because of our family's unexpected drive down the cancer highway, or if it was the house itself. All I know is I hated it here.

Dad spent his days at Mom's bedside, at appointments, and waiting for her to come out of treatments. He said he wanted to spend time with me, but I tried to be in bed when he got home. I couldn't stand to see him so alone, so tired, and so sad. He often opened the door of my room, just to peek in on me. If it was still early he came in and sat on the folding chair next to my bed. Sometimes he gently stroked the top of my head. He used to do that when I was little, and it still helped me to fall asleep. Sometimes we'd talk, sometimes we wouldn't. I think he just wanted to let me know he still cared. As soon as I drew up the covers, the door opened.

"I heard you get up," Dad said softly. "Dreaming again?" He left the lights off and sat on the chair. I think he was trying to hide recently shed tears.

I ignored the question about the dream. "How's Mom?"

"She's okay," he sighed. "Doc says the treatments are going well and her counts are coming up. It's slow, but they are looking better." He always tried to put a positive spin on the situation with Mom.

"I'm going to see her tomorrow," I yawned and curled onto my side to face him.

"That's fine, but after we get you enrolled in school," he said with as much authority as he could muster through his weariness. "You've been off for almost a month."

"I want to see Mom. I don't care about school right now. I can catch up later."

"Your mother would kill me if she knew you've been off for so long." Dad stressed. "Now get some sleep, we are going to enroll you tomorrow."

I didn't want to add to his problems, but I stopped short of agreeing with him.

"We'll talk tomorrow." Dad walked toward the light coming through the doorway. It seemed to make the shadows even darker. Although I strained to see the details of his face, blackness enveloped them.

"Dad…"

"Done talking," he said. "Sweet dreams." He didn't wait for a reply before he shut the door.

"Love you too," I whispered.

Chapter 2

It was mid-November and the morning sky was grey and dismal. Angry clouds spat rain against the glass of my bedroom window. I didn't have much of a view from my room; no sweeping vistas or the ocean shore of romantic daydreams. Instead I was met with cold, grey stone houses that littered the neighborhood.

We lived in a crowded, urban area, far from the familiar plains and prairies of Amarillo. Instead of wide open spaces, the houses here jostled for position. Some were shoved forward toward the street and others were nudged into the background, too grey to be noticed. Each generation of builders crowded in more and more buildings until the roofs brushed each other. Most were stone, like ours, but years ago others had been covered with cheap siding that was now the color of the stone. There was a bright spot though; we were so close to the hospital we were able to walk to see Mom.

As I continued to look out the window at the dismal autumn morning, a lady across the street caught my eye. She must have been on her way to work. As soon as she stepped out of her front door, she began tussling with her red umbrella. When it eventually opened with a violent twist of her wrist, it looked like a perfectly round drop of red blood cast on a faded watercolor painting. She finally got her act together and scurried toward the bus stop at the end of the block.

I turned away from the window, walked across the small room, and opened the closet door. Not much of a selection for a teenage girl. Dad put most of our things in storage including many of my clothes. We sold our house because we needed the money, but we had every intention of going back to Texas…as soon as Mom was better. I shuffled the hangers and they resisted on the rusty closet pole, squealing as they were forced into motion. I selected my pink and grey henleys that I intended to layer, and a pair of jeans.

I showered and dressed quickly. Even though I told Dad last night I didn't want to go to school, I had to admit I was kind of excited. Anxious and a bit nervous, I wondered what awaited me at my new school. A few touches of makeup brightened my pallor and I went into the kitchen.

Dad sat at a card table; milk dripped from his cereal spoon as he looked up at me. He smiled a tired, but familiar smile and dipped his spoon into the bowl. He wore his trademark Polo, but it was rumpled and worn like the man inside.

"Sleep well?" Dad asked.

"I had a few dreams...can't remember them though," I lied.

Chapter 3

For as long as I can remember I have had nightmares. My family had gone through a lot of trouble trying to manage them. Most doctors have a term called "night terrors" and attribute them to the overactive imagination of a child. According to these doctors, I would soon grow out of them; I am still waiting.

Most of my nightmares came from a terrible place, and as a release, I started to draw. I had been drawing ever since I could pick up a pencil. At first my parents discouraged my drawings because they weren't the kind of artwork most parents would hang on the refrigerator. Their efforts were soon put to rest. If I didn't draw, the nightmares just got worse.

As I grew, my drawing developed into painting, usually watercolor. I would only paint after I had one of my dreams, and I fixated until I was finished with it, often working day and night. When I completed a piece, Mom rolled it in tissue and put it away somewhere. I never looked at any of them again. Now that I think of it, I really never had the desire to.

Lately though, I noticed something is changing. All my life I have felt as if I were waiting for something… and whatever it is, it's getting closer. Lately, my nightmares have been wiggling through my defenses, like worms through an old apple. I had been having terrible dreams ever since we moved here. Sometimes they kept me up for hours and I usually woke more exhausted than I was when I went to bed in the first place. They were much worse than any horror movie I had ever seen. In fact, Hollywood would probably pay a nice sum for some of them.

In yesterday's feature, I was hiding in a deep closet. I was almost too terrified to move but I had to see what I was hiding from. Afraid to draw attention, I slowly slid toward the light streaming through a crack in the door. Things brushed the top of my head, and I was glad I couldn't see what they were. I peered into a dimly lit room.

It was my mom's hospital room, except she wasn't there. The scene was washed in shades of grey, like in an old movie. Everything was perfectly placed, awaiting inspection. Mom's drinking cup was sanitized for her protection, placed in a plastic baggie, and set near the sink. The work tray that was always full of newspapers and magazines was cleared and pushed against the wall. The bed was tightly made.

That was when a figure came into view. I immediately saw it was a thin woman. Since I was across the room, it was hard to tell how old she was. She wore a hospital gown, a well-worn one that tied in the back. She walked with a limp…no…it wasn't a simple limp. I looked more closely. The woman's leg was contorted at an unnatural angle. It had to be broken, and she dragged it behind her. Something urged me to sink back into the safety of the shadows, but I resisted and kept my eyes fixed on the scene.

The woman was hunched over and made a rustling sound when she moved. Immediately and with more speed than she seemed capable of, she began tearing apart the room. She seemed to be looking for something. Drawers were pulled out, and the contents dumped on the floor. Although it seemed impossible with her twisted leg, she bent over and peered under the bed. Dissatisfied, she stood up and in one sweeping motion, picked up the mattress and flung it against the wall. In the midst of her search, she stopped and suddenly focused on the closet.

As she ambled towards me, I could see her clothing was filthy and tattered. Her gown was tied crookedly and the hem was uneven and threadbare. She wore slippers caked with wet mud that fell off in clumps as she labored along. Long, tangled hair framed a once delicate face that was now pocked with rot.

My stomach heaved and I swallowed uncomfortably. As she got closer I saw her crooked smile, teeth uneven and packed with mud. My focus shifted to her eyes. They were cloudy and turned wildly in their sockets. Mud ran down her chin and spattered onto the floor like dirty snow.

"Key?" she questioned as she lurched. Her voice was labored, "Where's the key?" She staggered closer.

When I thought I couldn't stand it any longer, I put my hands over my mouth to stifle a scream, and I woke up, breathless and terrified.

Dad quickly ended my recollection by saying, "Trinity, I'm talking to you." He dropped his spoon into his cereal bowl with a clatter. He looked concerned.

I snapped back to reality. "Oh, sorry...I guess I'm just thinking about school." I couldn't think of anything else to say. "Everything's okay!" I smiled awkwardly.

Reassured, he returned my smile with one of his own. "No dreams! Good! Let me know if they are still bothering you. We might have to get that medicine again, so you can sleep."

"I'm fine," I lied. "No medicine."

"All right. Grab some cereal."

I poured some corn flakes into a bowl Dad set out for me. The milk followed, skipping off the flakes and swirling up the inside of the bowl. I was definitely not a nervous eater, and with Mom's cancer I must have lost ten pounds over the last year. Even though my stomach flittered, I pushed some cereal onto my spoon and shoveled it into my mouth.

"In a weird kind of way, I'm looking forward to today," I said as I chewed. Mom would have reprimanded me about having food in my mouth while I spoke, but Dad was oblivious.

"You don't know how glad I am to hear that," he said trying to smooth his dark, just washed hair. "I've been worried about you." He wore a slight smile that lilted on his lips like a butterfly, always ready to flitter away.

"I'm okay...really." I stated. "They're just dreams. Everyone has dreams...good and bad."

"I know," he said. "We don't want you to go through all that again."

"Dad..." I wanted him to stop.

I just want to make sure you're okay. You need your sleep."

He had no idea how bad my dreams were, and I was not about to let him know. "Like I said, I'm *fine*," emphasizing the word *fine*.

"Okay, okay. I won't harp on it," he replied. "As soon as you're done..."

I chewed and swallowed, “I guess I’m ready.”

Chapter 4

We sold our car to finance Mom's stay in the hospital, so I'd been learning the ins and outs of public transportation. We sat in the middle of the bus in the seats that faced sideways. Just across the aisle was an unkempt older man. He smiled at us a little crazily, and his eyes bore the hard knowledge of the homeless.

He wore a dirty red t-shirt that had seen better days. As he shifted in his seat, I could see the words, "Turnbull Prep" on the front. That was the name of my new school. I hoped all of its graduates didn't end up grinning at strangers on a public bus. Every few blocks, he'd utter, "Hey horsey!" Only he knew why. I was glad Dad was with me, or I would have been even more uncomfortable.

Soon we arrived at our stop and I followed Dad to the front of the bus. As I stepped onto the sidewalk, I looked at the only building in sight. It was foreboding; a beast of a structure that glowered at me. It was built of dark granite with ionic pillars guarding the door. Around the top of the cornice were angry gargoyles that clutched the ledges, eyeing everyone who dared approach. Large windows lined the building and heavy red drapes peeked at us through the leaded windows. They were hiding something awful. I could tell.

"Dad..." I said shaking off an odd wave of dread. "This is a school?"

"Honey, a lot of buildings in the northeast are like this," he said reassuringly as we ascended the wide granite staircase that led to the double front door. "It's must be a historical landmark."

I expected there to be a rope for a doorbell, like in the old monster movies. A tug of the rope would produce a stoic butler who led the lost traveler to his eventual, unnatural death. I grasped the sleeve of Dad's coat.

He continued, "Many of the schools and important buildings like museums and libraries around here were built then donated to the community. Industrial tycoons like Anthony Turnbull wanted to provide for the mill workers that he employed."

I was surprised he would focus on the history of such a spooky place instead of its dreadful appearance. "Dad," I countered, "he was responsible for the deaths of so many people in his steel mills, he had to do something to make himself look better. He donated to make people forget. Now he's a hero around here." I paused, "It was just PR."

"Hmm..." Dad mumbled. He hated when I argued, and I could sense the tension. I thought I should say something to smooth things over.

"Sorry," I stated. "I didn't mean to be belligerent. It's just that the school looks more like a prison, or an institution." I really couldn't give a crap about Anthony Turnbull or Andrew Carnegie, or any of the Industrial Revolution Pittsburgh millionaires.

"Maybe you could research all the good things Turnbull did around here instead of just the bad," Dad said. "Anyway, I understand this school is pretty special."

"How is this monstrosity so special?"

"Well, first of all, they gave you a scholarship, and I think you're pretty special."

"Dad!" I laughed. "Quit it!"

"Okay, seriously, this school is supposed to be an artistic marvel, inside and out." He stopped to study it for a moment. "It kind of reminds me of that old California house. What was it called? It was owned by some gun manufacturer."

"You mean the Winchester House?"

"Yeah. Look at this place...not as big as Winchester's, but definitely just as interesting. It took almost thirty years just to complete the interior alone."

"Sounds pretty great!" I said sarcastically. The cold building bristled at our approach.

"Their art program is first rate." He looked at me, hoping I would accept my fate a little more eagerly.

I quickly decided acceptance would be easier than resistance, easier on him anyway. I smiled. "I do like my art."

"I think we're pretty lucky they accepted you on such short notice and after the year had already begun." He sighed. "I am really glad you're here."

"Yeah," I agreed, still trying to put my father at ease even though I was doubtful. "And we don't have to pay for it."

"For this year anyway. You just have to keep your grades up."

"I'll try," I said as I looked at him and forced a smile showing my teeth in more of a grimace than a grin.

"Thanks," he replied.

As I walked inside, I found myself at the center of a wide marble hallway. It had an antiseptic feel to it, like a hospital. I almost expected to see nurses and gurneys rolling down the corridor. It lacked the warm, student-driven friendliness you usually sense in a school.

There were eight doors lining the hall. They were all identical, made of rich wood with a panel of frosted, ribbed glass on top. Each door was neatly labeled with uninteresting words like "OFFICE" or "JANITOR", or "DEAN". I wondered why Dad thought the school was so special. At least from the inside, it seemed like a pretty generic older building to me.

Dad selected the door labeled "OFFICE" and turned the polished doorknob. I followed him inside.

Unlike the hall, this room bustled with life. Three guilty-looking, teenage boys filled the chairs next to the door labeled "PRINCIPAL". Two secretaries sat at desks. One filed papers and another typed on her computer, not noticing that we walked into the room. The third person was a pretty, young lady who was arguing one-sidedly with a copy machine. She had no idea we were standing there. We waited about a minute before Dad cleared his throat audibly.

"Hello," Dad called. "Would you like me to take a look at that?" I knew Dad could fix that copy machine in less than 30 seconds.

"Well, if you can do something, I'd be most appreciative," she sighed and flopped her arms against her thighs in a motion of surrender.

"Sure thing." Dad walked around the secretaries' wall, approached the copier and immediately began pulling drawers.

In no time he extracted a crumpled piece of paper from a hidden compartment. He handed it to her.

"You're hired! Thank you!"

"Glad to help," he said.

"Now, you look like you need registration papers," she said as she walked from the copier to her desk.

"How did you know?' I asked politely.

"Well, you're the only teenager around here that's not in class," she smiled. "Oh, and we've been expecting a Trinity Pierce today, and you look exactly like her." She turned and shuffled through the file cabinet next to the copier and produced a neat folder of papers. She extended them to Dad with another smile, "Here you are."

Oblivious as usual, Dad took the papers. He turned and handed them to me. We took seats at the worktable next to a door labeled "NURSE".

Dad hated filling out paperwork; he usually left all of that to Mom, but without her, the duty fell to me. In my best printing, I completed each line. He sat next to me as I did so, and like all dads, he interjected obvious and already known information.

When I was finished, I gathered the papers and tapped their bottoms on the table to straighten them. "Here you go," I said.

He looked up, "You know you're the best!"

"No problem Pops," I replied. He stood and handed the paperwork to the pretty secretary.

"We'll contact you tomorrow," she said. "Her files just arrived today, so we'll be expecting her for her first day on Monday."

"Great," said Dad as he turned toward the door. "Thanks so much."

I followed Dad out the door and jogged to gain pace beside him. We rounded the corner that led to the outside door when I was hit solidly by something moving pretty quickly! I wasn't really watching where I was going and neither was he, but gosh! I lost my balance and found myself sprawled on my rear-end in the middle of the hall.

"I am so sorry!" the person said. My dad was already helping me up. I really was rattled and I tried to shake it off.

In a moment, the speaker came into view.

"I didn't mean to run into you! Please excuse me!" he said. "Are you okay?" He was very blonde, very tall, and very handsome.

Dad replied for me, "I think she'll be okay. You must be in some kind of hurry though!"

"I apologize," he continued. He knelt to help me up and extended his hand. "After school detention if we are late to class...and I'm late to class." He smiled at me. It was a smile that was sincere, apologetic and a little mischievous all at once. I had no choice but to smile back.

"There's never anyone in this hall..." he continued. "It's just..." he stopped when Dad held up his hand. "Are you sure you're okay..." he asked as he stood shuffling his feet and nervously clutching his books to his chest.

"She's fine," Dad replied, helping me to my feet. "Go on to class."

The boy smiled again, meeting my gaze with his own. His blue eyes were soft and I could have sworn I looked into them before. Certainly I met him somewhere...but how? Where?

He stood and adjusted his pack, his eyes never leaving mine. "Sorry," he whispered. When he smiled, his eyes brightened and my heart leapt. He began walking backward and managed a polite wave before he turned and trotted down the hallway.

While we rode the bus home, I wondered about the boy. Where had I seen him before? I just could not shake the feeling that I knew him...but that was impossible.

Dad interrupted my thoughts, "Are you sure you're okay? You seem off."

"I'm fine," I replied. To prove it, I bluntly asked Dad why he didn't mention Mom to the school.

"None of their business," he replied curtly. "We won't be here long anyway. When you start Monday, everyone who needs to know will know."

I thought about Mom, too afraid to ask if she was well enough to be released, or if...and I refused to let the thought of the possibility of her death cross my mind.

Chapter 5

When we got home, Dad flopped on the couch and took the remote. I knew he'd be asleep before he could even begin to watch anything. I picked up a worn, flannel blanket and tossed it over his knees.

"Thanks," he said thinly.

I plodded down the hall to my room. It was only ten o'clock in the morning, but I was exhausted. I guessed I had better get used to getting up early.

I stopped at my door and sighed, missing my old life and my old friends in Texas. I felt too tired to start all over again. Only seventeen and already worn out. I knew I had to tough it out for Mom and Dad, and I would try my best. It was just so hard sometimes. I reached and twisted the old plastic knob that needed to be pushed and turned at the same time in order to open. I thought of Dorothy opening the door to Oz, but this was nothing like that colorful land in the movies.

The walls of my room were painted yellow, a yellow I am sure was pretty and soothing to some little girl fifty years ago. Now these walls looked worn and sickly, shining brightly in some areas and dirty in others. The paint swirled in the corners and clung to the wall like an old bandage. I thought spending any amount of time in this room could drive a person rip-roaring crazy. As soon as I saw my room, I thought of a short story I read a long time ago called "The Yellow Wallpaper". Like the character in the story, I imagined myself creeping around the room in a month or two, hunched over...creeping...creeping...in and out of the wallpaper.

I needed to close my eyes, so I lay on my bed, and welcomed daydreams of my old room. They immediately began to blossom in my mind. I was comforted by things from my childhood...well-loved, stuffed animals, photographs of all of the people and places I grew up with, worn yet familiar toys.

I imagined I was in my old canopy bed. The floral pattern surrounding me was bright and light and the violets were in full bloom. My furniture was a polished white and everything was in its place. Sun streamed through an open window, and although it was late fall, it never got very cold in Amarillo. As I lay on my bed of dreams I remembered the miniature shelf that my dad built for me. Not much of a woodworker, it took him weeks, but it was a collection of tiny shelves that made up the floors of a larger wooden house. He painted it girly colors to match my room and hung it as a display on my wall.

My mom and I occasionally purchased a tiny miniature to place on the little shelves. I spent hours of my childhood arranging the miniatures perfectly. I had a jar of lollipops about the size of my little fingernail. I had tiny kittens that were placed around an even smaller saucer of milk. I had a miniature porcelain lamb that my mom gave me when I was three. I even had a tiny set of spoons that could be removed from a rack. Closing my eyes, I tried to remember all of the miniatures that rested on my shelves. I intended to get up in a few minutes and visit Mom at the hospital, but I fell fast asleep.

Finally dreamless, I awoke with a start and reached for the alarm clock. I always set it twenty minutes early, so it took a bit of forced concentration to calculate real time. It was five-twelve. I had been asleep for about seven hours. Dad had tossed a comforter over me that I shrugged off as I sat up. Darkness was approaching, but wasn't here quite yet…thankfully.

Standing, I physically shook off the sleepiness. I was still tired, but I wanted to catch up on the day. Sleeping longer could have been a possibility if my stomach hadn't awakened me. I realized I only ate a few spoonfuls of cereal this morning, so I went downstairs. It was as I thought; Dad was gone. In the living room a note lay on his threadbare recliner. I picked it up and read:

Sweetheart,

Went to see Mom. I know you wanted to go, but you need your sleep. We'll go together tomorrow.

Love you,

Dad

I was mad…no, not mad…frustrated was a better word. I wanted my mom.

Chapter 6

Cover the walls. I thought. I decided to cover those terrible yellow walls. Dad was still at the hospital and I was bored. I already made some macaroni and cheese that lie mummifying itself in a pot. Being a careless cook herself, Mom never taught me any culinary skills, so dinner was often macaroni from a box or some item that served to jazz up another.

I stood in the center of my bedroom and imagined the possibilities…not many in this small space. Another dirty, cracked plastic cover muffled the glare from the light bulb hanging above my bed. It was filled with burned gnats and crisped moths. I reached up and touched the plastic, noting to take it for a good scrubbing.

The walls were loathsome in the dirty light. Bright lemon swirled into sickly jaundice with no defining line. It looked patchy, worn, bleached. Try as I might to find an edge, I could not define the color change. It was already starting to give me a headache, even with this cursory inspection.

I brought several posters and many photographs with me that I stored in a small trunk under my bed. What was a teenage girl without her photos and posters anyway? I knelt on the floor and reached under the bed skirt with one hand. I curled my fingers into a fist and swung my arm under the mattress. The side of my thumb brushed something, and I instantly recoiled. I had touched something icy, not the way a storage box should feel. I hesitated, but again stretched out my fingers. They found the edge of the trunk, so I chalked up the icy sensation to my imagination. On my knees, I leaned way under the bed, grasped the sides of the box with both hands, and began wrestling it from its hiding place. As I tugged and pulled, the box shifted but moved very little. For a moment, it almost felt as if someone was pulling it back. Although the space under the bed was small, it took quite an effort to extract the case. I sat back on my heels.

Finally, my grunts and strains paid off. The trunk was old; my grandfather's. Supposedly, he made it himself out of walnut, so dark it was almost black. It had its share of chips and dings and the handle on the right side swung freely, attached to the trunk by only one screw. Two rusted, metal straps squeezed the middle of the box, the edges of which were neatly crimped. I grasped the oddly carved handle on the front and pulled it toward me. This time, it slid quickly; as if it were on ice. I almost tumbled backward but I caught my balance. I knelt and unlatched both clasps. As I lifted the lid, it complained with a loud squeak.

My photo albums were neatly wrapped in tissue paper. Before Mom got sick, we used to go on a website where you could build your own photo scrapbooks. She and I spent countless hours choosing backgrounds, cropping, and pasting. It took forever, but we always picked the best photos, the ones that really captured our memories.

I carefully removed one of the albums, pulled back the tissue, and opened it. It was the one with our vacation to Sedonia. As I turned the pages, memories came back in a warm flood. I stopped to gaze at a picture of Mom and Dad standing in the pool at the hotel. I took this one. As I remembered, a lump formed in my throat; one that was impossible to swallow. A tear that went unnoticed until now fell from my cheek onto the page. I quickly wiped it off before it could damage the paper. Overwhelmed with sadness, I shut the book tightly holding it as if it were an injured bird, and placed it back in the trunk. In the process, I inadvertently disturbed a container of some of my old watercolor paints. They were stored in an aging Tupperware container, yellowed and stained with the paint of my dreams. I hadn't touched the paints in years, but now might be the time. I pulled the box out of the trunk and popped it open. I was met with the stale, bitter odor of the paint; perfectly matching my own bitterness. I took a handful of the familiar metallic tubes and let them fall through my fingers.

Next I took a rolled poster that lay wrapped in a cellophane tube. I slid the paper from the plastic and unrolled the poster.

Ever since I was little, I loved SpongeBob Squarepants and here he was, grinning his buck toothed smile. I looked at him, all soft and yellow, a yellow that had no place in my ailing room. SpongeBob was the yellow of happy things...the yellow of buttercups...the yellow of lemonade...the yellow of school buses...the yellow of sunshine. My walls, on the other hand, were a miserable yellow...the yellow of cowardice...the yellow of age...the yellow of regret...the yellow of lost years.

Feeling triumphant over the room, I stepped to my nightstand and opened the drawer. I reached inside and produced a roll of masking tape and a box of push pins. Dad told me that in rented houses I shouldn't tape or pin anything to the walls, but I didn't care. This Yellow was alive and needed to disappear. The landlord could sue me later.

Since the walls were such a jigsaw of textures, I decided to use a little tape and a lot of push pins. Soon, SpongeBob stood frozen on the wall at the foot of my bed. His sunny smile instantly changed my mood; the misery of the walls was finally hidden. After an hour of rummaging in the trunk and rolling tape balls, I was finished. My walls were a collage of things I loved, from photos of Mom, Dad and my old friends, to my poster of SpongeBob and Patrick Star.

When I was finished, I surveyed my work. "Much better," I thought. "Much...much better!"

Chapter 7

Another thankfully dreamless night, or if I did dream, I didn't remember. Since it was Saturday, it was kind of late when I woke up. Examining last night's redecorating project, I was pleased with how my room turned out. I showered, dressed, and went downstairs. Dad was perched, one foot on the arm of the couch, tying his shoe.

"Hi, honey. Are you going to see Mom today?" he asked.

"Sure," I said. I really wanted to see her. I wanted to make sure she actually was doing better. Dad sometimes sugar-coated the facts.

"Are you leaving now?" I asked.

"Yup," he replied. "I'll wait for you though."

"Let's go then," I said. "I'll grab something to eat there if I get hungry."

We walked in silence until I decided I needed a little company, even if it was distracted. The grumbling of my empty stomach gave me a topic.

"Hey Dad," I stated. "I was wondering if you ever had a hospital milkshake."

"What's that?" he asked, still distracted by his thoughts.

"You know. The milkshakes they have at the hospital café," I stated.

"Oh," he sounded relieved. "I thought you meant some type of IV or something."

"No, Dad."

"In either case, I haven't tried one." We continued to talk about food, both hospital and airline until we reached Mom's hallway. Eastern Mercy was as pleasant as a hospital could be, especially the cancer wing. Although I was becoming a regular visitor, I forced myself to remain focused on the floor in front of me, not wanting to glance to my sides. To be honest, what I saw in the cancer rooms scared me.

When Mom first started being admitted to the parade of hospitals, I made some rookie mistakes. I often found myself glancing in open doors as I proceeded down endless corridors to my mother's room. The hopelessness of cancer was always there to greet me. Most patients were bedridden, their bodies curled into fetal positions. Others, frail and gaunt, sat on the edge of their beds. They looked tired and bored, longing to get outside, to feel the sun, somehow knowing they never would.

Once I passed a room where a frighteningly thin, old woman sat on the edge of a bed. Tubes and wires leashed her to a large machine that kept track of her misery. As I passed, she whispered my name…I heard her clearly. It was unmistakable and riveted my attention back towards her room.

"Trinity!" It was a light chiming voice. It did not fit the speaker at all. It reminded me of wind chimes, clear and airy on a summer morning.

I paused, suddenly frightened. Did I know this person? I couldn't. I didn't know any old women in any cancer wards. I had to find out why she was calling me, so I turned and reluctantly went back to her room.

When I got there, I peeked around the corner of the doorway. I was shocked. The room was empty…no bed…no tray…no old woman. I entered the room and looked around, even peeking into the bathroom…nothing. Maybe it was the wrong room. Maybe I imagined the whole thing…doubtful with my history.

I left and proceeded to my mother's room, trying to push the entire event from my mind. Throughout the rest of the day, my thoughts kept going back to the old woman. But that was a few weeks ago, and today my father was walking with me.

We reached Mom's room…832. She was asleep. Not wanting to disturb her rest, Dad and I quietly tiptoed in and sat in our prescribed chairs. Her food tray sat next to the bed, still untouched and probably quite cold.

Pale and tired, Mom slept with her mouth slightly open. Her features were shadowed and gaunt. Her cheekbones were sharp edges to her once soft face. Her skin seemed to be stretched over her bones since she had lost so much weight. It saddened me to see her so changed from only a year ago. The white sheet was pulled up to her chin like a premature shroud, and it rose and fell rhythmically as she breathed. Her usually unkempt hair was long gone, lost to radiation treatments, and she covered her baldness with black bandana dotted with smiley faces. It was a gift from a friend, intended to lift Mom's spirits. Wires hung from her arms that tied her to monitors and an oxygen valve was secured under her nose with a white piece of elastic that wrapped around the back of her head. There was even an item that resembled a clothespin that clasped Mom's index finger, monitoring who knows what. Above all, Mom looked vulnerable, like a featherless baby bird that fell out of its nest and waited for a rescue that would never come.

Dad and I watched her, silently on guard, for what must have been a half hour. Soon, she began to stir and mumble. Eventually, she opened her eyes, and immediately focused on me.

She wet her lips with her tongue before she spoke. "Up, please," she said in a sleepy whisper.

I scrambled for the bed control and pushed the buttons. "Hi, Mommy," I said.

"Hi, Trin," she replied with a weak smile.

She turned to Dad who sat eagerly near the window. "Hi, Daddy," she sighed, still tired.

He smiled and reached to squeeze her hand. It took a while, but Mom gradually gained a little strength. She still looked pretty bad, but today she seemed a little more animated than usual. Eventually, she sat up and folded her hands in her lap.

She smiled softly and took a rattled breath, "How do you like Pittsburgh?"

"It's pretty cool...literally," I replied with a shrug, not knowing what to say. "Honestly, Mom, it's just so dark!"

"Not what you're used to, huh?"

"No. The sun is always hiding behind some hill or tree or cloud," I complained a little, but tried to restrain myself. I didn't want to upset her or make her worry about me more than she already did.

“You know,” she said, gaining a little strength from her sleep. “I grew up right around here. If you can get past the sunshine issues, you’ll see the beauty of the place.” She paused and gazed wistfully out the window. “First of all, the hills and trees are lovely, so green in the summer and like delicate silhouettes in the sky during winter.” She stopped to gather some more strength. Dad and I waited patiently.

After a few moments she continued, speaking more slowly this time, “When I met your dad and moved to Texas, I thought Amarillo was the worst place in the world. It was just flat fields of boring yellow, but I got used to it." She stopped again and closed her eyes, remembering Amarillo. "Now I have come to love Texas, the warm climate, the desert, the grasslands full of bluebonnet, the canyons, even the juniper forests. The fields of yellow around Amarillo are beautiful in themselves, and when the sun hits them, there’s no friendlier color in the world.”

“You can say that again,” I said, feeling quite homesick. I thought of the Yellow in my bedroom, a stark contrast to Amarillo or SpongeBob.

We talked most of the afternoon about all kinds of things. Mom kept stopping to rest, but overall it was a pretty good day for her. When it was time for her to go to a treatment, Dad suggested a hospital milkshake. I enjoyed it like it was my last.

Chapter 8

Before I knew it, my official first day of school had arrived. I didn't get much sleep the night before because of the all the butterflies jockeying for space in my stomach. I rose with the sun...sun that was a rarity in Pittsburgh, so I took it as a good sign. I had the highest hopes for the day, yet in the back of my mind, the air was different. It seemed a bit heavier, the air a bit thicker, the temperature a little cooler.

I got out of bed and showered, savoring the warm water. I pulled on my favorite pair of jeans and a lavender long-sleeved t-shirt. My nervous stomach clenched when I bent to slip on my shoes, and I knew it would never allow breakfast. Dad was still asleep, so I grabbed my jacket and bookbag that lay slouched on a chair and tiptoed out the front door.

It was a cold fall day. Leaves hopped about my shoes like native dancers around a fire. The biting wind immediately gnawed its way through my thick shirt, giving me goose bumps. The sun was not as warm as it looked, so I slipped into my jacket. I made it to the bus stop just in time, and soon I was aboard a Port Authority bus. It slowly wound its way through narrow, bustling streets, trundling like a giant beetle toward Turnbull Prep Academy.

Before I knew it, I stood in front of the glowering structure. It stood strong, judging its newest disciple. As I climbed the many steps to the front door, I sensed its petulance. I imagined its slate shingles bristling with anger as I pulled the door open.

As instructed by my father, I stopped in the office and met Mrs. St. John, the guidance counselor. She was a slip of a woman, almost too ordinary to be noticed in a prep school. She was thin with very dark hair pulled into a tight pony tail. She wore a black pencil skirt and pale, green blouse that shrouded her already small frame making her look even more insignificant. She greeted me warmly with a slight hug, telling me how much I was going to love it there and what a great school Turnbull was. I wanted to believe her, but evidence soon told me a different story.

Mrs. St. John chatted about the school's lengthy history as we walked toward my assigned classroom, room 832, strangely, the same number as Mom's hospital room. We rounded the corner from the office and guidance suite and approached a set of double doors that led to the main body of the school. Mrs. St. John pushed the door open and I passed through. I stopped upon my first glance, stunned at what lay before me.

The room we entered was enormous. The ceilings were vaulted and soared at least thirty feet from the ground. Ancient wooden beams bent their spines and stretched in arches to support the peak. Darker wood was wedged between the ribs of the roof. It was a spectacular, robust structure and gave the impression that we were in the belly of an enormous monster.

The walls were a forest of wood. Rich, dark, classroom doors were heavily framed with wood of the same type. Each door was connected to the next with layers of carved crown molding and baseboard.

In the center of the room were ten long tables with about twenty chairs around each. The room was dimly lit by shaded work lights placed neatly in the center of each table. Above each table swaying on thick black chains, dangled iron chandeliers that composed of two simple circles, one on top of the other. Strategically placed on the black circles were oil pots that supplied fuel to the wicks in each. This wasn't a charming scene from Hogwart's, rather, these chandeliers looked like they were salvaged from some medieval torture chamber. As I looked about the unbelievable room, I saw that a few of the walls were lined with books; most of the others sported carved scenes on raised, wooden panels that soared toward the ceiling. I walked to one of the huge panels and ran my hand across the figures in the scene. Although they didn't actually move, each scene told a story. I quickly became lost in the relief.

Carved into this wooden wall was a scene of an old English hunt. Ten men were perched on horseback being led by a pack of dogs. Two of the men were blowing on bugles. Their cheeks bulged with effort. Several other men, probably servants or kennel-men, attempted to control the raging pack with thick chain leashes. It would have been a typical hunt scene, except for the dogs.

The dogs weren't your everyday hunting beagles; rather, they resembled large wolves. Their features were very pointed and their ears stood erect. They gnashed their teeth and spittle flew. You could almost see the fur on their thin backs bristling with anticipation. Their eyes were intense and wild and even lent a yellowish cast to the wood.

If you looked very closely, you would notice the people in the scene were also extraordinary. Their expressions were pock marked with terror. The kennel-men reeled with the strength of the wolves, and some of the horses bucked backwards with fear. The men on horseback screamed to maintain some order, but the scene bordered on complete chaos.

It was fascinating artwork, but peculiar and foreboding at the same time. I wondered what twisted mind executed this carving. I imagined an old man bent over a worktable chiseling wood. He wore green workpants and a white shirt stained with grime and sawdust. Tedious effort pained his hunched shoulders. He stopped working for a moment to recognize his creator. As he lifted his head, I could immediately see his face was twisted and thick. He wore heavy framed glasses that magnified his eyes. Even from my imagined distance I could see they were filmy with cataracts. The irises, which should have contained a rich color, were bleached almost completely white, leaving a pinprick of a pupil. He watched me, studying his creator with great interest.

Again, my imagination was getting the best of me. I forced myself to look elsewhere. I began to search for the doomed fox in the tangle of bushes at the bottom of the carving. He remained well hidden. I could have looked at the scene for hours, studying every detail and emotion etched into the wood.

"This is quite a wonderful place, isn't it?" interrupted Mrs. St. John.

"Uh, yeah," was the only reply that escaped my lips. I tore my eyes away and looked at Mrs. St. John. It was difficult, and I felt as if I had just awoken from a long sleep. Shockingly, she saw nothing out of the ordinary. This place was anything but wonderful!

"I always think of a medieval manor house, or maybe Arthur's Camelot," she stated as we resumed our walk. "We call this room the *Gathering Hall.*"

My head swiveled in every direction, and I drank in all of the detail. Medieval manor house! I was thinking more along the lines of Beowulf...maybe Hrothgar's Mead Hall. I imagined the monstrous Grendel approaching, hungry; hunting for a human meal. I noticed each carved wooden door and its frame had a theme or pattern.

I stopped to look at another carving, this one on a door. The door itself resembled the trunk of a gnarled tree and was framed by two smaller trees. Their branches stretched and met in a tangle of thorns above the door. On this door, a dense forest was carved in tedious detail. Every branch had a texture and the leaves even had faintly carved veins. When I looked even closer, I noticed sap was streaming from the trees like blood and collecting in haphazard pools on the forest floor. I touched one of these pools to see if it was sticky. It wasn't.

On this same door, I could almost see little things hiding in the thicket...fairy-like. Each time I focused on what I imagined was a figure in the trees, it faded into the carving. This had to be some kind of optical illusion! The faster I shifted my focus, the faster the figures hid amongst the trees. I could almost hear them laughing as I tried to catch them. Frightened and disturbed, I moved to the next carving.

Mrs. St. John was kind to let me explore the fantastic artwork of the school without hurrying me. She must witness the awe I displayed quite frequently. A river teeming with crocodiles, a windswept desert littered with corpses, a threatening storm approaching a small farm, children lost in a dark forest. "What is all this?" I finally asked, astonished.

"Well," replied Mrs. St. John, "the building was donated to the school back in 1907. It is very unusual, and there is very little known about the building before that. We do know, though that it served as a private mansion for the family of William Turnbull, a local steel tycoon in the mid-1800s. He donated it as a school, but we also know he was not responsible for its original construction. It seems the building is much older than that. No records are known to exist regarding the actual, original construction or the army of craftsmen that must have been imported to complete the beautiful, but quite unusual carvings."

"Gosh," I continued to gape and stare. House? Who could ever *stand* living here?

"The front office of the building was added in 1925 and that accounts for the differences in architecture," she continued. When the house was donated, an agreement was made to use it only as part of the school and to not have any type of tours or historical designation."

"And no one knows why?" I asked.

"Not that I am aware of," she said. "Then again I am a just a counselor and not privy to certain information. I do know that if these guidelines are not followed, the building would revert to the ancestors of the original owners."

"Who would that be?" I wondered.

Again, I stopped when I noticed new carvings along the baseboards, carvings of huge rats, life-like in every detail. They scampered between the classrooms. I crouched and ran my hand over one of them, half expecting it to nip at me.

"Those are our pets," said Mrs. St. John with a smile. "They are strange little things. The students have names for all of them."

"How many are there?" I asked as my eyes scanned the baseboards. I noticed the rats were perched everywhere, not just along the baseboards. They sat on the tops of doors, leering at everyone who entered the classroom. They nestled in the carved trees, scurried across doorframes. One was even eviscerating a formidable, wooden cockroach next to a rat hole carved into the baseboard.

"Funny thing is, no one knows," she revealed. "When we think we've found them all, one is discovered in a cupboard or in the corner of some obscure room. Last count was 157, but really, who knows?"

"They keep having babies," I mumbled too low for her to hear.

I made my way from rat to rat, engrossed in the detail. Every hair was carved into each body; the claws were as sharp as knives. The dark eyes glittered in the lamplight. It was incredible!

Mrs. St. John broke my trance by clearing her throat. I must have been staring at the rats for a long time. It took a bit of effort to shake off the hypnotic stare. Running my fingers along the wall I inquired, "Is this oak?"

"Mahogany," she replied. "All of it is mahogany."

"Goodness," I could have marveled at all of the detail for days on end.

"Anyway, you'll notice this is an enormous room, but a small school," she said, redirecting my attention. "There are only six classrooms of each level. Since this is a prepatory school, you may choose to stay here for up to three years, but your final year and a half counts at a collegiate level. With our reputation, most Turnbull Prep students are recruited by highly respected universities." I studied the layout of the hall. All of the classrooms lined the sides of the single, wide Gathering Hall.

Mrs. St. John abruptly stopped walking. "Here we are, room 832," she said. "You'll report to Mr. Arndt every morning."

I examined the door I would cross every day for God knew how long. It was the most unusual door I had seen so far. This one was covered with skulls. I paused, studying it intently. Some were large, some small. Some grinned sinister, toothy grins while others were frozen in eternal screams. Still others stared emptily in my direction, expressionless. I ran my fingers lightly across the work.

Strangely, it seemed as if the expressions on the skulls actually responded; they seemed to bow their heads and shift in the direction of my touch. I recoiled, pulling my hand away as if the door had burned me. My imagination again...I sure had a touch of the heebie-jeebies. Shaking off that ridiculous notion, I refocused on the faces. They were so detailed, so real!

Again, Mrs. St. John interrupted my amazement. "Here you go," she said as she held out a green piece of paper. I must have looked utterly confused. "Your schedule," she stated, her once warm smile beginning to weaken.

I reached absently and clasped it between my fingers. "Oh, sorry. I guess I'm just a bit…"

"Would you like me to go over it with you?" she interrupted.

"No, I'll be okay, thanks."

"Great. Mr. Arndt said he'd point you in the right direction." She moved to face me and gave my arms a squeeze. "You'll learn to love it here. See me if you need anything else, honey," and in a whispered tone she added, "even if it's just to talk. This must be so hard on you." She smiled, her face dripping with a mixture of empathy and pity. Then she turned and walked away.

I was alone in the huge place. It was completely silent except for the echo of Mrs. St. John's fading footfalls. For a split second I wondered why it was so quiet. Then I realized noise couldn't possibly escape from behind those overbearing wooden doors.

"Get going!" I said to myself. I took a deep breath, and reached for the doorknob. That's when I realized the doorknob itself was a small, grinning skull.

Chapter 9

I entered the classroom. The thud the door made as it swung shut sounded like the lid of a coffin being closed...thick and final. Like the outside Gathering Hall, this room also had high ceilings, but only to a height of about twenty feet. Tall, bent beams stood guard in here as well, reminding me of the poor titan, Atlas, cursed by bearing the weight of the ceiling. There was a bank of four very tall, thickly framed windows whose wooden tops arched at a peak, mimicking the curve of the ceiling. Dim Pittsburgh light struggled through the etched panes of glass.

The class was full of students. Some were working diligently at their desks; others were gathered in a group around a wooden table at the front of the room. A few others formed a line at the busy teacher's desk. They must have been working on something important, because no one noticed me when I entered the room. I looked around and quickly calculated five rows of five desks - twenty-five in all. I stood there for a few moments, taking in all the detail I could. I walked slowly towards the teacher's desk. As I moved, I felt a few, then more students stopping to look at me. With a distinct feeling of discomfort, I finally reached the desk and the students surrounding it stepped back to give me room.

Mr. Arndt looked up from his work. He was older, heavyset, and had a tired face. He had about as much hair left as Mom. He adjusted the thick, dark-rimmed glasses that teetered on the end of his nose, and said, "You must be Trinity. Welcome to Turnbull. Ravie, would you show Trinity where to put her things and find her a seat? You can take the rest of the period to introduce her to some of your friends, but keep it in check," he smiled kindly, but knowingly. "You understand what I mean, don't you?"

"Sure Mr. Arndt," a girl sitting in the row by the wall replied. She stood up and walked toward me. Her appearance was striking. She was about as tall as me, and had a slender build. She looked as if she could have been from India or Pakistan, or some other faraway place. Her skin was a milky shade of brown and her hair was short, spiky, and beautifully black. She wore a denim miniskirt with blue leggings and a pink long-sleeved t-shirt. An air of confidence surrounded her.

She approached, smiled widely, and said, "Hi, my name is Ravie."

"Trinity," I replied, lightly grasping her outstretched hand.

Ravie turned and led me to a large closet where everyone hung their coats and backpacks. There were no windows in there which lent a stifling feel to the room, as if someone was going to slam the door shut and keep me locked in there forever. Chunky pegs jutted from the thick wainscoting. I found an empty one, and flipped my coat onto it. As I did so, I noticed a wooden rat crouched behind one of the coats.

"This is the strangest place," I stated.

"Yeah…it is. One of the weirdest I've ever seen." She waited for me, leaning on the heavily stained door frame. Her arms were crossed and she smiled widely.

"Do you know a lot about this school?" I asked, wanting to know more about my odd, new surroundings.

"Not as much as I should," she replied. "They only let us know so much. I guess that's what makes this place so *charming*."

I didn't know if she was being sarcastic or not, so I let the comment fall. I followed her from the closet and into the classroom. She gestured to the empty seat next to hers. Mr. Arndt was speaking, so quietly slid behind the desk. I tried to listen, but my attention kept being pulled toward the carved detail in the room. It was all so amazing!

I sat through the next few minutes of class quietly staring at the walls. Soon, the students were working on their own again. Mr. Arndt told Ravie to introduce me, but it was obvious that she was very busy. She was working on a paper that, according to the assignment board, was due at the end of the week. She had a laptop perched on her desk and immediately began typing away as soon as she sat down. While she typed, I busied myself with my calendar.

I'm sure I looked occupied, but in reality I was still a bit shocked by the carvings. Ravie seemed nice enough, but she was under a lot of demands. I was sure by the end of the day we would either hit it off or go our separate ways. I wanted to get to know her a little better. I wanted to strike up a conversation, but I hesitated. She looked so busy.

After a few minutes, she stopped and looked at me, then smiled and sighed. "I'm sorry. Where are my manners?" She closed the lid of her laptop and whispered, "The hell with this! Trinity, where are you from?"

"Texas." I replied. "Amarillo." Images of bluebonnet, Cyprus, and plains of yellow grass warmed my memory.

"I bet you miss it," she stated. "I moved here five years ago...from Phoenix."

"I do," I said. "The sun the most. It's so gray here."

"Why do you think I dress this way? Someone's gotta bring a little color around here!" she laughed. "Honestly, I really miss the deserts and sun too. I thought I was going to go nuts here for a while." She paused and scanned the room. "Do you see that girl at Arndt' desk?"

"Which one?" I asked.

"The one in the green hoodie."

"Yeah." I replied unsure where our conversation was going.

"That's Andrea. She's from Puerto Rico. When she moved here, she had to sit under a sun lamp until she got used to the climate."

"Really?"

"Yup. Doctor prescribed."

"I wish I had one!" I laughed.

"Honestly, Trinity, Pittsburgh will grow on you. It's really pretty when it snows and the summers are great, especially if you're used to temps over ninety, like we are."

"So there is a light at the end of the tunnel?" I asked.

"Yeah, come April or May...or June," she laughed. "But there are lots of things to do. I'll show you around...maybe this weekend if you're not busy."

"That would be nice," I replied.

Ravie kept the conversation going. She really seemed to be a lively person. "Did your dad get a new job here? That's why *we* moved."

"You could say that," I replied, still not wanting to reveal too much about my family to this likeable stranger.

"That's cool. I know what you're going through. It's hard to be the new person."

She really had no idea what I was going through, but I was happy to have someone to talk to. "At my last school, it seemed like I knew everyone, but this is so different."

Ravie smiled. "Hey, I have a couple of good friends who would love to meet you. They're not in this class, but I'll introduce you later."

"Thanks!" I said with genuine appreciation. "I would like that."

"I remember what it was like being new," a pensive look crossed her face. "It sucks!" She smiled widely, showing her perfectly white, perfectly even teeth.

I laughed at her candor. "That it does," I said, but then I thought a little more deeply. I really didn't need to meet anyone new. My life was so hectic right now and friendships took a lot of care and nurturing...yet being alone was becoming all too familiar.

Before I could make any decisions, an irritating chime sounded over the intercom to indicate that it was time to change classes. Ravie gathered her things in a bundle, and I stood with an appreciative smile.

"Sorry," she sighed. "I have a lot of work right now. We have this paper due and this class is a pre-req. for organic chemistry next semester. If I don't get into that class, my dad will kill me."

"That's okay," I said. "Do what you need to do, and I'll just fall into step. I'm pretty astute."

"I just feel bad I don't have time to show you more right now."

"Don't worry about it," I said. "It will come." I decided to let things fall where they may. If I made a few new friends along the way, I thought that would just be a little bit of fortune smiling on me for once, and I could use all the good luck I could get.

We walked into the Gathering Hall and soon reached another one of the disturbing doors. This was a scene of war. The men on the door looked Egyptian; I could tell by their headdresses. They drove chariots headlong across burning sands towards the enemy. I stepped forward to examine the door more closely, and I was able to find the pharaoh. I knew because he wore a helmet-crown like Ramses did in the old Ten Commandments movie with Yul Brynner. I watched that with my mom one Sunday evening around Easter.

"Class is in here?' I asked.

"Yep."

"This is so weird," I said running my hand across the battlefield. As I looked more closely, I could see the splayed corpses that dotted the landscape.

"You don't have to tell me about weird. This place has been giving me the creeps since the day I got here."

"Me too," I stated, "but I also think it's fascinating. The more I look at them, the more I get wrapped into these peculiar stories. Don't you?" I looked at Ravie, genuinely interested in what she thought of all of this. She bore an uncomfortable smile and an uncertain look on her face. I didn't want to push her away so soon, so I made something up. "I had a great ancient history teacher in ninth grade. She made me do a research paper on the Hittite invasion of Egypt." I said this not because it really happened, but because I was a bit of a history buff.

"I hate research papers," said Ravie good-naturedly, "but it seems to me we have a little bookworm on our hands."

"I admit it. I am." I said blushing little. "Is it that obvious?"

"Yeah, but not in a bad way," she replied. She paused for a moment then continued excitedly, "You'll love Michael then. He's a great big hockey player. Looks like a dumb jock, but he's really smart..." She paused again, "I'll be the first to tell you that I have a total crush on him."

I smiled. Ravie was an interesting personality.

"Well, you might as well know too! Everyone does but Michael!"

My smile turned into a laugh, and Ravie started to laugh too.

She sensed my amusement, so she continued to jibe. "Typical man! A fabulous-looking girl is practically throwing herself at him and he can't get his fat head out of his book or pry it out of his hockey helmet long enough to notice!"

Still laughing, the irritating chime rang again.

"After you," Ravie said gesturing at the room. It was time for our next class to begin. I reached out and turned the doorknob that was carved like the wheel of a chariot. Like a wheel, it felt thick and heavy in my hand.

As I stepped into the room, Ravie continued to joke, but I had stopped laughing. I was It was as if I stepped from the Gathering Room and into the battle itself! The men and the chariots were life-sized in here and the violence was tenfold. The detail of the carvings was astounding. There were men falling from horses, others being shot with arrows. There were even several frozen in hand-to-hand combat. I could almost hear the soldiers yelling and the horses screaming. I could smell dust and blood in the air. This was obviously a history classroom. We approached a group of four kids who were leaning against desks, chatting quietly. Funny thing, no one took notice of the carvings. They were probably used to them; seeing them every day; they had become so familiar that they faded into the background.

"Hey," Ravie adeptly slid her way into the group and I followed. "Guys, I want you to meet Trinity.

I smiled. "Hi," was all I could muster. Suddenly someone touched me on the shoulder. I focused on him...slightly familiar at first, then a moment of total recognition. It was the boy who literally ran into me the other day.

"Hey," he said. "I remember you!"

"Oh, hi," I replied completely embarrassed; my face felt hot. I didn't know what to say.

"I had no idea you were the new person," he said. "I guess I didn't put two and two together."

"Listen," I began, afraid of starting off on the wrong foot, "I'm really sorry..."

"Sorry for what?" he asked.

"The other day," I continued, "In the hall."

"Totally *my* fault. Anyway, I ran into you...*literally*!"

My first impression was that he seemed really nice. Cute too with shockingly blonde hair, and what I came to call "Pittsburgh pale" skin. His jaw was square and firmly set and his lips lay in a slight grin. He was very tall and square shouldered. "I'm Gabriel...my name is Gabriel."

"Trinity," I replied. I was sure I was blushing. My face was so hot!

"Nice to finally meet you," he smiled. I got all goose bumpy just looking at him. I wondered what he meant by the word *finally.* More eyes were interested in us now. I could feel them scanning...judging.

One of the girls in the group leaned forward and lifted her hand in a friendly manner, "I'm Beatrice. Welcome to the machine!"

Everyone in the group groaned at her comment. I felt uncomfortable since I really didn't get the reference, so I smiled slightly, trying to be polite.

Gabriel saw I was feeling a little awkward, so he leaned over and whispered, "Nothing against you. Inside joke." His unfamiliar voice next to my ear caused chills to prickle up my spine.

"I'm sorry," Beatrice apologized. "We just call this school *the machine*."

"Why?" I asked, interested. This school was beginning to both frighten and intrigue me.

"In more ways than one," replied another boy. Like Gabriel, he was tall, but his hair was as black as mine. Some famous artist must have chiseled him from a block of marble. His complexion was smooth, and like Gabriel's, very pale. He wore an experienced look in his green eyes which made him all the more attractive. He was nothing short of incredibly handsome, but there was something else too. Something I couldn't quite put my finger on. "Nothing is ever the same here," he stated. "One day it looks one way, the next day another. I know I'm not making much sense to you, but you'll see." His lips arched in a knowing smile that defined his already perfect face.

"I think he's nuts!" interjected Gabriel. He pushed the other boy playfully.

I looked at the two girls and three boys in the group questioningly. Beatrice smiled. She had dark, blonde hair that hung to her shoulders in pretty, large curls. She was shorter than Ravie, and her smile lit up her face. She wore a black Turnbull Prep hoodie with jeans. "Shut up Kane." Beatrice said. "You're making her think we're a bunch of weirdoes."

"Well *you* are," the dark haired boy interjected.

Beatrice continued, "This, is Kane, cranky and funny...all in one package."

"You said package!" Kane and Gabriel immediately doubled over in immature laughter.

"Well, I'll lay it out for you," she said, completely ignoring Kane and Gabriel. "Besides the school itself, you have a couple of groups working here. There are the jocks over in that corner," she pointed at three boys who were sitting in a group of desks watching football highlights on a laptop. "They think they're cool, but they're not. Then you have your geeks over there." She pointed towards four boys who were busy kicking a ball of tape around the back of the room. "You've got a couple of other kids over there." She pointed to the group preoccupying the teacher. "They're okay. They don't bother anyone and no one bothers them. Finally, you've got the homecoming court." She pointed at two self-absorbed girls whispering to each other in the back of the room. Three other girls surrounded them. They giggled and smiled slyly. One of the girls immediately focused on me, whispering to her friends. I felt uncomfortable.

"They are something else," chimed the last boy in our group. I looked at him. He was the football type, tall, stocky and solid. He sported short dark brown hair and a square jaw. When he stood up to greet me, I saw he was well over six-feet tall, even taller than Gabriel. "You'd best stay away from them," he gestured at the affected group. "They're the mean girls." He smiled warmly, a smile that was genuine, kind, and familiar all at once. "I'm Michael."

"Hi," I replied.

Ravie, who was standing next to me, gave me a gentle nudge. This was the boy she had a crush on, the hockey bookworm.

Beatrice blushed at what she was about to say but continued her introductions. I was the only one who noticed. "Then you have these three dorks who only think about hockey." She swept her arm towards the boys like a model displaying a prize on *The Price is Right*. Gabriel leaned over and put his arm around her shoulders.

"That's everybody," said Ravie. Just then, the teacher called the attention of all of the students. Class was beginning. I glanced at my schedule. My art lectures were at the end of the day though; no studio time until next semester. We all took seats together on the window side of the room. I welcomed the sunlight, even though it was filtered by the constant mass of grey clouds.

Gabriel slid into the desk next to mine and whispered, "History...sucks." I looked at him. He was tall, even though he was sitting down.

I loved history, so I listened and took notes on the lecture, but I quickly realized this teacher did not want to be here. She was monotone and completely unanimated. No matter how hard I tried, it was hard to focus. My mind flittered about, looking for a place to roost, but finding none. I tried to focus...Mom...Dad...Home...Texas...nothing was working. I guess I did have a lot on my mind and I, right then and there, decided to cram one more thing on...Gabriel. For goodness sake, I just met him and already my stomach was crawling with those sometimes awful, sometimes glorious butterflies. I wondered what he was really like.

I strained to peek at him nonchalantly. I wondered what kind of car he drove. I stole another glance, and this time he caught me. He smiled gently, a soft smile that curled knowingly at the corners. I studied that curl and was led to his friendly eyes, slightly crinkled by the smile. Cool blue peeked from behind the lids as they widened. I turned my head slightly but did not look away. His smile faded and a look of concern crossed his face. He looked to his notebook, plucked a pen from behind his ear, and quickly jotted down a few words. He waited for the teacher to look the other way then handed me the note.

I read the paper. "*You okay?*"

I nodded with a slight smile. I pointed at my watch and pretended to yawn.

"Boring," he mouthed. He wrinkled his nose and nodded his head in agreement. I tried to focus on the remainder of class, but I failed miserably.

At the end of class, which took forever in coming, the students rounded up their belongings and filed into the Gathering Hall. There were about a hundred kids moving about the room. Some were sitting at the tables, others were chatting, in small groups, but most were moving into and out of classrooms. I got a chance to look around a bit more as I walked with my new group of friends. I saw a sea of unknown faces and heard unfamiliar voices.

Even full of teenagers, the room seemed empty. Voices and footfalls that would have echoed anywhere else fell dead from the walls. Although there were tall windows in the huge room, the drapes were drawn. The table lights should have provided some warmth, but the hall felt cold and unfriendly, as if the building itself didn't want me here.

Chapter 10

By the time I got home, I was tired, my head reeling with memories and excitement.

I visited Mom to talk to her about how school was going. I really missed her company. Up until now, I skirted her school questions with questions and comments of my own. I didn't want Dad to get in trouble for not enrolling me two weeks ago. I was careful not to tell her it was my first day, and I tried not to make the conversation all about school either. Mom seemed more animated than ever when we were talking about my new friends. I told her about Michael, Kane, Ravie, Beatrice, and Gabriel. We talked like old friends, and I even told her how cute I thought Gabriel was. She seemed to really enjoy hearing about them and how I was doing. For the first time in the past year, I felt happy. I didn't leave the hospital until late in the evening.

I walked home by myself. When I got there I checked the house thoroughly, like all teenage girls do, and found my dad fast asleep, sprawled face-down across his bed. I carefully laid a comforter on him, not wanting to wake him; then I went to the living room, flicked on the remote, and promptly fell asleep in front of the television set.

I awoke to someone shaking me gently. It was Dad. I didn't feel like talking and I was dead tired, so I pretended I was still asleep. When I didn't respond, he helped me up like a little girl and led me to my bed. He tucked me in, kissed me on the forehead and smoothed my hair. I reached up and hugged him, burying my face in his shoulder. "Everything is going to be fine," he whispered. "I promise," then he stood up and left the room.

I was alone, suddenly swept by an overwhelming feeling of sadness. My heart ached for Dad and I lamented the lost wholeness of our family. The soft face of my mother came to life in my mind. Her kind smile and warm eyes looked so far away.

My stomach lurched. I sobbed silently into my pillow until I fell asleep. I didn't remember my dreams.

Chapter 11

The next day I had a heavy load of art classes. I did not see any of my newfound acquaintances until the end of the day. On my way toward the front door I spied Ravie and Beatrice at the big tables. They waved and gestured for me to join them. I did so happily. I admitted I was glad to finally have a few friends.

"Hi," I said as I slid onto the seat next to Beatrice. Ravie sat across from her, but slid to her right slightly to include me in their conversation.

"Hey," said Ravie brightly.

"Why aren't you on your way out of here?" I asked. "You surely have something better to do than hang around here!"

Beatrice responded, "We're going out!"

"You're coming too," added Ravie. "We've decided for you."

"Well," I replied, "I was going to go ..."

"With us," Beatrice interrupted, finishing my sentence.

I didn't want to tell them about my mother and my family situation just yet. I thought for a moment while both girls looked at me hopefully. Dad would be with Mom, and I really didn't think he was expecting me to be anywhere today. I wanted to go with them, so I convinced myself that my mother would love for me to spend some time with new friends.

"Where are we going?" I smiled, giving in.

"Hockey game," replied Beatrice. "Ravie's got it bad for Michael so we're going to watch."

"I hadn't noticed," I said sarcastically rolling my eyes.

Ravie laughed, "You got it!"

They gathered their notebooks and stood up. "I'm really glad we caught you," said Ravie. She fumbled in her purse and eventually produced a mirror. She spiked her hair with her fingertips and checked her lipstick.

"Thanks," I replied. "I need a night out."

"You have to give me your number," said Beatrice.

"I barely know you, but I can already see you work too hard," added Ravie with a wide grin. "All work and no play makes Trinity a boring chick! "

Beatrice responded, "If I know one thing, Turnbull newbies are never…ever boring." Ravie nodded her head in agreement. "Maybe you'll find something you like at practice too!" she joked. I immediately thought of Gabriel, but unlike Ravie, I kept my new crush to myself. I wasn't even sure it really was a crush; maybe it was just a little fascination.

We walked to Beatrice's car, a brand-new yellow VW Beetle. Since I was tall, Ravie insisted I take the front seat, but even so, my knees brushed the dashboard.

"Sorry it's cramped," said Beatrice as she tossed her purse onto the back seat next to Ravie. "It was too cute to pass up." She adjusted the rear-view mirror after adjusting her own make-up again. The VW perfectly suited Beatrice's spunky personality.

"I'm fine," I replied. I wiggled in the seat. I could have used a few more inches for the kneecaps. "Just don't crash. No room for the airbag!"

Ravie giggled loudly from the back seat, "Girl, you do know who you're talking to!"

Beatrice responded, "Shut up back there!"

Ravie ignored her, leaning forward between the front seats. "Why do you think she has such an adorable new car?"

"Why?" I asked.

"Totaled the last one," revealed Ravie teasingly.

"Not my fault!" protested Beatrice with a nonchalant attitude. She waved her hand in the air, dismissing Ravie's comment. She placed both hands on the steering wheel and pulled onto the main street

Ravie explained, "Beatrice claims a big dog jumped in front of her car and caused her to swerve and hit a tree. Kane thinks the tree jumped out in front of her. I think she was putting on her makeup and decided to blame some poor dog."

"Whatever!" laughed Beatrice.

"Did the dog live?" I asked. Although I never owned a dog, I always wanted one.

"I don't know," Beatrice revealed. "After the accident, for a few minutes, it was lying in the road. Then, all of a sudden, it just got up and ran away."

"Maybe you just knocked it a little silly," said Ravie.

"I guess," replied Beatrice, "I'm glad it ran because it was huge!" Sitting beside her, I noticed she was gripping the steering wheel very tightly.

"Did you get out of the car?" asked Ravie.

"Hell, no! Not with that wolf-dog running around out there. It was late and dark. No one else was on the road. I wasn't hurt, so I just called the police and waited until they came."

"Sounds like a werewolf story, like the cheesy ones you see in the middle of the night on AMC," said Ravie."

I knew I saw that one with Mom. I think Jack Nicholson was the werewolf.

"You know it," replied Beatrice. "If I was getting out of that car, it was going to be with a cop with a gun."

"Full of silver bullets," I added.

"For sure!" Beatrice laughed.

Soon, we pulled into the parking lot of the ice rink and got out of the car. My knees were relieved. It had begun to snow lightly and the sunlight was very strange. It was completely overcast, as was usual in Pittsburgh, but the horizon around the setting sun was completely clear. The contrast lent an eerie glow to the cloud deck. It was as if I were in a tunnel and I could see the light at the end, but there was no way to reach it. I longed for that western light and silently cursed the clouds as the first shadows of twilight crept between the cars.

Oblivious to the atmosphere, Ravie asked, "How do I look?" She wore chunky heels, skinny jeans, and a tight white jacket over an even tighter blue t-shirt.

"Slutty," laughed Beatrice.

Ravie stopped in mid twirl and said, "Perfect!"

I laughed even harder. She really did look striking, but more like a model. I was amazed that Michael didn't notice her.

Chapter 12

I had never been to an ice rink before, much less a hockey game. When I entered, the first thing I noticed was a smell, kind of like plastic and sweat melded together. It was gross. The next thing I noticed was a whole lot of athletic young men. Most of them wore skates or rollerblades and some assembly of hockey equipment. They were all tall given the added height of the skates, and for the first time in my life I knew what it was like to be smaller than everyone else. I noticed suspenders holding up oversized shorts, really long socks over shin guards, helmets tucked under arms, and lots of Under Armor. Ravie looked in my direction and wiggled her eyebrows in girlish approval.

The next thing I noticed was that, even with my coat on, I was cold.

This was a huge building. Four ice rinks and one dek hockey rink were housed under one roof. Beatrice stopped at the rental counter and chatted with the girl whose job was to distribute skates. It was like the shoe rental at a bowling alley. Ravie leaned towards me and said, "Take it all in, girlfriend! You're only young for so long!"

"This is something!" I replied, scanning our surroundings.

After Beatrice finished her brief conversation, she said simply, "Canada" and pointed to her left. She knew exactly where she was going. We made our way towards the signs labeled "Canadian Rink." There were a bunch of players in Turnbull black and red gathered at the benches next to the ice. Some were lacing their skates, others taped sticks, but most of them just stood around talking.

"We're early again," said Beatrice. "Ravie just can't wait to get here to see Michael in his gear."

Ravie shuffled ahead of us and quickly corralled the dark-haired Kane. He nodded towards the locker room. She turned with a disappointed look on her face and shuffled back to us.

"Even now, we're *still* too late! He's already in there!" She gestured at the locker room.

"What do you mean, late?" asked Beatrice. The game doesn't start for a half hour!"

"That boy is obsessed," she protested. "He's meeting with the coach." She hung her head low and jutted out her lower lip in a mock pout.

"We'll see him afterwards," I said trying to make her feel better. We turned and walked past the players who were beginning to organize and make their way toward the locker room.

"Hi, Kane," Beatrice said.

"Hey," Kane nodded his head in a greeting and leaned on his hockey stick.

"Why so early, Rav? Looking for someone?" he teased. Before she could provide one of her trademark sarcastic answers, Kane stood tall, took his stick, and swatted another player on the forearm.

"Ow!" The player turned and complained loudly. "What was that for butthole?" It was Gabriel. He shook the sting from his arm and winced dramatically.

Kane grinned and gestured in our direction by cocking his head. Immediately Gabriel stopped complaining and smiled, a bit embarrassed. "Sorry ladies, I didn't know you were there. Did you come to watch Michael....oh, I mean...the game?"

Beatrice and I looked at Ravie simultaneously. "Why else do you think we'd be here?" replied Beatrice. She gestured towards Ravie with her thumb, like a hitchhiker who had been trying too long.

"What?" replied Ravie, faking innocence. "I'm just supporting the team!"

Gabriel turned toward me. Beatrice and Ravie continued their superficial conversation with Kane. He looked down at me with those stunningly clear, blue eyes. "Um...do you like to skate?" he asked awkwardly. Gabriel looked even more handsome than he did in school. He wore a black Under Armor shirt. I could see every muscle flex and stretch when he moved. Thick, black suspenders held up padded shorts. He had his jersey draped across the back of his neck.

"No," I replied honestly. "I've never been anywhere like this."

"Don't they have ice skating in Texas?' he asked. I had to really look up to meet Gabriel's gaze with my own. The skates must have added two inches to his already substantial height.

"They do," I replied. "They just don't have much hockey. I think Dallas has a team but no one really cares."

"Yeah...the old North Stars. That's too bad," he said. "Never should have moved."

I wanted to add, "Me too!" but I decided to keep that comment to myself. I didn't want him to take it the wrong way.

"Haven't you ever been skating?" He shifted on his skates and I glanced down at his feet. Those skates must have been made for hockey because the blades were so thick.

"No, never." I replied.

"Ever?"

"Ever."

"That's just all kinds of wrong." More of his teammates had made their way to the locker room and Gabriel looked around with a sense of urgency. "We have to go," he looked at me hopefully. "Will you be here after the game?"

"I can't promise because I'm not driving, but I bet we will be," I gestured toward Ravie.

'You will," he agreed. "She does this every game. Promise you won't leave." He turned with his smile and strode quickly to the locker room.

"I'll try!" I called after him. I instantly worried he would take that comment as a desperate one. I walked to where Ravie and Beatrice were standing. I was so self-conscious!

"Let's go sit down," said Ravie. "I love the part where they come out and skate in circles."

"The warm-up?" I asked.

"I'm already pretty warm," joked Ravie fluttering her hand as if it were a ladies' fan.

We walked through a scuffed plexi-glass door and into the rink area. It was even colder in here, so I was glad I had my coat.

I pulled it about me and buttoned the front. We took seats in the third row of about twenty risers. There were several other groups sitting to watch the game. I recognized some of the kids from school, and I assumed most of the adults were parents.

I had never watched hockey before, and I found it absolutely fascinating. It was the way they skated. I marveled at the years of practice they dedicated to perform something that looked so natural. I felt like I could just go out there with them and race, planting my jagged toe blades in the smooth ice and pumping my legs faster and faster. Even in my mind, it was quite a rush, almost like flying, going faster than I could ever imagine on my own legs, faster than anyone could run.

As I sat and watched, Beatrice tried to explain the rules. After a while, I thought I understood them pretty well, but I struggled a little with icing and line configurations. By the end of the game, I got most of it. Beatrice told me that Michael was a center on the first line, and Kane and Gabriel were wingers on that same line. That was part of the reason they were such good friends.

Before I could breathe, the game was over. We sat on the bleachers and waited. It took them a long time to come out since they had to shower and pack up all that equipment in those huge bags. Apparently, ice time was at a premium and we had already sat through part of another game. Beatrice told me sometimes games were scheduled after midnight on weekends. I guess you had to really love to play to be up for that.

The team filed out of the locker room. Kane, Gabriel, and Michael came out last. Immediately, Gabriel noticed us standing off to the side. He smiled slightly, waved coolly, and motioned for his friends to follow. Gabriel came straight toward me with a big smile. Ravie and Beatrice managed to intercept Michael and Kane just a few steps outside the locker room doors. I focused on Gabriel like a ray of sunshine piercing through gray, winter clouds. His blonde hair was still a little wet and he had an enormous equipment bag slung across his shoulder. He wore black jogging pants and a red Turnbull fleece. He saw me and cam over.

"So who won?" I asked.

Gabriel looked surprised. "Did you watch the game?" he asked, trying his best to mask his disappointment.

"Yeah," I gave in. "I'm just kidding. Congratulations!"

He laughed. "You had me going! Seriously, did you like it?"

"Yeah," I replied honestly. "I really did." Especially when he played, but I wasn't ready to tell him that. "I didn't quite get all of the calls and penalties yet, but I'm working on it."

"Yeah, some of our guys take an extreme amount of penalty minutes." He gestured towards Kane with his stick. "That idiot racked up eight minutes all by himself."

Kane saw that Gabriel and I were talking about him, so he strolled over to join the conversation. "Seems to me, I might be the subject here," he stated. I was surprised Kane was so animated after playing such a physical game and even instigating a fight.

"Trinity doesn't know much about hockey," said Gabriel, "so I was using you for an example...boarding, high sticking...the list goes on and on."

"Sure does!" replied Kane proudly. "I have to fight all your battles." He leaned towards me. "Doctor Hockey here can't do it himself."

Gabriel laughed and pushed Kane jokingly, then redirected his attention towards me. He pinched his chin with his index finger and thumb as if he were thinking deeply. "Zo, youf never been on skates...korreckt?" He used a ridiculously bad imitation of a German psychiatrist's accent.

I giggled at his silliness, "You got it."

"Gut," He grinned playfully. "Vee vill haf to get you some." He bent to look at my feet. "Size acht?"

"Neun." My stupid big feet! "I'll just fall down though," I replied. I noticed my heart was pounding in my throat. Just talking to Gabriel made me all excited and blushy.

"Ef you fall, I vill pick you up..." he paused thoughtfully.

I laughed. I hadn't known Gabriel a long time, but I felt like he had been around my whole life. I felt a little flirty, which was really unusual for me, but Gabriel wasn't the usual guy. "I think

I'd like that." I said. "But I have to warn you, I'm a complete clod!"

"Impossible," he responded with a chuckle. He leaned on his hockey stick thoughtfully. "Not you!"

"Yup, me! Believe it or not!"

With no warning, Kane whacked Gabriel on the forearm again. "Ow!" He jumped with surprise and shook off the sting again as well as the silly accent. "You're such a jerk," he laughed. "I'm going to deck you!"

""I'm scared," laughed Kane. "Come on, we gotta go."

I glanced toward Beatrice and Ravie. They stood with Michael by the exit. "Oh, I have to go too!" I said.

"I can't believe you got in the car with her," he joked shaking his head as we walked toward the door. "I'll have to let you in on her driving record sometime!"

"I heard," I laughed. "Ravie told me."

As a group we proceeded through the double glass doors into the parking lot. Wisps of snow curled lovingly around our feet. Gabriel, Michael and Kane carried their equipment bags and plodded towards their car like giant turtles.

Gabriel called back over his shoulder, "You're a lot braver than you let on!"

We walked towards Beatrice's yellow beetle. She popped the locks with her key fob and we all clambered in, eager to get out of the frigid night. Beatrice and Ravie were on me within seconds. "What was that all about?" demanded Beatrice. She started the car and turned the heat on full blast.

"Oh my gosh!" Ravie sported a huge smile brimming with questions.

"What?" I asked, trying to hide my own excitement.

"Gabriel is hot!" said Beatrice. "Every girl has had a crush on him at one time or another, but he's never dated anyone at Turnbull! Well, not until now!"

"Ooh…this is so exciting!" added Ravie.

"Oh, I'm sure he's just trying to be nice to the new girl," I said.

"No, no, no…Gabriel is nice to everyone. This seems like…it's a little more," stated Ravie matter-of-factly.

"For sure," Beatrice chimed in. She also sported a knowing smile. "He is hot and the best part is he likes you." Beatrice and Ravie quickly came down with a case of the giggles.

"Gossip time!" Ravie announced excitedly. "So what do you think of him?" Both girls turned and eagerly awaited my response.

I sighed. "He is awfully nice."

"And hot!" replied Beatrice.

"Yeah," I agreed.

"Do you want to know a little about him?" asked Ravie. I must have looked surprised because she quickly added, "Don't worry, nothing bad!"

"Sure." I really wanted to hear more about Gabriel, and I hoped it was all good.

She continued, "He came here in the middle of our sophomore year. Like us, he moved here from out of state, I think...Tennessee...Memphis?" Ravie glanced at Beatrice. "Help me out here."

Beatrice nodded and picked up right where Ravie left off. "He was kind of quiet for a while, but he found his way pretty quickly. As soon as he met Michael, they started to play hockey and everything just clicked for him. Now, he's probably the most likeable guy in the school. I hate to use the word "popular" because he wouldn't like that. Plus, everyone adores him. He always knows just what to say, just how to act, and most importantly, just what to wear." She continued, "He and Michael were really tight from the beginning."

"Soon after," added Ravie, "he started hanging out with Kane too. We all got together as a group about six months ago."

Beatrice nodded her head in agreement.

I thought for a moment. "So, Beatrice, Gabe, Michael and I all just came here within the past year?" It seemed odd that four of the six of us were fairly new to the area.

"It's not unusual though. There are always kids coming and going from Turnbull."

"It's a place that's always in demand," added Ravie. "It took me two interviews just to get accepted there. I'm just not the brightest bulb."

"Ain't that the truth!" Beatrice laughed.

"Pay attention to the road up there!" Ravie joked. "Plus, some kids can't make the grade and they are released or they drop out."

"But there's never an empty seat, right?" I asked.

"You got it," Beatrice replied.

We drove to my house first. Beatrice pulled to the curb and we chatted and joked for a while. Eventually, I excused myself into the cold, night air. It was close to midnight.

Dad was sleeping on the couch, so I turned off the television and covered him with a blanket. I tiptoed into my room and slipped into my pajamas. Although I was tired, I thought deeply about my new friends, especially Gabriel. Why did such a handsome, wonderful guy like me? I was so tired-looking, non-descript. I could picture him with someone beautiful like Ravie, or someone adorable like Beatrice...but not with ordinary, average me.

I wished I could lie in my bed like a normal teenage girl and dream about a very interesting, very attractive boy, but I was clearly not normal.

Plus...thoughts of Pittsburgh kept distracting me. It was such a strange place, so dark and so cold, but it wasn't just the temperatures or sunlight of late fall. It was the whole atmosphere of the city that possessed a chill. Every place, from Turnbull Prep to the grocery store to my own apartment had an eerie feeling about it...unwelcoming...callous. The only place I enjoyed was the coffee shop down the street...it had a corny name, *Hava Java*...or maybe it was just the caffeine that warmed me up and kept me going. Once again, I thought it was strange that most of my friends arrived here only recently, almost like Pittsburgh was beckoning them.

Chapter 13

Over the next few weeks, I spent a lot of time with my new friends, particularly Ravie. Anyone could instantly see she went well beyond very pretty. She was slender and tall with a graceful jaw-line, gently arched eyebrows and full lips. With her perfect model-like posture, she carried an air of confidence that commanded attention. Her designer clothing and handbags, and her devotion to style magazines and Hollywood tabloids indicated she was a slave to fashion and pop-culture. She had a new outfit practically every day that was edgy and very stylish. Sometimes it was a miniskirt, sometimes it was a ruffled blouse with long flowing trousers, and sometimes it was simply a pair of jeans and a sweater.

Although Ravie had an edgy appearance, her personality was soft and kind. We had the same love of books, reading novels almost constantly. She preferred romances and I always enjoyed a good fantasy. The day we met, we traded cell phone numbers and our conversations often lasted well past midnight.

Toward the end of my first month at Turnbull, Ravie offered me a ride home. I accepted hesitantly after a little prodding. It was awfully cold and I really didn't feel like busing it anyway. When we got to my house, I invited Ravie inside. Until now I had kept our friendship strictly at school and on the phone. Since it was obvious almost everyone at Turnbull had money, I was embarrassed to live in such a modest (and that was being kind) house.

We walked in the front door and, as usual, Dad was with Mom. We took seats on the couch and I offered Ravie a Diet Pepsi that she readily accepted. At first, I did not want to discuss the situation with my mother due to weariness on my part, yet I was sure the subject would come up...it had to at some point. I would tell everyone eventually, but I was uncertain if I was ready to do that. I didn't want my new friends to look at me like I was pathetic. I wanted them to know me for me, rather than for my sad situation they were glad not to have to experience. Then again, if they could still accept me, especially with all of my baggage, wouldn't that make everything a little easier? It was then that I suddenly decided to approach the issue of my family situation head-on, at least with Ravie. I was just going to be honest.

"Thank you for the ride," I said gratefully.

"Not at all," she replied smiling.

"Sorry about the house," I apologized. "Things have happened..."

"Why are you sorry?"

"Are you kidding?" I looked around for a moment before I spoke, immediately ashamed of my arrogance. "I guess...it's just not me."

Ravie gave the room a cursory examination. "It's better than a lot of places."

She was right. I knew I should be grateful for whatever I had. I guess it was just one more pill to swallow. If I had to swallow any more pills, I thought I'd choke.

"Anyway," I continued, "I think we need to talk. There are some things I'd like you to know...about me...about my family."

"Really?" Ravie asked. "Trinity, don't feel you have to tell me anything."

"I think it would make me feel better," I replied, hoping my words would ring true.

She nodded kindly. I think she figured there was something going on but she was too polite to ask. She waited until I was ready.

Ready to get to the point, I began. "My mother is very sick...dying, in fact, unless there is some miracle."

"Oh my gosh!" She cupped her hands over her mouth in surprise.

I swallowed hard and continued, "It's pancreatic cancer. Most people fight, but it moves quickly. We came here for an experimental treatment." I intended to tell my story in one monologue, saving any questions for later. "My dad quit his job to take care of Mom. We sold our house and many of our belongings, and what we didn't keep or donate, we put into storage. Renting this house was all we could afford."

Ravie looked surprised and sad. "If there's anything I can do to help, please tell me," she said emphatically.

"Thanks," I replied. "I really appreciate that. It's more of a waiting game though...waiting and hoping something...some treatment will work."

"This must be really terrible then," she said, "for all of you."

"It is."

"Have you told anyone else?"

"Just you," I replied. "Please keep it under wraps...just until I'm ready."

"Oh, I will...I promise." Her brow was furrowed with concern.

We sat and talked until well past sundown. Dad came home and introduced himself. He was tired, but put on his best happy face to impress my new friend. He joked halfheartedly before excusing himself to bed. He was just as glad as I that I had someone to talk to...someone my age...and someone female. After Ravie left, I did my homework sitting on the couch. It took me forever. My mind kept drifting to Mom and Ravie...and Gabriel.

Ravie was by my side almost the entire following day. I welcomed her companionship and empathy. We didn't have much time to talk, but like most good friends, we understood each other without much discussion. She rode me home again.

I had spent most of that evening in Mom's room with Dad. We were playing a game of Monopoly, which never was my favorite, and Mom was actually winning this time. Although Dad and I were dog tired, we stayed and played, happy to finally see Mom more animated and involved in the simple aspects of life, like a board game. Once Mom built a hotel on Park Place, I knew Dad and I were finished.

The move to Pittsburgh had been hard on all of us, but especially on my mom and dad. It wasn't a question of wanting to move, it was the necessity of it that hurt most. Mom was sick; she needed to be near the doctors in the city. Dad spent all of his time with her. The doctors told us not to give up hope, but I knew things didn't look so good.

Before Mom got sick, my dad was the type of man who never cried. He was too happy to waste time with tears. He was tall and handsome with a full head of dark hair. He smiled constantly and his smiles were contagious. Corny "dad" jokes were his expertise and most of them were so dumb you laughed simply at their senselessness. When he laughed really hard, he made a goofy whooping sound that made everyone laugh even harder.

If I was genetically related to my parents, I would probably be a model. Since I was adopted, I shared none of my mother's defined features, but, surprisingly, I did look a bit like my father. I had a long mop of black hair that swirled every which way. Try as I would, my hair would never stay in a ponytail, hold a curl, or otherwise look remotely attractive. I also shared Dad's blue eyes; except mine were a light color and his were quite dark. Most people thought we were really related.

With his wavy black hair and royal blue eyes, it was no wonder a lot of people said Dad looked like Superman. I watched the old movie once when Lois Lane died in a rockslide. Superman flew so fast around the Earth that he turned back time and saved her from a crushing death. Maybe that could save someone from a rockslide or car accident, but even if Dad was Superman, I still don't think he could save Mom from cancer.

Mom was a more serious type of person than Dad. She was very sweet and overly kind, but when she wanted to be funny, sarcasm was her game. I think her sense of humor was why she got along so well with Dad. Mom was very pretty, on the slender side, with thick brown hair she always held back in an untidy ponytail. Her messy hair contrasted with the graceful lines of her face. She had the defined jawline of a model and her skin was silky smooth. She was quiet and kind; a stark contrast to Dad, but his perfect match. She laughed at every one of his dumb jokes.

The highlight of the evening was seeing Mom and Dad joking around, trading jibes, like they used to. Mom's sarcasm was razor sharp and Dad's corniness was popping! The evening with my parents took me closer to the way things used to be before our lives were all turned upside-down. It wasn't until after 11 when she sent us home, not without a pang of regret. Dad and I continued our silliness all the way home, joking and laughing. It was good to laugh with my Dad, but our conversation still felt empty without Mom.

When we got home, we said our good nights and I crawled into bed without even changing into my nightgown. I lay on my back, too tired to sleep, lost in my own thoughts of Mom, Dad, and the evening. I tossed and turned, trying to find a comfortable position and soon I noticed something was pulsing against my hipbone. I reached into my front jeans pocket and pulled out my cell phone.

I had a text message:

T- cu2nit @ B's apt 7p?

I glanced at my alarm clock and saw it was already 11:37. I missed Ravie's message, but decided to text her anyway. I punched in the letters, awkward with sleep.

w mom c u 2morro. sry.

Chapter 14

The next morning I awoke before the sun. I had a nightmare, and it came back in a flood of sickening warmth. I was wet with sweat and my heart was pounding.

In this one I was in a dark, cold forest, a 'boreal" forest I think they are called. It was the type of forest you would find in Colorado or Alaska. The woods were dark and fragrant with pine trees, so thick a peek of the sky was rare. An occasional deciduous tree spat leaves upon me as I passed. It was nearing twilight on an autumn day and I, of course, was lost…

I was running. Something I knew I should never do if I was lost in a forest, but there was no time to wait for rescue. With night coming, I had to keep moving, an unknown sense of urgency pushing me. There was so much at stake. I made my own path, too pressed to take the time to search for an existing one. The heavy scent of pine was cloying, almost gagging. My feet became tangled in scrub bushes and thorny weeds slapped at my shins. My pants were torn below the knee, providing me very little protection.

Being lost wasn't my only problem; I soon realized something was following me, tracking me. Although I couldn't see them, I could hear them…muffled barks, bodies crashing through thickets causing the tall grasses to rustle and hiss. I imagined them… spittle flying, eyes rolling, tongues lolling, fur bristling with anticipation. They were the wolves…the wolves from the wall carving at school…the foxhunt…and they were loose!

I tried to find somewhere to hide, but there was nowhere to go! My scent was thick in their muzzles. In this forest, there was no hiding. They would find me if I hunkered in some thicket, and the tree limbs were too far off the ground to climb! I had to keep running…and praying even though I had given up on God long ago.

I recalled the wild look in the eyes of the wolves, and even more clearly I felt the fear in the faces of the handlers. The hair on my arms prickled as I ran. I was cold with sweat, and light was fading. I scrambled, looking for a tree to climb or something that would come to my rescue...nothing!

Now I could hear them panting! I pumped my legs harder. My lungs burned! I couldn't keep this up much longer. Suddenly I tripped but quickly regained my footing using my fingertips to steady my sprawl.

Daring to turn my head, I could see them! Shadows in the deepening gloom running between the trees. Their eyes were locked on me; a hundred eyes, yellow with fixed determination, lighting up the darkness. What kind of animals were these? I kept running. One was now off to my left about 20 yards. I looked at him as I ran, and he bounded playfully, like an enormous puppy, knowing he could be upon me in a few seconds.

Then something unspeakable happened! The wolf began to change...to transform! As he ran, his bounds became awkward. He stretched his neck, raised his face to the sky, and howled. His muzzle began to shrink and his gait became a little slower. I looked ahead, determined to make his error my gain. Panic, or adrenaline, seeped into my blood. What would he become? What could be worse?

I looked back cautiously; just in time to see the wolf go from four legs to two...he was now running on his hind legs! His muscular arms moved rhythmically with each footfall. He sped up, hurdling over small bushes like an Olympian, running diagonally toward me now. It was the silhouette of a human...a large man to be exact. He was running so fast, narrowing the gap between us. In no time I heard his panting behind me. He uttered a low growl, deep in his throat that was anything but human. Then I felt his hot breath on my neck. I tried... I tried...but I could run no faster! The ground rushed up and I sprawled face-first into the dirt. I was twisted around violently by strong hands gripping my shirt and hair.

Now I faced the sky. My chest heaved. Sweat mixed with tears ran down the sides of my face and around my ears. A figure entered my field of view. He was human and his face was mercifully hidden in shadow, but like the dogs, his eyes shone yellow. He leaned towards me; his features became clearer in the deep twilight. I knew him! Those perfect features were unmistakable! A confident smile curled across his lips…Kane!

"Trinity," he said. His voice was deep, almost a whisper. "I've been looking for you for so long. We *all* have been searching." He grabbed me by my hair, yanking me to my feet. He spun me around towards the other dogs. "Look!"

I gazed across the dimly lit clearing, and I saw the shadows of many other dogs, but that wasn't what caused my breath to hitch. At first it was the smell, familiar and coppery. I could almost taste the blood. Suddenly it became clear. The men…the men from the hunting scene on the door…all being slaughtered. Blood coursed across the ground and several of the wolves lapped at it eagerly. Even in the deepening twilight, I saw that a few of the men had their throats viciously torn. The wolves were attacking others who were not dead yet and they struggled and moaned. Drying gore spattered everything.

Kane pulled my head backward. I shut my eyes, unable to take any more. My head pounded with Kane's control, but I tried to twist away from the scene.

"Aw, Trin," Kane complained, "take a peek."

"No!" I replied through clenched teeth. I wasn't going to give him any satisfaction. I shut my eyes tightly and winced.

"But we did it all for you!" I pulled at his fingers with my hands, hoping for some relief from his grip on my hair. "Open your eyes, or I will pull it all out!" he growled. He jerked my head again, showing me his power.

Suddenly, He shoved me to the ground so cruelly my back began to spasm in waves of pain. "Trinity I swear this won't hurt…" He squatted next to me. Reaching with clawed human hands, he gently wiped the muddy tear mixture from my cheeks. I looked into his yellow eyes. Huge teeth peeked behind his perfectly shaped lips. He leaned toward me and twisted his claws into my hair once again, wrenching my head backward. I swung with my forearm in desperation, and I hit him swiftly in the side of the head. I reached and tore at those once-perfect features that came too close.

"This is going to hurt a little," he whispered. He grasped my wrists with his free hand and pinned them to the ground above my head. He squeezed them until I gasped, unable to bear the pain. Blood ran down his neck where my nails had found a target.

As he leaned over me, he opened his mouth. It gaped and stretched unnaturally to accommodate all of those teeth. He intended to feed. I squirmed, trying desperately to loosen his grip…losing hope…turning my face towards the woods, closing my eyes…I screamed, able to bear no more! I screamed and screamed myself awake.

Chapter 15

I took the earliest bus to school the next morning, not able to shake that awful nightmare. I had so many questions. Why Kane? I thought of Gabriel constantly, but Kane owned my nightmares. What did this mean? Why were my dreams so vivid again since I got here? For years, I kept them under control, but they were coming back. Should I tell Ravie? I didn't want my new friends to think I was a whack. Heck I didn't even tell anyone but Ravie about Mom yet. On the other hand, they seemed so understanding and friendly. I felt I had to talk to Ravie.

Before I knew it, I was close to my stop. It was so early, the sun hadn't come up yet, and I started to second guess leaving so early. It was too late to change my mind, so I got off the bus and stared at Turnbull. It stood tall and threatening in front of me, a stone titan with huge arched windows for eyes, the portico was a gaping hole of a mouth. A drape was pulled across the right eye, making it look like the building was winking at me. I walked up the steps and through the iron portal. I knew I had to find Kane today, right away. I wanted to make sure last night was really just a dream. I wanted to make sure he was okay.

Kane was one of those people who was so handsome; you couldn't stop looking at him. Sometimes it's the eyes or the shape of the face or the perfection of a nose that makes people attractive, but Kane was different. No matter how hard I tried, I couldn't pick out one feature that stood above the others. Then I realized what it was. Kane was perfect. He didn't even have a single blemish or birthmark. His skin looked milky smooth and he was clean-shaven. The lines of his face curved into a square jaw line enjoyed only by models and movie stars.

All of the girls thought he was hot, but he never dated anyone. Most of the time he was really friendly, but other times he seemed aloof and removed. Only a few times I had seen the icy side to his personality and a penchant for trouble. I overheard people talking about some issue Kane got into a few years ago, but it was never mentioned during any of our conversations.

When things weren't going his way, he wouldn't show up at school, sometimes for days at a time. Gabriel told me once that Kane's family life was pretty much non-existent, and that his parents kicked him out on a regular basis. When this happened, he had an open invite at Gabriel's house. During these times no one would approach him except Gabriel. His mood was brooding, quiet and ominous, like a distant storm. When he was in one of these dark moods, everyone seemed to notice instantly and gave him his space. I wondered how he paid for private school with a family who didn't care about him. Maybe he had a scholarship like me. I wondered, with all of his troubles, how he managed to not get kicked out of Turnbull. I made a mental note to ask Ravie.

Deciding stress was giving me a headache, I continued inside. Pausing at the door labeled "COUNSELOR". I considered stopping to reveal my dream issues, but quickly changed my mind. All they would do is call my dad and advise him to have me see a therapist to work out my anxieties with Mom's situation. I decided it was exponentially better to just keep walking and keep my mouth shut.

I entered the Gathering Hall really early for me and decided to hit the books to try to get my mind on track. Although studying came easy, I didn't want to fall behind, and I wanted to take my mind off of everything. There were only a few people in the building at such an early hour, but I did recognize one figure sitting at the long tables. It was Michael.

Michael was big, quiet and friendly...the brother I never had. He always had a kind word, but didn't offer up much information. He read a lot, always having a book tucked under his arm. I knew he was pretty smart too. No one could read that much and not be intelligent. Funny thing was I never saw the same book twice. Sometimes it was a classic; sometimes it was a sci-fi, sometimes history, and sometimes just a comic book.

With Michael, what you saw was what you got. I was a little hesitant to joke around with him at first because he was so quiet, nothing like Kane and Gabriel, but I soon realized he was just sweet. Ravie told me, in one of our many conversations, that Michael was one of the most penalized players in the hockey league, but I couldn't see him actually hurting someone; he seemed too kind. I approached his table as he sat hunched, pouring over some thick novel.

"Hey," I said in a hushed tone not wanting to startle him.

He looked up from his book. A soft smile crossed his lips. No wonder Ravie liked him.

"Trinity," he responded. "Why so early?"

I thought I'd reveal a little but decided not to. "Couldn't sleep," I said nonchalantly. "I decided to come in to study. How about you?"

"Early ice time," he replied. "Five o'clock. I decided to just drive myself here afterwards. Gabriel and Kane are still at the rink. They wanted to get in another skate."

"They seem so competitive. I'm sure they're trying to see who's the fastest."

Michael nodded, "You got that right!"

"Well," I said, "we can gossip a little or study for chemistry."

"Although I am a manly man," Michael joked, "I vote for gossip. I never study...unless you want to..." he added awkwardly.

"I hardly ever study either."

"I knew it," Michael responded. "I knew you were smart. I could see it in your eyes." He leaned back in his chair and folded his hands behind his head.

"What do you mean by that?"

"I can tell whether a person is smart or not just by looking into their eyes. I watch the expressions on their face to see how they answer a question or solve a problem, and usually, I am pretty accurate." He leaned back further and perched his huge feet on the table.

"Is this something you thought up?" I asked.

"Yup."

"Any scientific basis?"

"Nope."

“Figures. I think you just might be the smartest person here,” I joked with a hint of seriousness.

“Likely,” he replied, continuing my joke.

“Like I said, smart...and modest.”

Michael’s laughter broke through the silence that blanketed the room. “So, I’m still trying to figure you out,” he said. “I already decided you’re smart, but there’s something else. Something’s bothering you. You’re not letting us see who you really are. I’m curious to know what you’re hiding.”

He was good! “I guess it’s that I am pretty shy,” I responded with as much confidence as I could muster. “I’m not the easiest person to get to know.

“Nah,” Michael said. “It’s more than that.” He waited for an answer that never came. “But save it for another time. I don’t want to make you talk about something that you don’t want to.”

I was relieved. The conversation was getting a little uncomfortable. Michael did have an uncanny ability to read people, or was it just that I wore my emotions like a front-page headline?

“So when we’re not here, what do you like to do?” he asked. He shifted his feet to the floor and folded his hands on the table. He looked ready to listen.

“Well, I like to paint, I like to water-ski, and I like to read.”

“Water-ski?” Michael exclaimed. “No water around here ‘cept the frozen kind. We’ll have to get you on the ice someday. Ever been ice skating?”

“Not that much ice in Amarillo, but I think I went once when I was really little.” I decided to shift the conversation away from me. “What are you reading now?” I asked pointing at his novel.

“Dr. Jekyll and Mr. Hyde.”

“I read that!” I exclaimed. “I loved that book!”

“I don’t think I ever met anyone who has read this book before,” Michael responded. "People have heard of it – you know, the Hulk and all - but never actually *read* it."

Is this your first time reading it?” I asked.

“Nah, third. I am convinced Jekyll was a werewolf."

Chapter 16

Before I could decide whether Michael's reading choice was simply coincidence or something greater, someone spoke in the large room.

"HELLLOO!" It was Gabriel

"Hey!" Michael replied.

Gabriel came toward our table. "Did you see that game last night? Holy hell!" He gently rubbed my shoulder in a friendly greeting and took the seat next to me on the bench.

"I know! Man that shootout...five rounds!"

I had no idea what they were talking about. I still wasn't even sure if Texas still had a hockey team.

"Get out the polish...the cup is coming home!" Gabriel exclaimed.

"Man, the things I'd do if I ever got my day with that thing," said Michael.

"You will! And when you do, I'm coming over," replied Gabriel. "I got some ideas of my own..." He stroked his chin with his thumb and index finger in that pinching gesture.

"Enough!" I chimed in, fingers jokingly plugging my ears. "I really don't want to hear the perverted dreams of a couple of teenage boys."

"Well, we had no intention of leaving you out," said Gabriel slyly.

Gabriel was the glue that held the group together. Like Beatrice, he was friendly and silly, but not in a dingbat kind of way. He was a jokester, outgoing and gregarious...and gorgeous. I was attracted to him immediately, with his sly smile and his love of jokes. Once I heard Michael call him towheaded. Fortunately I knew that wasn't an insult, rather it was an older term that just meant really, really blonde. He played hockey every day and spent a lot of time after school in the weight room. Gabriel dressed stylishly, but it seemed natural to him, not forced at all. He didn't mince words, but no one minded his honesty. At times it was brutal and eye-opening, but for some reason, everyone respected an opinion when it came from him. Gabriel, hid nothing simply because there was nothing to hide. I don't think I had ever met someone so genuine in all my life. Just sitting next to Gabriel sent chills up my spine. I was beginning to have quite a crush on him.

"So we're going to Beatrice's tonight," Gabriel said to both of us. "Are you guys coming?"

Michael replied, "I'll be there."

They turned their attention to me, awaiting a response.

"I'd love to," I stammered, surprised. "But...where is it?"

Gabriel thought for a moment then said, "I'll pick you up, it will be easier than explaining how to get there...around six-thirty? Where do you live?"

"I can just meet you there," I said. I didn't want Gabriel to pick me up at my house. I was embarrassed to live in such a modest place, when I heard his was so spectacular. From what Ravie told me, he had the run of an ancient home in the east end of the city that used to belong to some banking millionaire. Gabriel's parents died a long time ago and he was raised by his uncle who left him a ton of money and a substantial art collection when he died.

"I insist," he said. "It will be so much easier."

"Come on, Trinity," laughed Michael. "We won't even call it a date!"

"Very funny, Michael!" I couldn't help but grin, then I had an idea. I'd have Gabriel meet me at the coffee shop on the corner. "Meet me at Hava Java's," I replied. "I'm going to study there after school anyway."

"On a Friday?" asked Michael questioningly.

"Great!" said Gabriel ignoring Michael's comment.

"Hi guys!" said a voice above us. I looked and it was Ravie. She nudged me into Gabriel to make herself a space on the end of the bench. I didn't mind at all. "What's this? A meeting of the minds?"

"Spike!" joked Gabriel. "Glad to see you so early!" He always teased her about her short hair.

"Shut up," she laughed. Ravie had a propensity for lateness, probably because it took her so long to get ready.

"You coming to Beatrice's?" she whispered to me. "You have to come this time."

"I think so," I answered.

"I got your message. Everything okay?" Ravie looked concerned. She mouthed, "Mom?"

"Oh, yeah," I replied leaning closely toward her. "She's really good. She was doing great last night." I left out the part about my dream. "I'm going to stop after school, then meet Gabriel to come over."

"Friday night! Gabe is picking you up? It's a date?"

"No, it's not," I replied, "just a ride. Dates can come later."

"Fair enough." Ravie shifted away and leaned back into the conversation.

After a while, we heard the bell chime. It was time to move to class.

After school that day I made a trip to visit Mom. She looked exhausted, but she perked up when I told her I was going to Beatrice's house with a bunch of other kids from school. Dad was still at home, so I decided to make the most of my Mom time.

"I am so glad this situation is improving for you," she said. Her eyes were ringed with weariness and she looked old and too thin.

"I just want to get you out of here and go home," I replied, then added, "I wish it were improving for you."

"Soon, honey. Just know that even if I come home, we'll be here with the doctors for quite some time."

"Don't say if," I said, "say when."

She ignored my comment and continued, "I know you miss your old friends and school, but it means so much to me that you are making friends here as well."

"Trying my best!" I said with a smile.

"Thank you...you don't know how much," she replied.

"By the way," she continued, "I've been dreaming about you lately. Is everything okay?"

My heart leapt into my throat where it fluttered uncontrollably. "Yes. I promise I'm fine, but what am I doing in your dreams?" I asked hesitantly, not wanting to hear her answer.

"I'm not really sure," she said. "In most of them you're hiding, like you always loved to when you were a kid. Except in these dreams you are hiding, and I can't find you. No matter where I look, you're nowhere to be found. After looking for some time, I get worried, as all parents do. I start to panic. I start tearing up the house, looking under beds in closets, even tearing drawers apart, looking for you." She continued, "The really weird thing is the whole time I am calling your name, I can't hear you answer. There is too much noise. That's when I wake up."

I coughed, half expecting my heart to leap out of my mouth and land on the bed. I imagined it flopping on the white sheets… bloody…beating.

"What's the noise?" I dared to ask.

"Well, I didn't know the first couple of times I had the dream. It bothered me a little until last night. I finally figured it out.

"So what was it?" I asked.

She replied, "Dogs…howling."

Chapter 17

My visit to Mom was short. I needed to be alone to think about things anyway, so I didn't argue when she insisted I leave, to go be with my friends. Dad was due to come keep her company anyway and with no treatments scheduled for the rest of the day; I figured they could use some alone time.

I walked to Hava Java's. I was supposed to meet Gabriel there at 6:30. I looked at my watch. It was only 4:30.

I decided to stop at home first. When I got there, I reluctantly walked to my room and looked longingly at my paint box sitting at the bottom of the bed. I actually considered blowing everyone off to stay home and paint. I quickly pushed that stupid notion out of my mind. I changed and freshened up. By the time I got to the coffee shop, it was 5:15

To my surprise, Ravie was sitting at a table. I walked over and stood across from her.

She smiled, "I was hoping I'd find you here. You never get my texts."

"Sorry, I turn my phone off at the hospital and I always forget to turn it back on." I slid out of my coat. "What's up?"

"Oh nothing," she said. "I just thought you could use some company. You have a new city, new family situations, new friends...it has to be difficult."

"I guess it is hard," I replied, draping my coat over the back of the chair. I sat down. "I just never stop to think too much."

"Please let me know if I can help, even if you just need some company," she looked concerned.

"Thanks." I replied sincerely. "I appreciate that."

"Okay, so don't worry. I brought my car and I'll be long gone before 6:30." She pulled a mirror from her purse and checked her hair.

"No big deal," I said. "You should stay."

'No way! I don't want to mooch in on your date."

"Not a date."

"Oh, come on!" she said. "He's in love with you!"

"With me?" I exclaimed. "Give me a break! We just met a few weeks ago!"

"Check it out," she said. "Ever since day one, he's been so protective. He doesn't even give any other girls a fraction of the attention he gives you."

"It's just because I'm new, and he's so outgoing."

"Nope," she replied. "I've known him for almost a year and he likes you! Anyway, you're perfect for him. He's a little outgoing and goofy, and you're more introverted and reserved. It's yin and yang!"

I blushed uncomfortably. "So which am I, yin or yang?"

"Definitely yin!" she replied. "Just leave Gabriel's yang alone! You just met him!"

I looked at her, disbelieving, and burst into laughter.

"A guy like him would never date someone like me," I sighed. "I barely even get a brush through my hair every morning. Sometimes I'm so tired."

Ravie looked at me, "Seriously?" She dropped he hands on the table dramatically.

"Completely. I am ordinary...nothing special...nothing to write home about."

"Shut up!" she took my hand and stuck her compact into it. Look at yourself, you're absolutely beautiful!" She spoke sternly. "Your black hair and your skin are like your own yin and yang! Now look at yourself!" she demanded. "Mirror…mirror…" Ravie gestured toward the compact in my hand with an accusing finger and a determined glare. "Open it and look!"

I looked at the compact. In gold script letters across the top it read *Sephora.*

Ravie," I responded, "I know I have my problems, but don't build me up like that! I look like a scared zombie every time I glance into a mirror."

"What?" she squeaked in disbelief. "A damn zombie! What are you talking about? I would love to have your looks!" she said. "Now open that compact!"

I snapped open the oversized, overpriced, plastic disc and looked at myself, still unconvinced. My eyes were a bright, clear blue color, like the color of a Tiffany box. I was always proud of my eyes. They were slanted upwards slightly, giving my face a look of liveliness, even though I felt dog tired. My nose was on the small side and I noticed for the first time that it was perfectly straight. My jaw line was smooth and clearly defined. It delicately cradled my chin and curled to my cheekbones that were quite high and rosy, providing a sharp contrast to my ice blue eyes. The slightly dark circles around my eyes gave me a haunted but not unattractive, quality.

Too bad we can't Freaky Friday ourselves!" I exclaimed with a forgiving grin.

"For real!" she laughed. "I would love if a hot guy, or any guy for that matter, had a crush on me!"

"Thank you," I said closing the compact and handing it back to Ravie. "I still don't believe you, but I guess I do need a little work on my self-esteem."

She smiled and tucked it back into her purse, "You look like Snow White, and you don't even know it!"

"Sorry,"

"Now, listen, they're all great guys, but Gabriel's got that spark...that confidence," she explained. "Just about every girl at school has a crush on him, whether they realize it or not."

"Well," I revealed, "Don't get me wrong, I really like Gabriel, and Michael is about the nicest guy I ever met...but I can't quite get a line on Kane." I paused. "What's his story?" I wanted to know how he fit into my dreams...why Kane?

"That, my friend, is a very hard thing to do," she sighed. "Kane.... underneath all those good looks is a boy who is too smart for his own good sometimes."

"What do you mean?" I asked.

"Well, he never leaves well enough alone. He is always up to something."

"Like what?"

"It's hard to explain," she said. "He's a pretty complex character. Sometimes he's in school, sometimes he isn't. He just doesn't seem to care. We're so close to college courses and he has to chance it." She thought for a moment then continued, "I guess he just likes to take everything to the limit…to see how far he can push something before it breaks."

"I didn't mean to pry, but how does he manage to stay enrolled in such a demanding school?"

"Actually, I think it's a combination of his personality and his limited work ethic. He just does enough to squeak by. His good looks and charm get him the rest of the way. He is a hard one to nail down."

"I don't know how to say this," I began, "but he scares me a little. I just don't know why."

"He never used to be that way. He was never moody or quiet like he is now. Just lately, he's been getting into some stuff…not anything bad…just…I don't know." She paused, "It's just he needs to slow down and stop questioning everything. He's so intense," she sighed and shrugged. "He's into something," she continued, "but I can't get up the guts to ask him exactly what is going on. To add to everything, Kane is Gabriel's best friend, so I'm sure Gabriel knows the whole story, but he'd never talk. "

"I saw they got along very well." I revealed. "I also noticed they're very competitive, at least with each other."

"They've been best friends since the tenth grade," she said. "Things have changed a lot since then, except their friendship. It's almost like they're brothers."

We ordered some snacks and talked while we ate. Soon it was 6:00 and Ravie got up to leave. She threw a fifty on the table.

"Don't resist," she said. "You needed a good meal, and what better than one a friend shared with you."

I didn't argue that point. How could I? "Thank you, and it's my turn next time."

"For sure!"

Chapter 18

I waited on pins and needles for Gabriel. Now I knew he liked me, and I was full of anticipation for the evening. I dated a few guys in Texas, but nothing serious. I could see Gabriel lasting a while longer, quite a while. As was my nervous nature, I thought I was jilted at just 32 minutes after six. I thought of poor Miss Havisham from Dickens' *Great Expectations*. I imagined myself wearing my wedding dress and guarding my wedding cake for 50 plus years. Maybe I just read way too much. Just in case Gabriel did show up, I tried to look nonchalant by sticking my nose in a book while I slowly sipped a cup of expensive tea.

My mind wandered, but kept touching on Mom's dreams. I refused to ruin my evening by thinking about it too much. I recited multiplication tables, mentally went through a list of linking verbs my sixth grade teacher set to music. I even tried to name the capital of each state. That tangled me up enough to get my mind off things. I was never very good at capitals.

At precisely 40 minutes past six, Gabriel walked through the door. I pretended to be absorbed in my magazine. Heck, I didn't even know what I was pretending to read. Gabriel took the seat across from me. I looked up and smiled my best smile.

"Hi!" he grinned. His blue eyes made him look young, charming, and irresistible.

"Thanks for picking me up."

"Anytime," he said. "Seriously, sorry I'm late. Have you been waiting very long?"

I smiled and lied, "No, I was studying and lost track of time anyway. You saved me from a periodic table death!"

"Happy to do so! Do you want a coffee?" he asked.

"I could go for another white tea."

"Done!" He stood and I watched him walk from the table to the counter, and returned quickly. A waitress would bring the order; she almost always did. As he walked toward me, I saw he was wearing faded Levis and a long-sleeved grey Carnegie-Mellon tee under his open black wool coat. He also donned a gray knit hat with a Pittsburgh Penguins logo on the front. It was pulled over his blonde hair that peeped out haphazardly from under the black trim. He took the seat across from me.

"I wouldn't have pegged you for a tea drinker," he said.

"Why not?" I asked a little surprised.

"Dunno," he replied. "You seem more thoughtful."

"What's that supposed to mean?"

"Well, to tell the truth, I think you can tell a lot about a person by what they drink. Think about it," he paused. "People like Kane, what you see is what you get...black...no sugar...no cream. Michael, on the other hand is big and fluffy, like a teddy bear, but strong...cappuccino. Ravie is all mocha frappuccino...sweet and eye-catching with too much whipped cream."

I laughed.

"You though..." he thought for a moment. "You seem sweet and delicate ...like a latte or café au lait."

"Interesting..." I replied raising my eyebrows.

"You know, though. If I spent a little more time analyzing, I may have guessed tea...delicate and balanced...and a little refined."

"Me?" I laughed.

"Just calling it like I see it."

"Guess what I have." He raised his cup. It was one of those insulated mugs, like you see for sale at Starbucks, but Gabriel's was red and black metal with a grinning red bull mascot on the side. It read *Turnbull Hockey.* "We'll see how close you get." He tried to look serious. The attempt made me smile at his honest effort. He tried really hard to be serious.

"Okay..." I was game. I thought for a few seconds. Gabriel seemed smart, straightforward, driven. Something with a lot of caffeine. A hint of sweetness or cream....something outside the box....Gabriel was no ordinary guy...I thought, looked around, then an idea popped into my head.

"Energy drink," I replied. "Monster...maybe?"

Gabriel burst into laughter. I began laughing too.

"You're saying I'm a Monster?" he looked at me playfully.

"Yes." I tried desperately to hold a serious face. I was not very good at hiding emotions with him though I had plenty of practice.

Gabriel tried to show his feelings were hurt. He stuck out his bottom lip, but a smile squirted through. "Funny thing is, you are so close!" he said.

I donned a triumphant smile, "Was I?"

"Mountain Dew, extra ice. I hate coffee!" We both burst into laughter again. I wasn't used to this.

Chapter 19

We finished our drinks and walked outside. Gabriel parked about a half block away. He pressed a button on the electronic starter that dangled from his keychain and the car hummed to life.

His Jeep Wrangler was probably the coolest car I had ever been in. I was never very materialistic, but this car was special. It was black and polished to a sharp shine. The hood was angled and sleek and ended with the trademark round headlamps.

He walked me to the passenger door and opened it. I thanked him and got inside. It was quite a step up, but comfortable. I never thought a car like this could be so nice! The leather seats were black and supple. The dash was also black and its lights glowed red in the deepening twilight, perfect Turnbull colors. He walked around the hood of the car, opened the door, and got inside. Without a word, he buckled his seatbelt.

"This car is nice!" I said getting comfortable. I ran my hand across the dash. It was polished to a sheen.

"Thanks!" he said. "My 16th birthday present. It was a choice between this or the Jaguar my uncle was getting rid of."

"What a choice!" I replied, not trying to sound too jealous. I changed the subject.

"So what is the official word...Jag-you-are or Jag-wire or Jag-war?"

"Whatever you'd prefer," he said. "Just don't use the proverbial Pittsburgh term please."

"What would that be?" I asked.

"Jag-off,"

I covered my mouth with my hands. "Does that mean what I think it does?'

"Most certainly," he replied. He cleared his throat and spoke as if he were the narrator of a documentary. "People around here have a certain way of speaking. Words that are nonexistent on other parts of the globe are invented and used in Pittsburgh vigorously. Words like *yinz, dahntahn,* and *nebby* have remained in vogue for the past forty years.

I giggled, enjoying his performance of the history of a word I had never heard before.

Gabriel continued, obviously enjoying his own sense of humor, "Ever since the mid 1980s…the Van Halen era…as anthropologists refer to it…people began using the term *jag-off* as an insult, often combining it with certain finger gestures to obtain maximum piss-off value."

I laughed. "So what are those other words you said?"

"Well," he replied dropping the act. "A *yinzer* is a person who has a Pittsburgh accent. *Yinz* is a version of the Texan favorite, *y'all. Dahntahn* is Yinzer for downtown, and *nebby* is a word that simply means you are being nosy. We drove for several blocks, Gabriel recited every Yinzer-word he could remember and I was thoroughly entertained.

"My Texas accent must sound really goofy then," I said. "I try to hide it, but I'm not too good at that I guess."

"More like refreshing," he replied. "I like the lingering vowels. It's not too common to hear a Texan accent all the way up here in Pittsburgh. It's different and cute on you."

"Thanks," I blushed. There was a short pause in the conversation.

"Not to change the subject, and I hate to tell you this, but Michael and I have hockey practice at 11:30. Unfortunately, he's going to be with us on the way home." He looked at me guiltily. He had no reason to.

"That's okay," I replied. I did want to be alone with Gabriel, but I couldn't see why he would think such a trivial thing would upset me.

"I hoped we could spend some time together, but it's just a busy season."

"It's no problem," I said, trying to convince myself that I wasn't disappointed. I felt like I could talk to Gabriel forever. We laughed and covered all sorts of topics. Soon, we arrived at Beatrice's house. With traffic, the drive was forty minutes, and I found myself wishing it were even longer. Gabriel pulled behind her car that was parked in the driveway.

"Wait there," he said. He turned off the ignition, got out, and walked to my door. Opening it, he held out his hand to help me get out.

"Hey guys!" It was Beatrice calling from the wide front porch. "Come on up!"

Beatrice was full of life and charm. Everyone just loved her like a little sister. She was short with bright blonde, curly hair. Unlike Ravie, Beatrice preferred jeans and a team sweatshirt to Gucci and Kate Spade. She coached elementary school kids in after-school soccer and was very athletic. She was looking forward to a degree in sports management, so she spent a lot of time on school teams and studying coaching strategies. Sometimes we didn't see her for days at a time because she had so many games to attend.

The first thing a person noticed about Beatrice was her constant smile; everyone was her best friend. Bouncing from conversation to conversation, she always had something interesting to say. She was constantly reprimanded in class for talking, and sometimes her friendliness allowed a bit of her silly nature to shine through as well. When she was particularly dippy, Gabriel would say, "Beatrice, your dingbat is showing!" Even though he must have said it a hundred times, she would pause a minute to comprehend what he just said, then she would laugh. She didn't care what people thought because they were going to like her anyway.

Gabriel followed me up the few steps to the front door. I opened it and stepped inside.

Beatrice's apartment was great. To the right, the living room was wide and comfortable with dark wooden side tables framing a heavily stuffed couch and loveseat. Gabriel helped me with my coat, added it to his, and slung them neatly across a chair by the front door.

We followed Beatrice through the kitchen and into a large game room with an enormous flat panel television hanging on the wall. In front of it was a u-shaped sofa.

“Nice, huh?” Gabriel whispered. He had followed me on my exploration of Beatrice’s apartment.

On the other side of the room were a large pool table and bistro table with six leather chairs surrounding it. I wondered how Beatrice was able to afford all of this. She lived by herself.

As if he were answering my thoughts, Gabriel whispered, “Beatrice’s parents live overseas. They give her anything she wants to make up for their lost company.”

I thought how utterly awful that would be; to be forgotten by all but my father’s wallet. I also thought it unusual for many of my friends to already be living on their own or even having parents who were never around.

“This is the reason we’re always at Beatrice’s,” said Gabriel. We walked to the bistro area where Beatrice set out bowls of snacks. We were still able to see the television quite clearly. The Penguins were getting ready to play. Gabriel offered me a Pepsi. I accepted, but I really wasn’t thirsty.

Beatrice, Ravie, and Michael entered the room and walked to the bistro area. Beatrice delivered drinks to everyone beginning with Michael and stood next to the table. Kane arrived a little later than everyone else.

“Kane!” Beatrice exclaimed.

“What’s up Candy Kane?” asked Gabriel. He stood up and shook Kane’s hand. Kane did the same and patted Gabriel on the back. Gabriel always called him “Candy Kane” and I think he got away with it only because it was coming from Gabriel. If that nick-name came from anyone else, I think Kane would have flattened them.

“Ah, nothing.” Kane revealed with a shake of his head. He did not smile. One of his serious moods.

Michael lumbered over to the television area, found the remote and flipped on the screen. Ravie shrugged her shoulders and bopped herself on the head in a joking way, showing the rest of us how dense she thought Michael was. “Game’s on.” he reminded everyone. Gabriel turned and leapt over the back of the sofa, like a puppy left off of his leash. Kane followed.

"Come on, Trin!" Gabriel called. He was definitely treating this like a date.

"Beatrice sat in the middle of the larger sofa, forcing Michael and Ravie onto the same section of the sofa. Although it seemed she did nothing on purpose, a discreet nod in Ravie's direction indicated she had planned the seating arrangement well head of time.

I hadn't noticed anything unusual until Ravie said something to Kane during one of the breaks between periods. "Kane, what happened to your neck?" She winced and pointed to her own neck.

Kane wore a large bandage that he tried to conceal with a black turtleneck. He looked at her blankly for a moment before speaking. All of the color drained from his face and he responded as if he had just awakened from a daydream. "Fight." His response seemed mechanical as if it were rehearsed. My stomach dropped.

She continued questioning, "Did Mason try to rip your head off again?"

"Yeah, but I deserved it. I was bugging the crap out of him," he smiled thinly. He seemed like he was trying to brush off the entire situation.

"You bug the crap out of everyone!" Michael joked. "It didn't seem like a big deal though."

"Man, you laid him out too!" Gabriel laughed. "I didn't know you got cut."

"I'm sorry I missed it," Ravie responded, "but I don't do midnight face-offs."

"Oh, I just slapped a bandage on it while I was on the bench."

"Looks like a mean one!" Gabriel got up to take a closer look at Kane's neck. "Why didn't you say something?"

Kane slapped his hand over the large flesh-colored bandage. "Just a scratch." Trying to distract the attention, he commented on the hockey game and everyone followed suit. What scared me was the fact that the bandage was exactly where I gouged him with my nails in my dream last night…Exactly.

We sat and watched the rest of the game. Well, they did. I couldn't. I was fixated on Kane's cut. Was that really a cut from a hockey fight, or did I do that? Why was it exactly in the place where I gouged him in my dream? My stomach was all flittery. I tried to relax, to calm down. I focused on the hockey, but my eyes kept drifting back to Kane's neck.

"I'd remember that cut anywhere!" I whispered to myself.

A few minutes before the end of the game, the score was 5-2, a certain loss for the Penguins. Beatrice stood and stretched, "Well, I've seen enough." She walked across the room to the kitchen, reached in the fridge and pulled out a sandwich ring on a big cardboard tray. She came back into the room and set it on the high table. I decided to help her out. It might get my mind off Kane.

I got up and asked politely, "Need any help?"

"Nah," she replied. "Keep me company though?" I took a perch on one of the bistro stools. Ravie arrived and sat on the stool next to me.

"I can't believe they're still watching that!"

I turned. Michael, Kane, and Gabriel sat on the edge of their seats, glued to the game. It didn't matter the outcome.

"So I've been curious all night. How's the date going?" asked Beatrice. She never beat around the bush.

I blushed. "He's really nice."

"Nice! He's like the catch of the year!" she said. "You know, he's never dated anyone...besides his hockey stick."

Ravie chuckled. "I think they all have!" she gestured towards Michael.

I laughed. That cut was probably just a coincidence.

"He must really like you if he's going to make room in the schedule," said Ravie.

"I hope so," I replied. "I do really like him."

"While we're on the subject, what about you?" I asked Beatrice.

"I've sworn off boyfriends," she said. "Now's the time to live it up...the best time of our lives! I can't be tied down...not now."

"Only you, Beatrice," said Ravie. "You crack me up."

"Thanks...I guess," she replied. But, you never know, I might have some prospects outside this little group."

"What's that supposed to mean?" I asked innocently.

Beatrice smiled and wiggled her eyebrows.

We all laughed. It felt good to finally have friends. I could talk about guys and fashion and movies to someone besides my parents. I did love them more than anything, and they tried really hard to fill the gaps of a teenage girl, but they were my parents.

I felt someone wrap their arm around my shoulders. I looked to my left. It was Gabriel. He gave me a little squeeze. "Hey," he smiled. "You look like you're having fun!"

"We are," I returned his smile.

I hate to break up a party," he responded, "but, we have to go. We have practice." Michael stood behind him, stuffing about a third of the sandwich ring into his mouth.

"Okay." I replied. "I guess girl time is over." I stood to get ready to leave. I didn't want Gabriel to be late.

"Let me drive you home," said Ravie looking at me hopefully. "They're just going to practice anyway. No time for anything else." She said slyly giving a hard glance in Michael's direction.

"What did I do?" he asked, oblivious, his mouth full of food.

"Oh absolutely nothing," she replied. I couldn't believe he was so dense.

I really was reluctant to go home to my room. I was having fun with my friends. Part of me wanted to go with him, but part of me wanted to stay here, to be comforted with company like a favorite blanket on a cold night. I weighed my options. "Do you mind if I go with Ravie?" I looked at Gabriel first and smiled shyly.

"Not at all, if you don't mind," he replied. "You should stay. All I'd be doing is dropping you off."

"I'd love to drive you home." interjected Ravie. 'I'm going your way and it will give us a little girl time anyways."

"As long as you're okay with that...oh and Beatrice isn't driving," teased Gabriel.

"I heard that," replied Beatrice from the other side of the room.

"I'm fine, thanks!" I replied.

Gabriel kissed me softly on my cheek. "See you tomorrow," he whispered next to my ear.

I stood and watched him walk to the door. It was like I was looking through a spyglass. I could only focus on Gabriel. Everything around him faded to gray, and I had those flipping butterflies again! Michael lumbered after him, sandwich in tow.

"Aren't you going, Kane?" asked Ravie.

He was still sitting by the television, staring absently in our direction. Maybe he didn't hear her, so she called again, "Kane?"

This time she caught his attention and he responded distantly. His attention was obviously somewhere else. "Oh, yeah...um...no, doc said no practice for a couple days...stitches." My heart started pounding. This *had* to be related to my dream.

Ravie stood and began to clean up glasses. Beatrice was loading the dishwasher. Kane still sat forward in the overstuffed chair. He absentmindedly scratched at the velvety fabric with his nails while staring at the television.

I stood, more by impulse than thought, and walked to take a seat next to Kane. He turned and nodded his head toward me. Gosh, he looked pale. He was about as handsome as guys can get, but today he looked worn out...exhausted...distant. A thin smile crossed his features like a cloud in a storm.

"Hi," was all I could think to say.

"What's up?" he replied slumping back.

"I guess you just look a little tired. I wanted to make sure you're okay."

He seemed to warm up a little, and sighed. He had an anxious look in his eyes. "I am tired. I don't know what it is."

"Do you want to talk," I asked, unsure where this question would lead. Kane was hard to figure. Sometimes he seemed so nice, but other times... I waited a few moments to see if he said anything else. When the silence became uncomfortable, I stood to leave.

“Trinity,” he said in a whisper, his eyes staring straight ahead. After a moment, he lowered his head and ran his fingers through his thick dark hair. As it lifted and fell it reminded me of the wings of a starling, black with blue undertones. “I have a question and I think you’re the only one who can answer it.”

My heart jumped. I was shocked. Something did happen last night and Kane knew it! Suddenly, I was afraid and I hesitated.

“Trinity?” he turned his body to face me. His eyes were hopeful.

I sat before I fell down. “I think I know what you’re going to say.”

“So you know what happened?” His gaze was no longer distant. It was stony and serious.

“No.” I replied honestly, regretting what I had revealed. “I just…”

“Tell me what you know!” he interrupted. His iron look was one I could not deflect. Was it that obvious I was harboring some information? Although I feared the outcome, I decided to tell him.

“This is going to sound strange…” I hesitated, unsure, but knowing I could no longer keep it to myself.

“Try me.” His jaw was set and he awaited my response with an unyielding glare.

My mind was racing as to what I was going to say. “Well,” I began, “last night I had this dream…you were in it…bad things happened…” I paused. A lump was forming in my throat. I felt like I was going to cry, but I couldn’t…not now…I took a deep breath.

Kane’s look seemed to soften, or I imagined it did. “Did I hurt you?” he asked.

I took a deep breath, “I don’t think so.”

“Well, I think you should see this.” He glanced towards Ravie and Beatrice to see if they were looking, but they were still engaged in a lively conversation.

I looked at him and winced as he pulled back the bandage; the wound gaped in protest. His neck was cut…no torn was a better word…just to the left of his Adam’s apple. Instead of a scab, the edges were ragged and red. The gash itself had taken on a purplish color. I noticed it was still oozing blood. I gasped and the room began to fade.

The next thing I knew, Kane was holding me in his arms like a sick child. Beatrice was holding a glass of water next to my right cheek. Thoughts pelted my mind like shards of ice. Did I gouge Kane like that? Was he really in my dream? Why did his cut look exactly like the one...just before he bit me? I was drowning in questions!

I sprang upright and almost knocked the glass from Beatrice's hand, but she was quick to recover. I reached for the water, grasped the icy condensation in my hands and drank it in little sips. Beatrice gripped my arm, looking anxious. I started to calm down, "I'm sorry, that never happened before." I crawled back into the soft sofa and surveyed the group. They were all still stooped or kneeling next to me, each one wearing a look of concern or empathy.

"I feel a little sick," I said weakly. I turned to Ravie, "Please...please would you take me home?" I knew I still had to discuss everything with Kane, but now was not the time.

She quickly gathered her purse and keys and in moments, she ushered me out the door. As I passed Kane, he whispered, "We'll talk tomorrow."

All the way home, Ravie tried to create a conversation in any way she could think of, but I blatantly told her I really didn't feel like talking. My thoughts kept going back to Kane's horribly gashed neck, and the fact that I did it. I *knew* I did!

I opened the front door and went directly to my room. It was time. I reached under the bed and pulled out the trunk. The old hinges groaned with effort. Quickly selecting the small, stained Tupperware box and a medium pad of watercolor paper, I carefully set them on the floor, took a spot next to them, and stared at the box of paints. I wondered if I should be painting at all, but it was an urge; I felt I had to paint. After a few minutes, I opened the Tupperware box. These were tubes of gouache, a thick watercolor with vivid pigments. I took a few in my hands and squeezed them gently...still soft. I felt as if they were old friends I haven't seen in years, comforting and welcoming. I read the names of the colors: yellow ochre...vermillion...burnt sienna...cerulean blue...viridian...even the names were beautiful. I went to the bathroom for some water.

I painted like I was possessed. I always did, never knowing what I was going to paint until the work was complete. Usually the images were so vivid and frightening I didn't even want to look at them when I was finished. Most people thought I was talented, but I used it more for therapy than anything else. I decided to begin, and without thinking, I immediately went for the tube of cadmium yellow.

I painted most of the night. When I was completely exhausted, I lay the tablet on the floor and crawled into bed. Countless tubes of paint were strewn across the carpet, but I didn't care. I'm sure my face and hands were smeared as well. For a moment, I tried to remember what I had painted, but I couldn't. I let it go and fell asleep. The nightmares returned.

Chapter 20

I was trapped underwater. Thick weeds covered the surface like a carpet and it was murky, hard to see. I was holding my breath, desperately looking for a way out. I tried with all the strength I could muster, but the vegetation was too heavy to push away from the surface for more than a moment and a quick taste of air. There was nowhere to get leverage. Every time I pushed, I just sank deeper into the water. I had to get to the edge, but which way should I swim?

I struggled and managed another gasp of air when I saw a shadow. Something was in the water with me. I stopped to look and saw a large dark figure coming towards me. At first I thought it was a fish cutting smoothly through the water, but then I saw more as it got closer. It wasn't streamlined at all; its long body swung rhythmically from side to side, more human than fish-like. It was so hard to see in the dim water...

I awoke, sitting upright. I couldn't see in the dark, so I lay down, chest heaving with fear. I didn't know what to think. After a few moments I was able to catch my breath. The nightmare faded away and was gone in moments. I grasped at the details, but they evaporated like smoke. I lay motionless. Why was I having such horrible dreams? Maybe it was stress, but why were they so lucid? Was there a connection between my dreams and school? Was it my friends? Was I losing my mind? I lay sleepless for hours, refusing to be taken again by my nightmares, but my refusal meant nothing.

Chapter 21

I woke early the next day, eager to see the sun. Even though I lay awake for hours, sleep steals you quietly. I sat up in the early morning light and saw something scattered on the floor.

The posters that I had so meticulously hung were ripped from the walls. They lay in tatters like a broken piñata on the floor. Ribbons of paper dangled from pieces of tape and bent push pins. The dirty, Yellow walls crept through in vengeful glory. I felt sick. SpongeBob's happy, yellow face lay on the floor except for a shred of an eye and a buck tooth still sticking loyally to the wall. "An eye for an eye, a tooth for a tooth" I thought almost hysterically. Photographs of friends and family lay ruined and strewn across the floor. Most were punctured, but others were slashed.

I got out of bed. How did this happen? Was someone here last night? Was this some kind of joke? Even more questions! If someone *was* here, they would have to have done this in the dark. My paint tubes were still strewn across the carpet and interestingly, not one tube of the paint tubes was stepped on. I kicked the tubes to the sides of the room, and then picked up the SpongeBob poster. His yellow body was twisted and crumpled. I examined it ruefully before I dropped him to the floor.

Another, equally frightening thought entered my mind. Had I done this in my sleep? I heard of people sleep walking, but never anything like this. Did stress cause this? I couldn't let Dad know! He'd make me stay home and rest, but staring at these walls was the last thing I wanted to do. I gathered the posters and photographs and made a neat pile on the floor. I intended to salvage what I could, but for now I had to clean it up before Dad woke. I gently slid the pile under the bed then I dropped to the floor. I sat thinking for a long time.

After a while, I remembered the painting. The tablet was still open to the page I was working on last night. Maybe that would give me some kind of clue. My hands were shaking, but I ignored them.

I had painted a scene of a storm at sea. It was very murky and dark with the violence of the storm smeared in heavy swaths of grays and blacks. A small schooner was battling for survival. The people on board wore yellow rain jackets and the horror on their faces was more felt than displayed. The focus of the painting wasn't the struggling boat or even the people on board; rather it was the monstrous storm that churned the waters. I was shocked at the mayhem depicted in the painting.

As I looked more closely, the detail of the sailors came to life. Six little figures struggling against an unholy gale. I painted myself and my friends all on that doomed ship! Why had I done this?

Chapter 22

I was late to school that day, so I opened the door of skulls onto a classroom that was working quietly. Excusing myself with a whisper, I handed Mr. Arndt my tardy slip from the office. Without looking up, he took the slip, and handed me a test.

"Thanks," I replied halfheartedly.

Noticing my tired tone, he looked up from his work; glasses perched on his broad nose. "You okay?" he asked.

"Yeah," I whispered, "I'm okay."

Mr. Arndt was one of the only adults in school that knew the situation with my Mom. A look of pity, or was it concern crossed his face. "If you need anything, just say so," he said quietly. "It's difficult right now, but I know you'll be okay."

"Thanks," I said, forcing a smile that probably looked more like a grimace. How did he know I would be okay? He had no flipping idea what I was going through, and Mom wasn't even my first thought any more. I wanted to blurt out..."How do you know Mr. Arndt? You know nothing about me! My dreams are coming alive and this school sucks! All you can say is you'll be okay. What if nothing is okay, Mr. Arndt? What if the world is a pile of crap and you're sitting smack on top of it?" I was becoming hot with rage.

Instead, I took my seat and looked at the test...chemistry...multiple choice. I began circling answers, but after a while it just became random. I couldn't focus. Although I tried to comprehend the questions, my mind wandered. I kept dwelling on the events of the morning. Engrossed in my thoughts, I didn't hear the bell.

"Hey," I heard a voice above my head. I looked up. It was Ravie.

"Finish up...let's go." She was smiling, but when she looked in my eyes, her smile faded quickly. "What's wrong? Are you still feeling sick?"

"I just didn't get enough sleep."

"Do you want to talk? Is your Mom okay?"

"Not right now," I replied as I stood up. I turned in my test and followed Ravie into the Gathering Hall. There were kids everywhere. We walked to one of the long, wooden tables and sat down.

"So what's going on?" Ravie asked.

"I had a bad night," I replied.

"I feel like I need to help you," she said allowing her hands to fall in her lap.

I looked at my friend. Her brow was wrinkled with concern, a concern I was getting tired of seeing, yet it was this same concern that I appreciated when I was feeling pretty low. I needed to tell someone what was happening. This wasn't at all about Mom. It was about *me*.

"Ravie," I said on the verge of tears, "It's just getting worse." I wanted to tell her everything. "I think I'm going crazy."

"Trin," she said; her concern deepening. "You're going to be okay."

"Everyone keeps telling me that, but it's not true! Nothing is going to be okay...nothing!"

Ravie sighed...helpless.

"Can you come over after school?" I blurted out.

"Anything, honey," now she looked alarmed. I knew she thought something happened with Mom.

"Please don't tell anyone else...please?"

"I won't," she said solemnly.

For the rest of the day, I was distant, lost in my thoughts. Had my dreams suddenly taken shape? *Was I crazy?*

I purposely buried my nose in books, though not one word from them entered my mind. All of the "what ifs" received due diligence, but I made no decisions on how to proceed with my thoughts. Maybe if I shared them with Ravie, she could help me sort through everything, or just run screaming, thinking I was having some sort of delusional episode. I decided it was worth the risk. I thought she would at least listen.

At lunch I took a seat in the rear of the Gathering Hall. I tried to remain as invisible as possible, but almost immediately Gabriel and Michael stopped by to talk. They were worried about me. They wanted to know if I was okay. They wanted to know if they could do anything. My answer to all of their questions was honest and straightforward, "We'll talk later."

Gabriel looked alarmed and sad at my reply. Wisely, he didn't push me for a response. They knew I had a tough time at Beatrice's last night. He began to walk away, then turned thoughtfully, and came back. He bent over and kissed me lightly on my cheek. I smiled softly in return.

"I'm so sorry I left last night," he said looking deeply into my eyes.

"It's not your fault. I just need a little time. I think I need to talk to everyone...soon...but not just yet."

Michael, quiet as usual, just smiled kindly. I wondered if he knew anything about my nightly horror fests. It didn't seem like it, but Kane knew. I was certain of that.

They left and took seats at a nearby table, almost as if they were guarding me. I appreciated their concern. I sat quietly and looked into my book, thinking. Beatrice stopped by a little later. "You okay," she asked.

"Fine," I lied. "Can we talk later?"

"Sure," she seemed surprised then smiled and rubbed my back in a gesture of concern. Then she walked away. At this point, Ravie was the only person I felt I could reveal everything to. I hoped that even if she thought I was nuts, she wouldn't toss me aside.

After school, she met me at my locker. We walked to her car and drove to my house in an uncomfortable silence. She was getting to know me well and knew I would talk when the time came. I wasn't one to be forced.

By car, the trip to my house was a short one. Luckily she had a small car and managed to squeeze into the only available parking place on the crowded street. I led her up the stone walkway and inside. As usual Dad was at the hospital and there was a box of Kraft Macaroni and Cheese and a can of tuna on the counter.

We took seats on the couch facing each other. I asked her if she wanted something to drink and she politely refused. "Let's just talk," she said.

I didn't know how to begin the conversation, so I was glad she started talking first.

"Trin, you've only been here a few months, but it seems we've known each other a lot longer." She looked at me sincerely. "I hate to see my friends suffering, and your pain is pretty obvious."

"That's nice of you to say," I replied politely.

"Is it your Mom?" she queried.

"No, she's doing okay actually," I said. "That's not why I asked you here." I knew she thought my problems stemmed from my mother's illness. Boy, was she in for a shock!

"I know you have a lot going on right now and I..," she paused, and corrected herself, "we all want..."

I interrupted her, "I have to show you something. Please follow me." I led her to my bedroom. As soon as we entered, I stopped. I turned and faced her. She looked surprised. This wasn't what she expected.

"Look," I said. "I want you...no, I need you to tell me if I am crazy. You're about the only person I can believe at this point..." I took a deep breath, "...and that includes *me*."

Ravie had a puzzled look on her face, but she let me continue. "I need you to look at something and tell me what you really think."

Not giving her a chance to answer or to back out, I knelt on the floor. I reached under the bed, this time not caring what made my hand an after school snack, and slid the entire poster pile out from under the bed and into the middle of the floor.

"Trinity...," Ravie began.

I stopped her. "Look, You might think I'm nuts, hell, you probably will, but I am asking you to just listen to me. I don't know what caused this to happen, all I know is it *did* happen... I need to know if it's you guys, this house, that weird school, or if it's just me."

She stood silently, looking alarmed, but genuinely interested in what I had to say. "I've been having really bizarre dreams, since I was little. But ever since we got to Pittsburgh, they've gotten so much worse. There were never faces in the dreams until I started hanging out with you guys."

I continued, gathering steam and courage. "This morning I woke up to this mess." I pointed at the pile of papers stacked on the floor. "A couple of weeks ago I hung these on my walls. They were not only something familiar to keep me company, but also they covered the disgusting color of the walls."

A look of genuine concern seeped across Ravie's face. I had to make my case quickly, before she wrote me off. "This morning…this is what I found…all across the floor. At first I thought someone…you guys were trying to scare me, but now I believe it's much more than that."

Ravie stooped and picked up a few photographs. She examined each one closely and let them fall from her hand to the top of the heap. "Trinity," she stated looking at me very seriously, "we didn't do this, if that's what you're thinking!"

I ignored her and knelt next to the pile. "Then I thought this all might be me. Am I so stressed about all of the changes in my life? Am I subconsciously causing all of these problems for myself? I don't know….Ravie…" I pleaded. "You have to help me!"

"Okay," she stated, shaking her head, "Okay. Let's look at this. It's obviously got you very upset." She sat cross-legged on the floor next to me. I had expected her to leave in a huff, but she took the logical approach, wanting to really see what had me in such a state. With a look of concerned determination, Ravie began piecing together the SpongeBob poster, picking out all of the pieces and reassembling them on the floor.

I decided to explain some more. "I sat and thought about this all day. After a while of analyzing everything that is happening, I realized I was hearing tearing sounds in my dream last night. Now I realize the tearing sounds were the posters and pictures being torn off the wall. *I* did it! It's the only explanation…"

"Hold on," said Ravie interrupting me in an urgent voice. "Look at this!" She pointed at a rip in SpongeBob's yellow cheek. "Trinity," she continued...I really think..."

"I'm nuts!" I finished.

"Trinity, no," she continued holding up some photos. "Look at these...these puncture marks." She pointed to a few of the holes. "Do you see how they're volcano shaped? And the tear in the poster? It's creased from the back!" She picked up another picture.

"Trinity, look at this picture! This is you and your parents! Look at how the paper is slashed! It's like whoever tore each of you right down the middle!"

I noticed one picture lying in the middle of the pile that was untouched. It was still unmarred, perfect. I picked it up. Ravie stood next to me and watched. It was a picture of my mother when we were camping in Arizona. It was taken right before Mom started to feel sick. I picked it up and examined it closely, holding it up to the light streaming in the window. Something was written on the back.

I flipped it over.

"Oh my god, Trinity!"

A message was scrawled across the back in red ink. It read simply:

"I am coming for you."

We stared at each other. She went to the wall and ran her hand up and down the cracks. She looked very closely.

I stared at her, trying to comprehend what she was saying and doing. "Trinity...I can't believe I'm going to say this...but these pictures were torn from behind! Look at the wall. There are marks, raised marks, like scars on the walls! You just can't see them right away because of the swirls in the paint!"

She crawled to the corner of the room and examined the bottoms of the walls. "Trinity, down here, there are places where the scrapes broke through the plaster. Look!"

I slid next to her to examine the evidence. Plaster dust and chips littered the floor. I noticed even the dust had a yellowish tint. Did this evil color soak all the way through the plaster? The walls were split in places and the plaster dust heaved out of the cracks. The cracks themselves were convex. If they were scraped from the outside, they would have to be concave!

"Something's in the wall!" she said. "Something in the wall tore these...from the back...something inside the wall!"

Chapter 23

I tried to stay out of that house as long as possible, so I was everywhere. I spent a lot of time at Ravie's, sat at the coffee shop, and I visited Mom as often as I could. She was still in the cancer unit. The treatments were working, but her white cell count was still way too high to be able to leave the hospital. She was in better spirits though, but we had to be careful not to visit her if we felt ill or had even the slightest sniffle.

Over the following week, I went to school but kept mainly to myself. I talked to Ravie mostly, but stayed away from the rest of my friends. I outright avoided them, and things seemed different, not as warm, not as welcoming. I know the chill was coming from me. Hell, I was not as warm, not as welcoming, and not as friendly. I didn't want anyone pulled into this...or to get hurt...or killed...in my dreams.

Ravie caught up to me one day after school. Together, we walked through the Gathering Hall to the outside. Although the air was cold, Ravie smiled warmly.

"Trinity, everyone is so worried about you."

"I know," I sighed.

"Gabriel is just about out of his mind. If he calls me one more time to see how you're doing...I swear..."

"I'm sorry," I said. "I'm just trying to figure things out on my end." I stopped and looked at her pleadingly. "Sometimes I feel like I'm going to break."

"I understand. God, Trinity, I saw what you saw! I saw those posters, and you have to sleep in there! I don't know what you're going through, but I do know you can't live like this...especially on your own." She continued, "Trinity, I think everything that is going on is related...the dreams, your posters...maybe even your mom!"

My ears pricked at the mention of my mother; it wasn't the first time I put her into my endless equations.

“Please, come out tonight. We all need to talk together. You should tell everyone what’s happening!” She pulled on the sleeve of my coat and grasped my forearm. I stopped walking. She held my hand, he brow furrowed with concern. “We can help you work through this! We’re not against you. I think we can help you, and you can help us!”

She looked at me intently and sighed. “Trinity, I have to tell you something as well. I didn’t want to share it, because I didn’t want you to think I was weird.”

I laughed. “Weird! That’s funny…me thinking someone else is weird.” I thought about it for a moment. Ravie looked uncomfortable and I immediately regretted my words. “I’m sorry, Ravie. I didn’t mean to laugh at you. I just was always the weird kid.” I sighed. “I apologize.”

“That’s okay,” Trinity looked relieved. She stopped for a few moments to gather her thoughts. “Like your dreams, I’ve always had *feelings* about things.”

“What kind of feelings?” I asked, immediately intrigued.

“I don’t know. It’s hard to explain,” she said. “I just know when something is going to happen.” She looked at me intently and honestly.

“Good things or bad things?” I was even more curious now. A small part of me thought she was poking fun at me, but a bigger part, an overwhelming part, believed she was telling the truth.

“Both,” she said thoughtfully, “and lately they’ve been very strong…overpowering.”

“Did they get worse around the same time I got here?” I asked.

“Actually, I’d have to say not worse, but much stronger; a little over two months ago.”

I knew it. I had to be some kind of catalyst for all of this. “What are your feelings like?” I asked, interested to see if she experienced anything like I did with my dreams.

Her hand went to her stomach. “It feels like butterflies, like when you’re on a roller coaster, but that’s not all,” she paused. “I hear voices, tinny, urgent voices, like wind-chime whispers in a storm.” She looked frightened.

“Please go on,” I said. I knew all about those butterflies.

"I don't know. It's like I've always had inklings but never full blown urges of what to do. I only started actually hearing the chiming voices lately, in the past few weeks. It's like a door is opening and I'm realizing things for the first time." She looked at me intently, "Either I know what is going to happen or..."

"Or what?"

"I'm crazier than you think," she stated.

"Oh, I don't think you're crazy," I said.

"I wouldn't lie to you, Trin."

"Me either," I replied. I looked at my new friend. My mother always told me to look in my heart when I had a problem. My heart would always tell me the truth. I looked into Ravie's eyes and closed my own. I took a few deep breaths and cleared my mind. My heart knew Ravie was sincere. "Have you told anyone else," I asked.

"Just Kane."

I asked, "Why not everyone?"

"It doesn't feel right," she replied. "I think we both need to talk to him."

I didn't want to be the only one laying my weirdness on the line. "Okay, but why Kane?"

"He has some ideas," she replied, "about the school. Ideas I think you need to hear."

"Will you come tonight?" she looked at me pleadingly.

"Yeah," I replied. "Where are you going to meet?"

"We're going to get some pizza. Just come. I won't ask you to say anything about any of this...unless you want to."

"I could use some pizza."

"I'll pick you up at seven," she smiled.

Chapter 24

Ravie arrived at my house a little early. She knocked on the door and I let her in. For once Dad was home and practically flew to the front door to meet her. The joker in him was always happy to see a new face and share a few laughs.

I talked to Dad whenever he happened to be home, about my friends and about school. I never let him know the weird stuff that was going on. I wanted him to think everything was just fine. I wanted him to focus on Mom.

We small-talked a bit and in his usual gregarious manner, he told some corny jokes then excused himself to the kitchen.

"Be careful, girls. It's Friday night. Don't stay out too late!"

"We will, and we won't, Dad, "I assured him.

"Good! Home by midnight or the Big Bad Wolf will get you!" he laughed maniacally.

Just the mention of a wolf sent chills up my spine. Ravie and I walked to her car.

"Your dad seems sweet," she said.

"He's the best!" I replied. "I wish you knew him before all this." It was then that I realized how much I missed my father. He's just a shell of himself."

Ravie stopped. "Trin, I wish I could see what was going to happen next. I want to tell you your mom is going to be fine. " She shrugged her shoulders. "I just can't see anything about you...it's like a fog surrounding the facts...I'm sorry."

"That's okay...really..." I said then added, "Anyway, I don't want to know."

We arrived at the pizza place right on time. Pittsburgh isn't known for its pizza, but this place was special, Scooby's. The best part about it was there were televisions throughout the restaurant, and you sat on couches to eat. Even if there wasn't a hockey game on (a real rarity) they had all kinds of video games and consoles you could play while you ate. It was great, not just for the pizza, but it gave you a sense of being in a friend's comfortable home. Something I quietly longed for.

Beatrice was sitting on a large couch, awaiting everyone's arrival. With her usual bright smile, she welcomed us and offered us a cup and a pitcher of Pepsi. The restaurant was crowded and I was glad to have the company, even if most of the faces were not familiar. We sat and talked lightly about superficial things such as the people at school and chemistry class.

Soon Gabriel arrived. He wheeled into the room like he was late for a hockey game. He immediately took the seat across from me. He looked at me and his eyes locked on mine. His broad smile faded quickly. "God, what's going on, Trinity?" As usual, Gabriel didn't mince words. He reached out and took my hands in his. "It's just that you look so tired."

"If you only knew," I mumbled.

"What can I do?" He looked at me pleadingly. "Please don't push me away!"

"I…I don't know," I replied.

After a few moments with my friends, I realized how much I missed them. I needed them if I was ever going to get through my stay in Pittsburgh. It was then that I decided it was time to talk about Mom. Maybe I should start attributing all of this weirdness to the obvious source.

"I think I need to talk to all of you," I said softly.

"I'll get everyone," said Gabriel. He gave my hand a squeeze before he got up from the table. I hadn't noticed, but Michael and Kane had arrived while I was talking to Gabriel. They sat quietly by the door. As soon as Gabriel stood up, they came over to the couches and took a seat.

It felt like we were all sitting around a stuttering campfire awaiting the proverbial scary story. Too bad it wasn't just a story.

I had been practicing what I might say to everyone. "Okay," I said. "First of all, I'm sorry I've been so distant and scarce lately, but I had a lot of thinking to do." I took a deep breath, "There are a few things I think I should tell you. I ask that you don't share them with anyone. My family is pretty private and I really don't need to deal with more than I already am." I continued. "My mother has pancreatic cancer. The chances of survival are about twenty percent. So far, she has outlived the doctor's predictions and she is holding her own."

My friends looked at me in disbelief.

"We moved here," I continued, "so she could get some drug treatments. She's reacting positively, but nothing miraculous has happened."

"God," said Gabriel. "I had no idea."

"I'm so sorry," Beatrice chimed in.

I continued, looking at each of them. "We had to rent a horrible little house in the East End because my dad quit his job to take care of Mom. We sold a lot of our things, even our car, but we're okay."

Michael spoke up this time, "Trinity... If there's anything we can do."

"Really, there's nothing. I just thought you should know." Everyone looked at me as if I had just announced my own mortality. "I just get tired sometimes; other times I need a little space." I continued. "On the bright side, my mom is getting a little better. Her counts are coming up, but it's a slow process...with no guarantees." I sighed and continued, "I finally feel I know you all well enough. I've been here over two months, and I didn't want you to think I was some kind of weirdo or goofball. It's just that I'm...I'm just not myself."

"Trinity, you should have told us sooner," said Beatrice. "We could have helped you more...been there for you."

Michael chimed in, "Anything you need."

Kane sat motionless. He still wore the bandage on his neck. It was over a week since my dream of the wolves.

Gabriel leaned over and hugged me gently. He whispered in my ear, "Ask for anything and it's yours." He backed up and gave me a look of concern.

A lump was forming in my throat, and I struggled to hold back the tears. My throat burned. I looked at the ceiling and breathed deeply. The tears trickled paths down my cheeks anyway. I wiped them away and swallowed that gagging lump of self-pity.

We sat around and nibbled pizza, but no one was overly talkative or very hungry. I knew I started the evening off with a real downer, so it was going to take some time to recover our usual jovial mood. After a while Michael flipped on the hockey game, and at least the boys were engaged. Kane remained eerily silent, even for him.

I hoped he would come and talk to me. We left our last conversation when I passed out. He never approached me in school or anywhere else during the week, although he never left my thoughts.

I waited until Gabriel was occupied with Michael in some in depth sports conversation. I was determined to get to the bottom of this. I approached Kane as he sat on the couch staring blankly at some ESPN hockey program. Absentmindedly, he reached to his neck and touched the bandage.

He spoke first in a whisper so his friends couldn't hear. "Meet me by the rest rooms." He got up before I could reply and walked toward the back of the restaurant. I waited a few minutes and followed.

He was waiting at the end of a long, dimly lit hallway next to a pair of water fountains. He looked scared. "Trinity, I have to tell you," he took a deep breath then paused, his gaze intensifying. "It isn't healing."

I studied his perfect face. He was frightened and tired, dark rings circled his green eyes. His pallor was that of a dead man. He didn't ask, but I winced as he peeled the bandage back. The wound gaped in protest. It was still torn, the edges still ragged and red.

"God, Kane! Have you seen a doctor? That was over a week ago!"

"Yeah, I'm on all kinds of antibiotics, but nothing is working. They can't figure it out." He carefully repositioned the bandage over the cut and pressed the tape back into place.

"I'm sorry. I didn't know..."

He grinned, something I wasn't expecting. "I've been doing a lot of thinking," he paused. "At first I was scared, then angry, but just last night I realized how stupid I was being."

"What do you mean," I asked.

"Trinity, you didn't do anything. You can't come into my dreams."

I struggled to keep it together. "Yes, I can! I ripped that gash in your neck...in my dream!"

I felt a wave a dizziness followed by a wave of guilt, crashing one after another into my body. "I am so sorry, Kane!"

He wrapped his arm around my shoulders and held me steady until I began to calm down. I needed his support even more than he knew. He looked at me intently and honestly.

"I'm sorry if I made you feel like this was your fault. I should have never done that."

"But it is, Kane. It is entirely my fault!"

He responded with another smile, "We need to talk some more...just not here."

"Soon!"

"Tomorrow," he stated. "I'll call you tomorrow." But things happened and he never had the chance.

Chapter 25

Luckily, Dad didn't wait up for me because it was almost midnight when I got home. The conversation with Kane had me spooked and I really didn't want to go to bed. I knew I would lie awake, thinking. I was afraid to go to my room, but I had no other option. I couldn't turn on the television because it would wake Dad. It always did, and I just didn't feel like talking to him about my evening. I couldn't even sleep on the couch for fear of him finding me there and shooing me off to my horrible room. While making my decision on my sleeping quarters, I decided to look at my cell. There was a message. It was Gabriel.

I dialed my voicemail. He wanted me to call him when I got home and I debated the lateness. I decided to call anyway. I needed something to take my mind off of this place.

I pushed the buttons and he answered the phone immediately, only after a half-ring. He seemed concerned, and we talked for a few minutes. He asked if he could come over.

Although my dad was asleep, I agreed. Sitting on the front stoop was technically home anyway. He asked to wait for him at my front door since he didn't know the exact house. I looked out the living room window even before I had hung up the phone. I had that tickle of anticipation in my stomach; I couldn't wait to see him. I thought deeply about this new boy. What role did he play in all this?

Gabriel arrived in his black Wrangler a little later. Luckily there was a parking space two doors down the street. I grabbed my coat and quietly crept downstairs and across the living room. I opened the front door and peeked out in time to see him stretch out of his car. Even from a distance, he was tall and athletic. His white-blonde hair caught the moonlight like a halo.

I walked on to the porch and sat on the stoop. It was cold, so I put on my wool coat and wrapped my arms around my knees. Gabriel caught my eye and smiled sweetly. He made a couple quick strides down the sidewalk and jogged up the few front steps. I stood to greet him.

"Hi," I said.

He smiled and gave me a polite hug then gently pulled me closer. "I couldn't stay away any longer. I've been worried about you."

I pulled my head back and looked up into his face. His eyes held mine, and I smiled warmly. Wrapping my arms around his black flannel coat, I held his shoulders. He was much taller than me, so I rested my cheek on the warmth of his neck. He gently placed one hand around the back of my head and stroked my hair. After a few moments of just being held, I looked up at him.

"You okay?' he asked.

"I am," I replied confidently. He had the uncanny ability to always make me feel safe.

I welcomed his warm, sweet breath as he leaned toward me. Our eyes were fixed on each other and we shared a long, sweet kiss. I still couldn't believe he was really here.

Gabriel's hand moved from the back of my head and traced a slow trail down my back. I was goose bumpy all over. He held me around my waist and pulled back, looking intently at me.

"God," he whispered, "I've been waiting for that!"

I smiled up at him.

"So let's talk," he said.

I moved and sat back down on the steps. He followed my actions. I scooted to sit closely next to him in the cold. He curled his arm around my shoulders. Butterflies again.

"What do you want to talk about?" I asked.

"Everything," he replied.

My shyness was coming out. I didn't want to seem awkward, so I did what I always did, I sat quietly. We remained that way for several minutes until Gabriel decided to break the silence. "Trinity, I'm going to be honest. I feel like I've known you for a really long time even though I just met you."

Funny thing was I felt exactly the same way. I lifted my head, my eyes meeting his.

He continued, "I want you to know you can call me anytime."

"I know," I replied, grateful for his concern. "And I will."

Gabriel squeezed my shoulders gently, and we sat looking at each other for several moments. In the moonlight, he looked like an angel, perfect in form and beauty. I studied his face. The first thing that caught my eye was his cheekbones. They were smooth and chiseled. His lips were full and red against the light color of his skin and when he smiled, the ends of his mouth curled warmly. His nose was perfect, not upturned, or too big. It looked as if someone plucked it from an ancient Greek statue and placed it on his face. His chin was strong and angled. I followed its curve and came to his eyes which were the most calming shade of deep blue. The outer edges turned slightly upward, giving him a mischievous look. When he smiled, they crinkled into arches. His lashes were long and outlined his eyes like the kohl on an ancient Egyptian. His hair was the lightest, whitest shade of blond and a little long. It was tousled, which just gave him a purposefully unkempt look.

Gabriel was so handsome. Again I wondered, *why me*? He could have any girl he wanted. My thoughts began to make me doubtful, wary, and uncomfortable, so I pushed them from my mind. I wanted to enjoy the moment with him...alone. I guess we had been looking at each other for a long time, so he leaned over and stole another kiss. This one was short and sweet, but just as enjoyable as the first. The butterflies in my stomach would not calm. I smiled at their tickling.

"How's Mom?" he asked.

I quickly came back to Earth. "Actually better today. I can't wait to have her back home."

"I'm sure if things are looking up now, they will only get better," he said convincingly. "I wish I could meet her. The way you talk about her makes me feel she is someone very special."

"She is...to a lot of people."

We sat for a few moments and watched the snow thicken on the grass and the cold car windshields. "I love nights like these," he revealed.

"Actually, I never thought about snow until I came to Pittsburgh," I said.

"Seriously?" he replied, amazed.

"Yup. It doesn't snow much in Amarillo." I thought for a moment. "Usually it is enough to stick to the grass then it melts pretty quickly."

"Do you like it? The snow?"

"I guess. But the darkness here is the hardest thing to get used to. Actually, Amarillo gets over 250 days a year with sun. "

"Really? This is my *favorite* time of year," he replied.

"It *is* beautiful like this." I closed my eyes and enjoyed the moment. "I never thought snow would make noise."

"Hmm...it's funny that's what you notice...the sound of the flakes as they hit everything. When we get great, big, soft flakes, it is perfectly silent. That's the best kind of snow."

I imagined the city blanketed with fluffy flakes. In my mind, it was lovely. "I guess I don't have a favorite kind...well not yet."

"You will," he replied. "There are all kinds of snow."

I responded by smiling thoughtfully as I watched the flakes fall. I knew he was looking at me, and that made me feel good, like someone was interested in me rather than all of the drama going on around me. For once I wasn't an afterthought.

After a few moments Gabriel spoke, "Trinity, I really came by to tell you how sorry I am that I didn't drive you home from Beatrice's last week. Kane told me you got sick."

"It wasn't a big deal," I said. "I think I just forgot to eat. I got a little dizzy."

He looked away as if something were bothering him. "I'm afraid to ask this right now," he said, "but I will because I feel I have to," he paused.

"Go on," I said, alarmed at what he was about to reveal.

"Do you trust me?" he asked, almost reading my mind.

"Of course," I said immediately. I was certain I did. I didn't even think about it. I just continued to wonder why he liked me and not someone prettier. "Why do you ask that?"

He responded, "I guess there are thing a guy just needs to know about a girl."

I smiled and looked at him intently. He returned my gaze.

"You ready?" Gabriel said suddenly gently reaching out with his hand extended toward me. I didn't know we were going somewhere.

"I can't go anywhere. I…"

He interrupted, repeating, "Do you trust me?"

I replied by holding out my hand which he took readily and gave a slight squeeze. "Come on, I have something for you." He led me down the street. It was awfully cold and it had begun snowing bigger, quieter flakes that twirled to the ground.

We stopped at his car and he turned to face me, holding both of my hands in his. He grinned excitedly, really making me wonder what was going on.

"Close your eyes. Don't peek!" But I wanted badly to peek. I was one of those people who welcomed a preview of my Christmas presents; often spying in my parents' closet and under the bed just to see what they got me. This was torture, but I kept my eyes shut.

"Okay, you can open them," he said a few seconds later.

I opened my eyes and Gabriel stood in front of me holding a delightfully wrapped box. It was a little larger than a shirt box and wrapped in glistening gold foil paper, topped with a graceful white organza ribbon.

I was astonished. I didn't know what to say. I wanted to be gracious, but I was at a loss for words. Gabriel smiled widely as he held the box out for me to take. Snow swirled around his face and the perfectly formed flakes clung to his black woolen coat for just a moment before they melted. His gaze was light and flittered across my upturned face like one of those lilting snowflakes.

I returned his smile with a look of surprise. Finally I managed to squeak out one word, "What...?"

"You're going to need these," he interrupted.

"You don't have to…"

"Shh…" Gabriel gently brushed my lips with the tip of his finger. "Open it," he said excitedly.

"It's a beautiful package," I said.

"A beautiful package for a beautiful girl," his smile was unwavering.

He still held the box and I stepped toward him. I pulled at the feathery dance of ribbon and it fell to the ground. My heart was flittering in my chest. What could be inside?

I pulled up on the golden lid. The gift inside was covered with shimmery white tissue paper. I crinkled it back gently.

It was a perfect thought. Lying inside the box was a pair of white figure skates. I touched them and gazed up at Gabriel. After a laugh he turned and set the box inside the open car door. When he turned back, he had the white skates grasped by their laces in one hand and he had his black hockey skates in the other. "Come on," he said offering his arm once again. I took it willingly.

He stopped for a moment to shift his clunky skates over his shoulder. Wrapping his free arm around my shoulders, we shuffled through the snow together. He led me down the street and around a bend. Turning, we walked quickly down a dimly lit side street and into a small park full of trees. I would usually have never followed a boy here, but this was Gabriel. I trusted him with all of my heart.

"Not many people know this is here," he said. "It freezes over pretty quickly."

We stopped next to a small pond with a walking bridge gracefully arching over the far end. There was a narrow path lined with old fashioned gas lights that meandered around the pond. It lent a lent calm warmth to the scene. The entire park was surrounded by pine trees that reached toward the blackness of the snow-dusted sky.

Snow collected in patches on the pond while other spots glistened in the gaslight. The needled trees were beginning to decorate themselves with the falling snow. I stopped to enjoy the quiet area. It was like something from a fairy tale, or maybe straight out of a Dickens' novel. I could even hear the quiet hiss of the gas lamps and the snowflakes glancing off of the frozen pond. This was a scene I would remember forever.

"I had no idea this was even here. It's beautiful!" I smiled.

With a leather-gloved hand, Gabriel brushed the snow off of a wooden bench and gestured for me to sit down. I obliged and he slid closely next to me. "Put your shoes under the bench to keep them dry." He set my skates in front of me and removed his own shoes. I hesitated, unsure.

"I've been wanting to teach you to skate," he paused and looked at me.

I was surprised that he remembered me wanting to know how to skate. "You're sweet, but is this safe?"

"It's frozen solid by now. Anyway, it's only two feet deep in the middle."

Why not? I thought. I bent and removed my shoes and slid my feet into the unblemished, snow-white skates. They felt clunky but comfortable.

"Lace them as tightly as you can without cutting off your circulation. It will keep your ankles rigid," he said.

I followed his suggestion and with a little help, I was laced up in no time. Gabriel was already standing in front of me. When I finished, he held his hands out for me to take. He grasped them firmly and I managed to maneuver myself into a standing position. He moved to my side and held his arm out for me to take. He wrapped his other arm around my waist. With his support, I began hobbling toward the ice.

It felt as if I was wearing big, beefy, Frankenstein boots. I wondered how anyone could look so graceful on these things. After a few steps, I realized I didn't need much help on the grass, but the ice was going to be a whole other story.

We reached the pond and Gabriel turned to face me again. "Keep your ankles stiff and your knees loose. If you get too tight or scared, you're going to fall. The worst that can happen is that you fall on your butt...not so bad."

I laughed a little nervously. He placed his hands under my forearms and led me onto the ice. I was hesitant, but I welcomed my first step. I tried to keep my knees loose and my ankles stiff, but I clung to Gabriel like I was drowning.

"Loosen up. Hold my hands." I let go of his forearms and placed my hands in his. He began gliding backwards and I started stumbling forwards. He let me gather my courage for a few moments before giving me any instruction.

Adrenaline made me brave, so I took my first shuffle and glide. It worked! I was only going about a millionth of a mile an hour, but I didn't fall. I was skating! Gabriel let go of one of my arms. He skated backwards so effortlessly. I wished I was as good as he was.

"You're doing great!"

"Thanks!" I replied with a huge smile. I continued to amble like a toddler. Soon, Gabriel let go of my other arm and I was on my own. He circled in front of me, holding out his hands in case I wanted to grasp them.

"Now try pushing off using the side of your skates," he said.

I tried...and teetered. I jerked my upper body to catch my balance and swayed too far to compensate. Just as my feet went out from under me, Gabriel was there in a flash. He caught me around my waist and helped me regain my footing.

"Thanks!" I said.

He laughed politely, "That's why I'm here." Again he held me by my forearms. As I started to get going, he let go of one arm and then the other. This time I was able to push off four times before he needed to make a save.

We continued like this for several minutes, and before I knew it, we covered the distance around the pond.

"Look," said Gabriel, "you made it!"

"I'm better than I thought!" I replied excitedly.

"Ready to go again?"

"Sure!"

"This time," Gabriel instructed," try not to look at your feet. You want to get a feel for the ice rather than concentrate on where your feet are going."

"Okay," I replied. I focused on Gabriel's confident smile. His blonde hair almost as white as the surrounding snow. He skated in front of me slowly, patiently. I appreciated his silence. He didn't bark out a ton of instructions or offer too much drippy encouragement. He just skated backwards, allowing me to learn on my own. I came close to falling several times, but each time he was there to catch me. We were soon done with our second lap.

"Need a break?" he asked.

"I guess," I replied. I was having fun, but a little break from the tension I was feeling in my thighs was a good idea. He led me off the ice to the bench. Again, he dusted the snow off with the palm of his gloved hand. We sat closely together.

"That was fun!" I exclaimed.

"Yeah," he replied. "I love to teach people how to skate. It's like opening a door they never knew existed."

"Thank you," I looked up into his finely angled face. "This is a perfect distraction."

"I figured there was some situation brewing, something you couldn't tell me."

"Yeah." I paused. "I just don't want people to feel sorry for me. You know, this might sound weird, but having a sick mom is kind of like being an amputee."

"What do you mean?"

"I can hear the whispers and the 'poor things' and the 'that's-too-bads'," I continued. "The pain and distraction are obvious and they get tiresome pretty quickly."

"I can imagine."

"I remember when I was in second grade there was a kid in my class," I paused, remembering. "His mom was really sick for a while and then she died. I remember not wanting to go near him or even talk to him because I thought death might be contagious." I looked into Gabriel's calm, blue eyes. They reassured me with their kindness and concern. "Isn't that stupid?"

"Not at all," he replied. "You were just a kid."

"Yeah, but I still remember that. Now I know how it feels." I lowered my head and looked at the ground. "It's almost like I'm being punished for treating someone so badly."

Gabriel immediately removed his black leather gloves. "Look at me," he whispered gently. He took my chin gently in his fingers. "Everything will be okay."

I felt his warm, sweet breath and I inhaled. I wanted to believe him. He seemed so sure.

He leaned toward me and brushed his lips softly on my cheek. I turned my face toward those lips and we shared a long kiss. We lingered, sharing the warmth of each other's breath in the cold night air. I could have stayed there forever. Hours may have passed, and I wouldn't have cared. We were completely lost in the moment. Gabriel kissed me again.

It continued to snow, harder now, with big, fat, lazy flakes falling like tickertape to the ground. Gabriel shared my delight by catching a few flakes on his tongue. Every time he laughed, I could see his breath freeze on the air.

"How about one more skate before we go?' he asked hopefully.

"Certainly," I replied. We walked to the ice. This time I felt much more confident; maybe it was the joy from this unexpected, heart-stopping date.

Gabriel stood on the ice and held his hand out for me to take which I did so willingly. He pulled me towards him and I didn't resist. I took a glide and was sure some of his confidence was rubbing off on me.

Gabriel pulled me along, he moving backward and I forward; our arms bridging each other's bodies. He picked up a little steam then suddenly and unexpectedly stopped. I squealed and had no choice but to glide right into him.

He caught me with a sweeping gesture, one arm around my back. He took my right hand in his left. We stood like a pair of ballroom dancers.

"Do you trust me?" he asked grinning.

"What are you doing?" I asked. "I can't dance! Especially on ice!" I grasped him even more tightly as I struggled to keep my balance.

"I didn't ask you if you could dance," he said. "I asked if you trust me."

"Of course I do!" I replied. His strong arms supported my back and he held me closely.

"Do you remember when you first came to my game and you told me you always dreamed of skating? Feeling like you can fly?"

"Sure," I replied. "I think being able to skate is amazing, but it takes practice! I can't just..."

"So do you trust me?" he interrupted.

"Yes!"

"Then just follow my lead. Skate with your heart. Don't pay any attention to your feet."

"I'll try!" I replied, full of doubt.

Gabriel began skating backward, supporting me firmly. "Close your eyes," he whispered.

It was hard. I closed my eyes, but I kept peeking. The second we'd pick up a little speed, I'd open my eyes and grasp onto Gabriel.

"I thought you trusted me."

"I do!"

"Then keep them closed," he laughed.

This time we picked up some more speed. I could feel Gabriel making turns. I tried to keep up.

"Use your heart. It will show you the path."

I decided to try it. I stopped thinking and started feeling. I willed my clumsy feet to follow his gracefulness. We were going faster now. Snow was freckling my face and it tickled. Faster still!

I found that as I relaxed, I began to see Gabriel, even though my eyes were closed. I could see where his feet were going. I began to mimic his footfalls with my own. As I concentrated, I saw more of what I had to do, and skating got easier.

"You got it!" said Gabriel. "Keep it up!"

I did what he asked; keeping my eyes shut tightly. I could feel us picking up speed, slowly at first, then faster. He held me closely. It did feel as if we were flying! My feet were moving in rhythm with his and soon we were those ballroom dancers, turning and gliding. Snowflakes kissed my cheeks and the cold air ruffled my hair. It was incredible!

Gabriel whispered in my ear, "Don't be afraid. Just keep moving. Keep seeing with your heart!"

"Okay," I replied excitedly. "How is this happening?"

"Shhh...now...open your eyes."

I was afraid to see what we were doing, but excited as well. I opened my eyes. What I saw was nothing short of astounding. I gasped, but kept moving. "Gabriel!" was all I could muster.

We moved around the ice effortlessly. I didn't know how, but my feet knew exactly what to do. I didn't even have to think, I just knew...like an instinct. It was as if someone wound me up and I just went, doing what I was programmed to do. I was having the time of my life, yet I didn't know how! I looked around in amazement, and then I looked to Gabriel.

He gazed down at me knowingly, holding my body against his. He too moved effortlessly, not needing to watch where he was going. Not needing to see anything at all. He smiled; his expression was kind and full of love. I rested my cheek on his chest and we danced through the snowy night.

We must have skated for a long time. To my dismay, our speed began to slow. My heart raced in rhythm with his. Soon, we stopped completely and I looked into Gabriel's kind eyes...eyes that sparkled with the knowledge of what had just taken place. He hugged me closely and kissed me softly on my forehead. Hand in hand, we silently skated toward the bench. It was again blanketed with snow. Gabriel again brushed it aside and we sat. I had to ask, "How did I do that? It was like we were Olympians!"

Gabriel replied thoughtfully, "Trinity, don't question wonderful things; just allow them to happen."

I looked at him, "But..."

"But nothing," he laughed. "You're a natural!"

I realized I would get nowhere with him, so I decided to stop asking. We really didn't say much for the next few minutes. My mind was busy; amazed at how I could suddenly skate so well. I didn't want the night to end, but it was time. I had to get some sleep. I didn't have to tell Gabriel, he was already unlacing his skates as if he knew what I was thinking.

Even though I put my shoes under the bench, they were full of snow. I turned them over and tapped them on the bench. They were cold when I slid them on. I wiggled my toes and waited for Gabriel to gather our skates. He stood and took my hand.

We strolled silently through the snow. There must have been three or four inches along the sidewalk. Slinging our arms around each other's waist, we headed home.

Gabriel spoke first. "This is probably going to sound pretty weird, but I'm so glad you decided to trust me," he stopped carefully choosing his words.

I suddenly felt very cold, as if a wave of ice had enveloped us both. Yes, it was cold outside, but I had never felt a cold as deeply as this. Surprisingly, it didn't seem to faze Gabriel.

"Why wouldn't I?" I asked.

"Well...how should I say this," he paused and thought for a few moments. The seconds seemed like hours. What was he going to say?

"There are big things coming, Trinity, and I need you to be ready."

The cold turned into a fist and squeezed my heart. "What do you mean?" I asked, suddenly frightened.

"Well...strange things are happening," he paused again, "with all of us...at school...at home...I just want you to be careful."

Why did he say that? I was afraid to ask questions. I wasn't sure if I wanted to know more. Gabriel's warning frightened me. More so that he knew peculiar events were taking place, and I didn't even tell him about my dreams. I wondered what was going on with him. Could a few dreams really be so bad? I thought of Kane and answered my own question...Yes, yes they could.

Gabriel and I sat on the porch steps for some time. It must have been close to three-thirty when he left with my kisses. I wished we could just be regular teenagers, with nothing unusual going on, going to a regular school with ordinary lives. I would welcome that warmly.

Ending my rambling thoughts, I decided to go inside. Gabriel had frightened me with his candor and honesty, but I welcomed his warmth and concern. It was a difficult act to balance. I slowly closed the door half expecting my father to be sitting on his chair, waiting to see where I had been. Luckily, he was still asleep. I decided to bypass the couch and tackle my room head-on. I wanted to catch some sleep if I could, but Gabriel occupied every thought I had. I hung my damp coat, careful not to clang the hangers in the closet.

As I opened the door to my room, I was met with the Yellow. It was alive...sneering at me as it perched on my walls. It was as mean as ever...and sarcastic...pretending...holding out its arms to welcome me...but having a sick heart.

I turned off the light, forcing the Yellow's absence. I lay on my bed, thinking of Gabriel, analyzing what he said, especially the part about strange things going on. I also thought of Kane. I had to help him, but how? Eventually, my eyes became heavy and I dozed.

Nightmares grasped me right away, like hungry animals. I dangled into the deep where all dreams come from. Anything could just rise up and swallow me. I was immediately captured and pulled down...down.

Chapter 26

I was in an old house, obviously abandoned. Windows were boarded up hastily, and what was strange...they were boarded up from the inside. There was no method to the hammering. Nails twisted into the wood. Some found their mark and held the wood to the frames; others were attempted then abandoned for no reason. Still others bent with the impact of the hammer and were pounded into the wood anyway. Anyone could tell it was a hurried job. I could see the last rays of twilight struggling through the gaps in the boards. They stretched in long, dying stripes on the floor.

I looked around. I must have been in a sitting room or parlor. The house was Victorian in architecture because the windows were tall and arched at the top, and the room was thickly trimmed with ornately carved woodwork. Heavy velvet drapes hung from gilded rods above the windows for so long, the nibbles of mice and the rot of time caused them to begin to slump. They clung to the rods like suicides that changed their minds, grasping for life. Braided gold trim dangled in tatters around the edges.

There was furniture that must have been elegant at one time with its pastel, velvet cushions and ornate, wooden armrests. Now most of the pieces were covered with sheets, yellowed with time and dusty with cobwebs. In places, moths had feasted on the cotton. In other places, the threads, unraveled with the passage of time and the weight of the sheet itself, threatening to fully expose the furniture.

The wallpaper behind the furniture clung to the walls in some places, but in others, the glue had dried up long ago. This caused the wallpaper to sag in great billows, like an old woman's blouse. The color was a faded yellow with a murky, floral pattern. Too familiar, I thought.

Sometimes even though you're alone, you know you shouldn't touch things. Even in this dusty, forgotten place, I could feel someone watching me...waiting for me to make a mistake...to make an unwanted noise, to touch something I shouldn't.

I looked to the floor. What would have once been delicate green and brown carpets were faded and riddled with holes. I could also see piles of small black specks which I assumed were mouse or rat droppings. They carpeted the room.

I crept across the parlor, afraid to wake up whatever evil thing slept in the house, wincing with every floorboard that creaked. Although I was there only a few minutes, I already saw the shadows on the floor lengthening and the light dimming. I made my way to the closest window and peeked between the slats.

The sun was on the horizon, beaming its last rays of light on the landscape. From what I could see between the boards, it looked like I was in a large, grey clapboard home. The ground was quite a distance below, so I assumed I was on the third story. A rusty fence made of iron spikes surrounded the gently rolling grounds. There were very few trees surrounding the house, but a dense forest waited for someone to cross beyond the fence, waited patiently.

As I peered more deeply into the twilight, I could see people on the ground...shadows...darker than the surrounding woods. They scampered among the trees...impatient. Their silhouettes blackened like ash against the last burning rays of the sun. Who were they? As I watched, the sun flashed its last brilliant rays of gold then sunk below the hills in the distance. At that precise moment, the people began to chatter and screech.

My heart pounded in my chest, but I kept looking. Some figures rose up on thickening legs and arched their arms in unnatural poses, hands waving wildly in the air. Others lifted their faces toward the sky and screamed. Still others stretched on the ground and convulsed violently. One thing was abundantly clear...they were changing!

One particularly large man leapt onto the iron bars of the fence and grasped it with hands that ended in claws. Pushing with his legs, he leapt over the spikes topping the fence. He chattered at his success. Others began to follow. I recognized them! These were not the wolves...they were much, much worse! These were the rats carved on the baseboards and crown moldings at school! Dozens of them! They were almost as large as the wolves, and their beady yellow eyes were fixed on the house.

As I watched, one smaller brown monster that was half-rat, half-human was in such a hurry; he leapt prematurely and was unable to clear the spikes. I gasped as he impaled himself through the thigh. As his body slid down the spike, he kicked with his one good leg and clawed at the fence. His teeth gripped, latching onto posts, trying to free himself. His body turned from rat to human, then back to rat. I had to move! I had to hide!

I scurried into several rooms, searching quickly. I wanted to be inside something, out of any open space. I was on the edge of panic, but I had to keep a cool head. There was a loud bang downstairs...then another...and another! They were throwing their bodies against the boards! With a sickening sense of dread, I realized why the house was boarded from the inside! Now, I could hear nails screaming, resisting the bodies that forced against them. I scrambled, knowing I only had a few moments before the rats, or the people, or whatever they were, got inside.

I ran into a bedroom. There were the tattered remains of a yellow, floral canopy dangling from a square wooden frame. Under the canopy was at one time a sumptuous queen-sized bed. Mice had made nests in the soft mattress filling. Their sudden movement startled me. Sensing my presence, they scrambled in great numbers across the bed. Some even preferred the openness of the floor in their mad dash to safety.

More crashes from downstairs.

Spying a built in wardrobe in the corner, I raced to it and flung it open. It was enormous, going back at least six feet. Blessedly, there were still old coats hanging inside. I didn't want to imagine what was living inside the pockets. I parted the clothes and wiggled my body to the rear of the wardrobe. I reached and shut the door but for a crack. I needed to breathe and I needed to see when they came for me. Crouching in the rear of the deep closet, I listened to more crashes coming from downstairs, cringing with each one that passed.

It took longer than I thought but the final crash did come. Immediately after, I heard the scrabbling of claws on the downstairs floors…and the whipping of their ropy tails. They were inside!

Holding my breath, I was afraid the moldy smell of the clothing would make me sneeze and give my hiding place away. Would they find my body, or would the rats devour everything? I imagined them ripping at my flesh and gobbling. How long would it take me to die from rat bites?

I sat for a few moments that seemed like hours. I went over whether I should stay put or if I should make a break for it. If I ran, where would I go? I pushed into the farthest, darkest corner of the wardrobe and prayed for Narnia to appear. Thoughts of peeking out of the door tempted me. I had left it open ever so slightly, and I moved slowly, scooting my rear-end across the wardrobe floor. I leaned just far enough to get a clear view out of the crack.

Soon, I heard them clipping and squealing in the hallway. I held my breath and strained to hear what sounded like a human voice as well. Was it true? Was someone directing them? It was a man's voice, but try as I might, I couldn't hear the details of what he was saying.

Slowly, I pulled some of the coats off the hangers and piled them on top of me. I was lucky the wardrobe was huge and I had enough room to do this without opening the door. I pulled the top coat down far enough to be able to catch a glimpse of part of the room.

I looked just in time to see the first of the rats scuttle into the room. God, it was huge! I put my hands over my mouth to stifle any gasp that escaped. My skin crawled, and I pulled the coat up to my nose. If they found me, surely there would be nothing I could do.

Suddenly I felt a sharp pain on my arm. I glanced over to see that a large mouse was rather angry with me taking up residence in his closet, so he decided to give me a nip. With a shiver of disgust, I swatted it away with the back of my hand. I peeked out the door once more.

Many more rats were tearing the room apart, screeching and squalling, knocking over dressers and ripping up the bed with their muzzles. They left nothing untouched. A few minutes later, a human shape entered the room. It was a man and he was speaking in squeals and screeches, gesturing wildly at the rats.

A big brown rat strutted towards the wardrobe. I pulled the coat over my head once again and sat perfectly still. With its claws, it pushed open the door. I could hear his pause as he surveyed the small space with its sharp eyes. Did he know I was here? I awaited his call that indicated prey was located, but one never came because the man in the room started barking his rat orders again. As quickly as they arrived, the rats suddenly left. I waited until I heard them scrabbling down the stairs. I waited a long, long time. I wondered who had called them away.

I couldn't stay in the closet forever; I needed a better hiding place, one that didn't leave me so vulnerable. I clambered out of the wardrobe and stood on the hardwood floor. Tiptoeing, cringing with every step, I peeked around the doorway into the hall. No one was there. In the dust on the floor, I could see huge tail scuttles and smears of dust.

Like one of the rats, I scampered down the hallway, peering intently into each room, looking for a hiding place. I peered into the last room, and that's when I saw it! A chain hung from the middle of the ceiling, and around the chain was the outline of a small door. There was an attic!

I did not know if I should pull the chain or not. Opening the attic would probably draw attention, but should I risk all of that noise? I had to do it!

I jumped up and just tipped the chain with my fingers. I tried again. This time I got a fistful of cold, thick links. As I landed, the door yawned open. Dust and cobwebs spilled onto my upturned face. Instinctively, I bent over and brushed them away with my sleeve. Stairs had popped out of the opening like a tongue mocking me. Again I jumped and pulled on the first step. They tumbled out in sections and landed with a thud. Wincing at the din, I listened for the rats...nothing! I put my foot on the first rung and tested its strength. Although I was thin, it groaned but held my weight. Without stopping, I clambered up the stairs.

When I reached the top I checked out the attic, making sure this was somewhere I wanted to stay. Despite the layers of dust and cobwebs dangling from almost every surface, the room looked fairly harmless. I bent down and pulled the stairs back up into the room. It was almost pitch black with the door closed, and my eyes adjusted to the darkness slowly. On the tops of each wall was a ventilation slat that let in a little moonlight. I made my way to them to look outside.

I peered out carefully, afraid of knocking the decaying boards to the ground far below. All was quiet among the trees. No rats...were they all in the house? I turned from the window.

After a few moments in the darkness, I was able to spy a metal pull chain hanging from the center of the large room. I slinked to it and gave it a yank. Light instantly flooded the room. I winced at its brightness, and after a few moments, I welcomed it.

There were a few pieces of furniture covered in drop cloths. A grandfather clock, enveloped in a shroud of cobwebs and dust, stood judging me from the corner. A parade of ancient toys and a broken-down antique baby carriage crept along the back wall. Other items stood, partially covered in rotting cotton sheets. The mouse droppings were evident here as well. They covered just about everything.

I decided to make myself comfortable. I had no intention of leaving until the morning, so I pulled a cloth off of an old sofa and sat down. I put my head in my hands and ran my fingers through my hair. I didn't know what to do, but at least the feeling of panic was starting to subside.

Looking around the room again, I spied a weapon. I quickly selected an umbrella from a cylinder stand and pushed the rusty button to open it. As it opened the old nylon wings shredded with age, leaving me holding the steel skeleton. It was too awkward to maneuver, so I cast it aside and kept looking. I rummaged through boxes and pulled the cobwebby covers off of everything. In one aging cabinet, I found a dull Swiss Army knife that I stuffed into my pocket. I found nothing else that could be used as an effective weapon.

An old wooden high chair in one corner of the room gave me an idea. Rushing to it, I picked it up, and pried one of the legs off of it. To test it, I swung it like a baseball bat. It made a whooshing sound, and it felt heavy and sturdy. I took my place on the couch again. After a few moments, I slid back into the seat and closed my eyes. As I rested I thought of many things to calm myself...Texas...Mom...Gabriel...Ravie...Kane. Instead of feeling calm, I thought of the rats. It felt as if I were waiting for them to find me. I had to come up with a plan.

Suddenly sensing something was wrong, I opened my eyes. I hesitated, not wanting to see what was there, but I looked to my right. Perched on a cedar chest next to the arm of the sofa was an enormous, white rat. It scrutinized me with its beady, pink eyes and took a few hops towards me. I recoiled, fearful of its audacity. Its eyes glinted as it stretched to sniff the air around me. Now I could see many more rats, hopping from surface to surface, perched on the windowsills, sitting on the toys. They were everywhere. I didn't even hear them come!

Someone standing behind me wrapped their hands around my neck. They squeezed slightly, just tight enough so I couldn't speak, but I could still manage to breathe with some effort. I tried to claw the hands away, but it was no use.

"Trinity...I've been waiting so long..." The voice said hotly into my ear. It sounded like an iron blade, strong and sharp. I squirmed and kicked, but the strong hands squeezed even tighter, completely cutting off my air. I relaxed and so did the hands, albeit just slightly

The voice began speaking again. "You are very special." He buried his face in my hair and inhaled deeply.

I wanted to distract this stranger, to get his focus away from me. "Who are you?" I managed to whisper "Why are you doing this?" I struggled to pull the claws from my neck with no success.

"I am coming for you," the voice deflected my question. "I need you."

I had to keep my wits. I was starting to see black spots before my eyes. He was squeezing my throat so tightly. It was only a matter of time before he choked me or even snapped my neck. His hands certainly were strong enough to achieve either option without much effort. Distraction was my only chance.

I started to sob. It was hard to breathe, but it was the only thing I could think to do. I felt his hands release a little then one dropped to my shoulder...It was working.

I had to take advantage…now was the time. I grasped the chair leg and swung it backwards over my head. To my astonishment, it hit my intended mark! The second his hands released me, I leapt forward and spun around. I brandished my chair leg towards my attacker. I could see him, human, crouched next to the couch, holding his head. I had to remain calm. I walked toward him, intending to strike more blows, to disable him.

I approached quickly, planning to put my body weight into the swing. The chair leg came down towards the back of his head. While I was in mid swing, he deftly reached out his hand and caught the leg. He stood slowly, and raised his face. It was covered in blood! My first blow did strike the side of his head and caused a gash. The blood wet his blond hair and ran in rivulets down the all too familiar contours of his face. I stumbled backward with realization… "Gabriel?" I let go of the chair leg, and it clanked to the floor.

"Trinity, why did you hurt me?' he questioned innocently. "I was trying to help you." He opened his arms. I resisted the urge to rush to him. "Please…help me!" He dropped to his knees.

I knew I shouldn't...but I did. I couldn't stand to see him there, bloody and helpless by my own hand. I reached into my pocket and clutched the Swiss Army knife tightly in my fist. I dropped to my knees on the floor and studied him. His blue eyes pierced the curtain of blood that covered his face. As I looked into them, I realized this wasn't Gabriel. He reached toward me and grasped my arm. I let him pull me closer. He held me tightly in a lover's embrace. I watched over his shoulder, emotionless as the rats came from the shadows.

Before he could stop me, I raised my arm and plunged the knife into his back. Immediately he let go and leapt to his feet. I sprawled backward and scurried away from his grasp as he released a shriek of pain that could only be outdone by the devil. He whirled, trying to reach the knife. It was buried to the hilt just below his left shoulder blade.

He howled. His features melted from human to rat then something in between. Gabriel, or the creature that looked like Gabriel, suddenly stopped. I expected him to fall down, but he didn't. He turned in my direction. His eyes locked onto mine and immediately he bounded over furniture and other obstacles toward me! There was a sneer on his blood-streaked face. I turned and bolted for the stairs. I pushed on them with all my weight. Before they could even give slightly he was upon me. The weight of both of us on the stairs in the floor caused the trap to open. We fell through the hole and crashed to the floor below. As soon as we hit, I scrambled away from him.

All my efforts were in vain. In one leap, he had me. There was no more talking and no more time. He sank his claws into my biceps and crouched, mainly human in form, over my chest. I grimaced with pain, but refused to scream. Tearing my gaze away I saw dozens of rats emerging from the shadows of the hallway.

"I love you, Trinity," he said, his breath hot on my cheek. As soon as those words left his lips. I heard the chatter of hundreds of rats, screaming with excitement. I felt a bite and a tug on the side of my neck.

When I awoke, I thought I truly was dead. The dreams were becoming more defined and more vivid. Unlike most dreams that fade with each moment I was able to remember almost every detail. It took me a few minutes to relax and breathe normally.

Slowly, I got out of bed and padded off to the bathroom. It was early morning, just after sunrise, but I reached for the light switch nonetheless. I needed light any way I could get it, and in Pittsburgh, often the only source was from a filament. I looked into the mirror and was stunned at what I saw. My knees buckled and I fell to the floor.

Chapter 27

I awoke to cold tile digging into my cheek. I opened my eyes. Remembering what had stunned me there in the first place, I sat up and slowly got to my feet, like a dead girl rising from her tomb. I stared into the sink, purposely avoiding the mirror. Closing my eyes, I resisted, imagining what I would see. I already smelled the coppery truth.

It was as I feared. Blood pocked my face and spattered my hands! I looked closely in the mirror. My shirt was soaked. It was drying to a burgundy color in spots and was darkest around my collarbone. Dare I look? I had to at some point. I took a deep breath, leaned toward the mirror and pulled back the collar of my pajamas. Blood oozed from a large bite on my neck.

I had to clean myself up. It was early and Dad wouldn't be up for another hour. I took a shower and began to bandage myself. I carefully washed the wound with soap and peroxide. It took some time to make the butterflies from tape and place them strategically along the gash and to cover it in gauze. I wrapped in a towel and went to my room.

I forced myself to look at my bed. It was in shambles. The sheets were spattered red, but there was something else. Lying in the middle of my bed was the Swiss Army knife, covered to the hilt in blood.

Chapter 28

I quickly cleaned up my room, packed the sheets into a cardboard box, and shoved it under my bed. I told Dad I had cramps. He, like most men, would never argue with that. Luckily the one turtleneck I owned wasn't in storage, and it was black. It covered the bulge of the bandage nicely. I packed some first aid supplies in my bag – bandages, tape, peroxide and gauze – anything I might need in case blood started to soak through.

On my way to school I felt numb. There were two explanations to what had just happened. I had cut myself with the knife or…I had cut Gabriel. No matter how many times I ran the scenario through my head, these were the only answers.

I walked into the Gathering Hall. I had to find Gabriel. There were very few students sitting around, studying. I checked the time on my cell. Ten o'clock. Most people were in class and would be for some time. I couldn't bring myself to sit still today. I would just think too much as usual. Gabriel was one of the few kids in school who should be on break right now. I looked around the Gathering Hall, but he wasn't there. I headed for the bathroom. I could sit on a windowsill in there and think for a while; between classes I could find one of my friends. I opened the glass door that read "LAVATORY" and entered the hall that divided into two doors labeled "BOYS" and "GIRLS". Sitting on the floor in the hall was a familiar shape. It was Kane!

He looked up with tired eyes and smiled weakly when he saw me. I walked toward him and sat on the marble floor. He put his arm around my shoulders. "I guess you heard," he stated as he looked at me.

"Heard what?" I asked, suddenly alarmed.

"About Gabriel."

"No," I said. Fear seeped into my stomach and my chest felt tight. I shifted to my knees in front of him. "Tell me!" I grabbed the sleeve of his black hoodie in a nervous fist. "What happened?"

"Ravie has been trying to call you all morning. Is your phone on?"

"Forget about the phone! What happened?" My heart felt like it was going to pop out of my chest.

"God, I have no idea. Gabe must have gotten home really late last night. Someone attacked him before he got into the house; stabbed him in the back."

"What?" I asked, shocked. "Is he alive?"

"Yeah...he is...barely. A neighbor heard the sounds of a struggle and scared them off with his dog. Gabe was just lying there, bleeding."

"Where is he?" I grasped Kane's shirt more tightly.

"Presby. Trinity, only family is allowed in."

"I don't care!" I said. "I have to try to see him!" I stood and began to pace.

"Ravie already tried," he replied. He stood, grasped my shoulders, and looked into my eyes in an attempt to calm me. "*No one* is allowed in."

"Kane," I said. "Listen to me. It was the rats! I was there!"

He looked at me, "What do you mean? You were there?"

"Kane, I dreamed that last night...well not exactly that." I continued. "I had a dream I was in a house and people were trying to get in. The really weird thing was they acted like werewolves, but they looked like rats. They changed from human to rat to human again. Gabriel...or something that looked like Gabriel...was one of them. He trapped me in the attic!" I stopped. "Kane, can you come to my house? Right now?"

"I suppose, but...," he paused. "What the hell, Trinity?"

"Look!" I pulled my turtleneck down and showed Kane my bandage. "Something killed me in my dream last night! At first glance, it looked like Gabriel, it really did, but when I looked really closely...I mean really closely, into his eyes, I saw it wasn't him! Come on! Drive me home. We'll talk along the way."

Kane's hand immediately went to the bandage on his own neck. He stood up and followed me through the Gathering Hall.

"We never talked about my cut. Trin…is this the same thing?" We headed for the front door, caught a couple of sideways glances, but no one stopped us. I think they were afraid to. We got into Kane's truck and he began to drive.

"So let's talk." He glanced at me with an icy intensity. "Tell me what's going on!"

"Kane," I began, "I think *you* know something, and *I* know a hell of a lot. We just have to put it all together before something even worse happens! Gabriel is lucky he is still alive, and I had something to do with what happened to him." I debated whether to tell him the truth or not. I quickly decided I had to if he were to trust me, to help me.

"Kane," I began. "Ever since I was very young, I have been able to see things...I guess you could call them *places...*in my dreams. I know these places are real, but no one else can see them."

"Keep talking," said Kane as he drove. His jaw was set.

"I know this is going to sound weird, but hear me out." I said. "When I was little, the doctors called my dreams *events.* I guess you could say I can see into what I believe is another world or existence…or something. I've seen things you'd never even imagine." I sighed. "I can go there when I paint."

Kane glanced at me as he drove, "What?" He shook his head in disbelief. I knew he didn't understand.

"Honestly, up until recently, they've been just visions. I see things…*places...*when I dream. I think sometimes I actually go to these places when I'm asleep. I have been dreaming a lot lately, of awful places...nightmare places. I paint them too...paintings. You have to see them!" I stopped, choosing my next words carefully. "When I was young, my mother had me to all kinds of doctors, but the dreams kept on coming. I started to draw what I saw. I have tablets and tablets of drawings and watercolors. When I was about twelve, the dreams just slowed down, until now.

Kane looked really frightened, wide-eyed and pale. "God, Trinity. If you're telling me the truth, what does this have to do with me and Gabriel?"

"I don't know...yet..." I continued, "Anyway, I dreamed about you, and I think I dreamed about Michael and now Gabriel. During each of the dreams, something was terribly wrong. I still don't understand any of it."

"What about Michael?" he asked a little more softly.

"Michael seems like nothing happened I can't really remember that one, and I'm not sure why. Then there was you...until last night when I hurt Gabriel." I continued, "Nothing ever crossed the dream-reality line until I got to Pittsburgh...until I met you guys."

"So this just began recently?"

I nodded.

He glanced at me seriously as he tried to focus on the road. "You're kidding...you have to be," he insisted. "But somehow, I know you're not." He looked distraught...wild-eyed...familiar.

"I wish I were kidding. I wish this was all a huge joke...but it isn't," I explained. "You have to understand, this is who I am. I've always been able to see these places."

"What do you mean, *see* places?" he asked. He had a fearful but knowing look. "Is it like seeing ghosts?" he asked.

"Kind of," I paused, trying to think of a way to explain. "There are people...people from somewhere else...I know they're not ghosts...they want to tell me something, but they can't, so they use my dreams." I thought of what to say next. "Kane, sometimes I actually go to those places, especially when I paint. It's hard to explain. I guess I'm compelled to paint...sometimes until I almost pass out. It's like I am in a trance or something. Like I'm here, but I'm not really here."

"Trinity, my mind is telling me you're crazy, but my heart is telling me to listen to you." He took a deep breath and continued, "I always go with my heart." He looked mistrustful, wary, and for the first time since I've known him, unconfident. When I looked at him, I saw a scared boy. We drove for a while in silence. We both needed time to digest the conversation.

"When we get to my house, I have to show you something I found last night. I think it's pretty important."

"Ok..." he said uncertainly.

I knew my father wouldn't be home, so we went inside. Not stopping for niceties, I led Kane to my bedroom. "Ignore the ugliness, please," I requested.

"God, Trinity! This color is creepy. How do you stand it?" He ran his hand across the wall and I could swear the Yellow darkened in anger.

"I can't," I replied. "I hate this place!"

"I can see why you're never at home. It could drive you crazy," said Kane. "It kind of sucks you in…all swirly and ugly at the same time." He studied the paint closely.

"I think it may have done that already," I replied. "Here," I said, trying to distract him from the hypnotic glare of the paint. I sat on the floor and pulled a cardboard box out from under the bed.

Kane tore his eyes from the wall and rubbed them with his finger and thumb, "I think that already gave me a headache." He sat cross-legged on the floor next to me. I stopped for a moment and shut my eyes. I took a few deep breaths.

"You okay?" he asked.

I opened my eyes and studied his face. He looked softer than he had in the car. His toughness had withered and was replaced by fear. His black hair was tousled and he was unshaven. Dark circles encompassed his tired eyes giving him a vampiric look.

"I just don't know if I believe this myself." I stated.

I sometimes imagined what I would do if I had one wish that would come true. What would I wish for? How would I word the wish as to not be misconstrued or to end up with something I really didn't expect. I had the perfect words for this one. "I wish I had a normal life." I said softly.

I took one more deep breath and began. "When I woke up this morning, I was covered in blood. I assumed it was mine, but now I know I hurt Gabriel." I continued, "In my dream, Gabriel was chasing me. He was like the king of the rat-people." I opened the box and pulled out the rumpled, bloody sheet and set it aside.

The knife I found in my bed lay in the bottom of the box. It was an old Swiss Army knife; the wooden handle was nicked in several places and the varnish had worn off the middle. I lifted it carefully and handed it to Kane. "This isn't mine," I said.

He examined it closely, turning it over in his hands. "Trinity, if I didn't believe the crap going on here, I would say you're crazy." The shaft of the knife was covered in blood, dried to a dark brown. Kane fingered it for a few moments then set it on the carpet next to me. "Where did you get that?" he asked.

"Why?" I asked warily.

"I would recognize that knife anywhere. It belongs to Gabriel."

Chapter 29

Kane studied my face intently for a few moments before he spoke. His usually smooth brow was wrinkled with worry. "I might as well tell you this too. I got a call from the hospital this morning. They have been trying to contact Gabriel's family all night. They took his cell and started calling numbers." Kane paused pensively. "Trinity, there aren't any numbers on his cell…for family I mean. The only numbers he has are his friends…*us*…no one else! I thought about it all night. I know his parents are dead, but there has to be someone."

"Are you sure?'

"No one can find his family, not the hospital, not the police."

I paused to think, but nothing made sense. "Why do you think he doesn't have any numbers?"

"I think there is a lot more to Gabriel than any of us really know."

"Well, maybe he has two phones or something," I said

"Even if he had all the money in the world, I doubt a nineteen-year–old has two cell phones…and no parents or siblings or cousins or anything."

"God…" This was really scaring me.

"So I thought about this last night. Beatrice's apartment is all laid out…you remember?" he asked.

"Yeah."

"I've known her for two years…never met any of her family either. They don't come to visit and she never mentions her parents. She says she has a sister, but you would think she'd show up at some point."

The more Kane said, the sicker I felt. "What about Ravie and Michael?" I asked.

"Never been to Michael's. He's always been a little private, but I never thought anything of it. He just says he has an apartment in the North Side with his mom.

He continued. “I’ve known Ravie since we both got to Turnbull. I know her brothers and her mom. I've been to her house, and I know she’s okay.”

“You just figured this all out?” I asked.

“Just this morning. I’m not the smartest guy in the world, but if I ever get my act together, I think I could give a few of the nerds at school a run for their money.” He forced a smile. “Honestly. It took a bit of putting two and two together, but it was like the sun came out from behind the clouds and lit up the facts. They were just lying all over the place, and all I had to do was pick them up.”

“And then there’s me…even I am a transplant. I moved here when I was seven.

“There has to be a reason why all of us are *not* from Pittsburgh. It’s almost like the city called us here.” I said softly.

“Trinity, when I talk to you and you explain what's happening, it feels like I’ve found a lost piece of a very old puzzle…a piece I’ve been searching for…well, for my whole life.”

I was afraid, more so then I have ever been. “I’m sorry I ruined everything for you…for Gabriel. Maybe if I had never come, we wouldn’t be…”

Kane took my hand and held it gently, “None of this is your fault, Trinity. There’s a reason these strange events are happening with all of us, and I think we’ll figure it out very soon.”

Suddenly, with a great sense of urgency, Kane said, “We need to talk to Ravie.”

Chapter 30

I wanted to see my mother while Kane looked for Ravie. She wasn't answering her cell. Hospital rumor was Mom might be released in a week or so. Dad was elated. He was coming back to his usual jovial self, whistling around the house and telling more and more stupid jokes. Since my mom's treatment was experimental, I knew we would have to stay in town while the doctors monitored her. But it was a ray of hope, and a pretty bright one at that.

The hospital was a short walk from my house, but I decided to make it a longer one. I needed time to myself, some fresh air...no matter how cold...time to think. There was so much happening right now, and so quickly. Although I loved my mother deeply, my thoughts kept going to Gabriel. What the hell happened last night? No matter how deeply I thought or how many explanations I built, they were all flimsy, transparent. I thought deeply as I covered blocks upon blocks in longs strides. I found it was easier to think clearly if I kept moving.

Maybe the blood came from me. Maybe the knife fell into my pocket while we were skating. Maybe it nicked me in my post-date euphoria and I didn't notice. Maybe I was kidding myself.

Perhaps I dreamed the whole thing, even Kane telling me that Gabriel was in the hospital. Perhaps the stress from my mother's situation was blurring into my social life. Perhaps Gabriel was fine and at school and not injured at all. Perhaps I was kidding myself.

Could be that I bled in my bed sheets. Could be I incorporated that into my dreams. Could be I was rationalizing a perfectly methodical occurrence. Could be I was kidding myself.

I had to find a way to get in to see him.

As I walked, I began to focus on the more obvious answers. I had no explanation for the blood or the knife in my bed, so I decided to look at the answers that lie figuratively strewn in my path. Why was I dreaming about my friends? That question, I could not answer...but I knew there was something I needed to know...something was missing.

That led me to an obvious question...why Gabriel? Why not me? Was someone...or something trying to get to me and using my friends to do it? My stomach sank. That had to be it! I was the one with the crazy dream history. I was the one with the evil house. I was the one with the bloody knife in my bed. This had to be the right direction. I was the *catalyst* for all of this activity.

I continued walking. Why couldn't I use them to build some answers? I was missing a foundation upon which to lay my facts; I just had to find what it was! All I was coming up with was more questions...questions that nested in my thoughts...questions with no direction....questions without relationships. All of these events had to have a common thread. Why couldn't I find it? I tried to follow each thread to a reasonable conclusion, but I just became tangled in the webs I wove. Why did Gabriel get hurt in my dream? Why did he want to kill me? Was this a precursor of what was to come? Would he kill me in reality and the "good boy" act was just that...an act? What was Gabriel really up to? I refused to believe he was anything but the wonderful person he showed me.

And most of all, what was with my surroundings? Was something living in the walls of the Yellow bedroom? Would it reach out and get me one dark night? And what about school, the carvings, the underlying dark details that everyone but me failed to notice?

My mind...maybe that was it; I was going crazy, simple, easy explanation. That must be it, yet I knew it wasn't the answer. I watched the cracked concrete sidewalks stream below my feet...passing with nothing but searching thoughts and more questions. I felt overwhelmed, exhausted.

I was walking for a while when I remembered where I was going in the first place...Mom! I had to get to the hospital. I jarred myself out of my meditation and looked at my surroundings. At first, I didn't recognize where I was. Had I walked until I became lost? Nothing was familiar except some graffiti on the forgotten wall of a large brick apartment building. It was almost completely shrouded with dead weeds and a broken down chain link fence. I felt a strange need to touch that graffiti. I didn't know why.

Stepping over the weeds, I pulled aside the obscuring, rusty fence. The graffiti was actually a series of letters that spelled out a word, and I knew this word! It peeked at me through the weeds when I passed by on the bus to school. I always thought the blue color was unusual. It almost glowed. I had always wanted to come here and see what it was all about, but I never had the reason to, until now.

Every letter was large, about ten feet in height. I soon realized each letter was perfectly shaped. The letters arched, spires in artistically sculpted blue shades of spray paint. The words resembled the skyline of a city, full of twists and towers. In fact, it was some of the most intriguing art I had ever seen.

I stepped back from the wall to see what the letters read. Although I already knew, I wanted to be sure. Vines, half dead, still embraced most of the wall. I grasped their brittle branches and tugged hard. After a few attempts, letters began taking shape. First an A and an M. I pulled harder. They resisted, but after some struggling I saw an E…an N...a T…a final A. "Amenta," I whispered.

Chapter 31

The sound of my whisper grew. Other voices joined my own, whispering like tiny chimes, "Amenta...Amenta!" they twittered and tinkled. I walked to the wall and gently placed my hand on the faded paint.

Immediately, I felt a pulse of energy, like blue electricity surging through my body. There was no pain, just boundless bright energy. It coursed through my veins like my own blood. It felt powerful and glorious, like I could solve all of the problems of the world singlehandedly.

"What is Amenta?" I asked as I placed my cheek against the cold wall. I clung to it like a weed myself, wanting to put as much of my body as I could on that exhilarating energy.

"Welcome Trinity," the tinkly voices said. "Welcome!"

I should have been afraid, or at least doubtful. Here I was, hugging a wall, listening to fairy voices in my head. Instead, I embraced what was about to happen with open arms. I closed my eyes and the voices sang with excitement, themselves a cacophony of energy. The energy pulsed with my heart beat. In seconds I faded into the bricks of the wall.

I instantly knew I wasn't next to the building any longer. I also knew I wasn't on Platform $9_{3/4}$. I felt warm sun on my cheeks and a cool breeze lifted my hair from my shoulders. It danced through the air along with the voices, singing in a strange language that was distant but somehow familiar.

Excited, I opened my eyes and drank in my surroundings. Amenta was absolutely breathtaking. There was no where on Earth this beautiful; there couldn't be. The sky was a purple-blue and I stood in a wide field on the edge of a deep forest. A green field brimmed with strange red and orange wildflowers. Their scent kissed the air. They swayed in the breeze, dancing and whispering. I examined them closely, beautiful, but unlike any flowers I had ever seen. Some resembled roses, but without the thorns, and the edges of each petal were fuzzy like the feathers of a flamingo. Others mimicked the simple form of a daisy, but the petals were the orange of a blazing sunset. There were even flowers within flowers, ones whose stamen were tiny flowers themselves. They were unbelievably beautiful.

I turned to the east. The forest was lush, but not dark like the mischievous Grimm forests of fairy tales. I would be okay if I lost my way in these lovely woods. I knew there weren't any witches with candy houses or poison apples in there; no wolves to feast on young girls that lost their way; no houses of rats or anything of nightmares. This forest was too lovely…and familiar, like reuniting with a forgotten childhood friend,

These trees were light and friendly. Sunlight danced on the ground while the trees whispered their own welcome in the breeze. I could hear a stream babbling nearby except I couldn't pinpoint exactly where it was. It sounded cool and inviting. I imagined the sweetness of the water cascading down my throat. I wanted to rush into the woods; to find that stream and lay beside it for hours, staring at my own reflection like Narcissus, until I too turned into a graceful flower.

I turned around and saw violet hills in the distance. These hills marched to majestic purple mountains on the horizon. They were capped with snow that glistened even at this great distance. In the foothills I saw a towered, white city, regal and elegant. The voices told me the city was called Djeba, the Throne of Horus.

While I debated whether to meander through the forest or to approach the city, I saw something strange, something that did not belong in this beautiful place. It caught my attention immediately. Lightning against the mountains. Storm clouds, dark and looming began boiling over the mountaintops. These clouds were swift and angry and they were approaching rapidly.

The voices stopped their sing-song tones and took on an alarmed note. "Careful, Trinity! He comes!" My heart began to beat rapidly. I stood still, hoping those clouds would disappear, but luck was not on my side. They continued to roll over the mountaintops and pour into those lush valleys like a plague of black locusts.

“Go back! Go back Trinity! He can’t follow you…not yet!” The voices raised their alarm. The wind began to pick up quickly. It became icy cold. In seconds it began screaming in my ears, and I shrieked. Lightning scarred the sky with blazing streaks.

“How do I get back?” I screamed.

“Close your eyes and feel the wall again! Go through the wall!”

I stood in the field and spread my arms wide. It took an enormous effort to stand blindly in a field like a lightning rod reaching to feel an imaginary brick wall. I knew any second I would be struck by a well-aimed bolt of electricity and turned to ash. I wanted badly to curl into a ball and wait for the storm to pass

Suddenly I felt scratchy brick against my cheek. I opened my eyes, and I stood again hugging the cold brick of the apartment building. I stumbled backwards and the first thing I realized was that it was night. I must have been hugging this building for a few hours.

Reality hit me like that same wall. Gosh! Mom knew I was going to come and Kane was awaiting my call. I bet they were both worried! My cell phone buzzed messages into my backpack. I had to call.

I quickly unzipped my backpack and opened it. I gasped at what was inside as laughter tinkled in my head. Reaching in, I grasped two fistfuls and smiled as I brought them to my face inhaling their wonderful scent. My bag was completely stuffed with the wonderful flowers from the fields of Amenta.

Chapter 32

I walked in the direction of my house as quickly as I could. I decided to call Mom first; I made the excuse that I had fallen asleep at the library. She sounded disappointed, but agreed that tomorrow would be a better day for a visit. Dad was talking in the background. I couldn't tell if he was talking to someone else, or if he was talking to Mom about me. Either way, I think I was in for it when he got home. I told her I was going to study at the coffee shop for a while in case Dad needed me. I convinced her it was just past eight and I had a big math test coming up.

I hated lying to my mother; after all, she had never lied to me. I would make up for it later; I didn't know what else to do. I could tell them everything and ask them to trust me, but all that would accomplish would be an appointment with a psychiatrist, not the time I truly needed to figure out this mess.

Dad usually stayed at the hospital until 9:30 or so, so I had enough time to make it to Presbyterian to see Gabriel, or at least get a report on how he was doing. I decided to call Kane.

He picked up the phone instantly. "God, Trinity! Where have you been? I've been trying to call you for hours! I thought you were going to see your mom."

"I was," I replied. I decided not to lie to Kane. He would know I didn't fall asleep at the library or the coffee shop, or anywhere else. He was too smart to fall for that. "Can you meet me?"

"Yes! Ravie is with me."

"Bring her along. We're going to see Gabriel, but I only have about an hour before my dad gets really upset."

"Trinity, I told you no one is allowed in,"

"I know, but I have to try!" my voice cracked with frustration.

Kane sighed, "Where should we pick you up?"

"Actually, how soon can you be at my house?"

"Give us ten," he replied.

I hung up the phone. My house was still a half-mile away, but I walked quickly and soon saw it. There were so many bad vibes emanating from that place that I decided to wait on the porch. I just couldn't go inside and be greeted by the loneliness that place loved to heap upon me. I sat on the stoop, frozen butt cheeks or not, it was better than being in there.

Just before I began analyzing everything again, Kane pulled up. I slid next to Ravie on the bench seat of his truck. He looked over his right shoulder, and his eyes widened. Ravie also turned in her seat to greet me.

"Trinity, you look like hell!" she exclaimed. "Where have you been?"

I laughed. "Actually, I'll explain later. Now we have to see Gabriel."

"Trinity," this time it was Kane who spoke. "They'll never let you in to see Gabriel looking like that. You look like a crazy person."

I hadn't looked at myself since my visit to Amenta. I reached over Ravie to adjust the rear view mirror so I could see myself more clearly. Kane kindly turned on the dome light. I leaned more closely. My face was smeared with dust from the brick wall. My hair was a windblown mess. Luckily I threw my makeup bag in my backpack that morning and I always had my brush. I took both out and began some adjustments while we drove to the hospital.

"So now what is going on?" asked Ravie a little impatiently.

"Well," I smiled, ignoring her question. "Is this better?"

They both glanced at me and Ravie replied, "A little."

"Much," said Kane.

We arrived at the hospital and pulled up to the visitor's entrance. He left the car in the 15 minute spot. Ravie and I didn't argue. We didn't expect to get in anyway. I turned and looked judgmentally at Kane's scruffy military green coat.

"Don't worry," he said peremptorily, "I'm a charmer." He smiled and I could see how he could get what he wanted, as long as the information person was a woman.

We approached the information kiosk, and Kane put on his most innocently handsome smile. He asked for Gabriel's room number. Ravie and I smiled alongside him, trying to be as nonchalant as possible. The lady punched in Gabriel's name on her computer. "Hmm..." she said. My heart leapt. "It looks like he signed himself out just a few hours ago."

"Was anyone with him?" Kane asked.

'"I'm sorry," she replied. "The computer doesn't give that information. All this says is he signed out at...five forty PM."

We turned and ran for the door. "Thank you," Ravie called over her shoulder.

We scrambled into the truck. Kane was backing out even before Ravie even had the door shut, but she didn't complain. We headed for Gabriel's house. Kane drove quickly. He always drove quickly, but this time it was intense. I could tell he was really worried. "What the hell?" he asked rhetorically.

"I'm not sure," replied Ravie. "When I talked to Beatrice this morning, his condition was grave.

"Why didn't you tell me?" My heart was in my throat.

Ravie turned to me. Her eyes were sad and guilty. "They wouldn't let anyone in, Trinity. I swear."

"I would have figured a way in." I replied angrily. "You guys don't understand, I put him there...it was me. Me!"

"You want us to believe you went to his house and stabbed him?" asked Ravie.

"No," I replied. "Not like that! It was a dream...a dream that came true!"

"Trinity," said Ravie, "I'll be the first to admit, there is something about you...something surreal, but I cannot believe you have the capacity to try to kill somebody....even in a dream."

"I don't," I replied, unsure and confused. "In my dream, Gabriel tried to kill me, so I stabbed him...but it wasn't him...I woke up...went to school..." I began to break down; tears cut a warm, salty path into my cold cheeks. "Kane told me he was hurt! Who else could have done it?"

I turned to Kane. "You, you should know! Look at that bandage on your neck! That's where I tore your skin. I know you had the same dream I did. I reached out of my dream and did that to you!" I paused. "You know I did!"

Kane touched the bandage on his neck. Immediately it became red with blood.

"Oh god, Kane," It's bleeding again!" said Ravie, alarmed.

"I'll get it later," he said. "We're almost there." We turned onto Gabriel's street. I had never been at his house, but it was exclusive and elegant. How could someone be attacked and stabbed in such a high-end neighborhood?

Kane shut off the car and bounded up the front steps, waiting for no one. The house was dark. He banged on the front door. Ravie and I quickly joined him. After a few long minutes, we heard an inside lock being undone. The door opened to a sleepy eyed Gabriel. I gasped with delight and hugged Ravie.

"Hi guys," said Gabriel. "I guess you heard what happened." We all gently pushed our way inside.

I forced my way past Kane and carefully placed my arms around Gabriel's shoulders. He smiled and welcomed my excitement with a kiss. I stepped back quickly, and worried about causing him any pain.

He smiled, "Come on in."

He turned on a few lights and we entered the living room. The furniture was overstuffed leather and not like a bachelor pad at all. It was excruciatingly neat and tidy. No photographs or knickknacks graced the tables. It was comfortable, but impersonal...odd, but not cold. Spartan was the right word, not reflecting Gabriel's warm, caring personality at all.

Sitting regally by the fireplace was an enormous, black dog. He watched us, knowing he was handsome...and intimidating. After a few moments and sniffs of the air, he put his head down, unconcerned.

"Please sit down," he said. "I was just getting some sleep. I had a rough day." I wondered how he could be so nonchalant with all I had put him through.

I sat on one side of the sofa and Kane sat on the other. Ravie made herself comfortable in an oversized recliner. Gabriel perched on the arm next to me and immediately took my hand in his. I was happy he did. I looked at him. He looked tired but good; better, much better than me. His hair was tousled with sleep and he had a delicate pallor.

Kane piped in. 'When did you get a dog?" He gestured at the animal on the hearth

Gabriel held his answer but offered an introduction. "This is Anubis." He walked to the dog and knelt beside it.

"So you look pretty good for a guy who was all but dead this morning! What the hell happened?"

"I really can't say. I don't remember much," he paused, thinking deeply. "I know I met Trinity for a skate, I remember getting home…then…" He paused again in thought and shook his head, frustrated, "I just can't get it all."

Ravie raised her eyebrows and nodded at me. I hadn't told her about the skate.

Gabriel continued, "When I got home last night, I was attacked as soon as I got out of the car. I do remember, they came from behind me and moved like ghosts. Luckily, I can fight." He took a deep breath. "They only got me three times...in the forearm, back, and side. They didn't hit anything vital, but they did nick an artery in my forearm. That's why the doctors were so concerned. I lost a lot of blood." Gabriel stood, walked to the dog, and seemed to become a little lost in his recollection. "I remember the dog barking. I know he helped me, but I don't remember how."

"Didn't anyone else come?" asked Ravie.

"Eventually, after the dog barked for a while. The houses are pretty far apart here, and no one pays much attention…unless something irritates them like a dog barking." He scratched the dog's head and it responded by nuzzling Gabriel's hand. The dog's ears stood erect and his muzzle was long and pointed like a Doberman's.

"Anyway," he continued, "All they had to do was stitch up a few things and give me a little blood. I came around pretty quickly. They wanted me to stay the night, but why? I feel tired but fine."

Ravie opened her mouth to protest his leaving the hospital. Gabriel stopped her, "I promised I would come back tomorrow to check for any infection."

I looked at him doubtfully.

"I will!" he protested. "I promise, and I don't break my promises."

"Did you find out whose dog?" asked Ravie.

"Mine," replied Gabriel matter-of-factly. "No collar, no leash, no chip, no history. I'm keeping him." Gabriel ran his fingers across the dog's back.

We sat in silence for a few moments looking at the strange but regal dog. Gabriel then addressed us directly, "Trinity, Ravie, Kane...I've been thinking a lot about this." He became suddenly, deadly serious. He stopped petting the dog and stared at us. That look commanded our attention. Gabriel was usually jovial and brimming with smiles. This was a whole other side to him, a side I had never seen, a side I never wanted to make angry. He looked powerful, and angry. A vein in his temple pulsed as we sat in awe around him, awaiting what he had to say. Even Kane sat assiduously attentive.

"Listen to what I have to say very carefully," he began. We obeyed. "I don't know who attacked me last night, but this isn't the type of neighborhood where people get mugged in their driveways. Someone planned this attack. They were waiting for me."

"Who?" asked Kane?

Gabriel ignored the question and continued, "I just want you all to be careful. If someone knows my schedule, they also know yours. I have my ideas about what's going on here, and I'm pretty sure you are not the targets."

"Gabriel, don't take this the wrong way, but I have to ask...Are you into something we should know about?" Ravie asked. "It's nothing illegal, is it?"

"Of course not!" Gabriel laughed and revealed a little about himself. "When my parents died, they left me everything. There's a lot of stock and a lot of money. I think they were after whatever they could get, and if they spent enough time learning my schedule, they might be back."

"Really?" asked Kane. "I figured you have some money but enough to kill you?"

"Yeah," he replied. "I just don't like to show it around."

I was glad Gabriel seemed to be okay, but I wondered what his real story was. I wasn't buying the rich kid gets mugged story. This had something to do with my dream, and I think Gabriel knew the whole story. Our lives were all twisted and tangled together, whether we wanted them to be or not. It was like one of Mom's soap operas. People only revealed things when they had to. Although I loved Gabriel with all of my heart, he was keeping something very important from me; something that would change my life...all of our lives.

We didn't stay long. Gabriel looked tired and none of us wanted to intrude on his space. Instead of heading home, confused and answerless, we decided to adjourn to the coffee shop. We needed to talk. Things were getting stranger by the minute.

Chapter 33

When we got there, we ordered and sat at a booth in the farthest reaches of the shop. The three of us sipped our drinks awkwardly, each not wanting to be responsible for opening the can of worms that sat in front of us. *"Once the worms get out, it's almost impossible to get them back in," my mom used to say.*

After a few moments, Kane leaned forward. "So," he said, "here's one more thing to think about."

"More?" I complained.

"Do you know why we call school *the machine*?"

"What?" I asked for clarification.

"I thought you would have figured it out by now. You seem pretty observant. He waited a few seconds for an answer I did not supply. I was just trying to process all of this new information, and here was something else.

"On your first day Beatrice said, 'Welcome to the machine.'"

"No," I answered. "Why do you?" I had no idea where this conversation was going.

He looked at Ravie for support. She smiled and shrugged her shoulders. He paused, took a deep breath and continued. "At first kids called it the machine because all of the classes seem programmed, the teachers seem bored, and Turnbull keeps pumping out graduates. But I call it the machine for a completely different reason.

"Why, then?" I asked.

" I'm just going to say it...call me batshit crazy if you want...but, they move," he stated. "The carvings *move*."

"What do you mean?" I asked, suddenly intrigued.

"The carvings on the doors, throughout the whole school, they move!" He was adamant. "It's so slight no would ever notice. Not unless you've been there for years or if you're looking for something unusual, would you *ever* notice they move."

"I'm sorry," I began. "I don't..."

"It's true," interrupted Ravie. "I never noticed either until Kane pointed it out to me. It was just about the time you started coming to Turnbull. Hell, I've been here four years and I didn't believe it until I started watching it myself. They *do* move."

Kane's face was stony once again. I turned in my seat and looked at Ravie, my eyes pleading for support. She denied nothing but said, "Okay Kane! Now she thinks *we're* crazy!"

"You really see the carvings move?" I asked. "When I first got to Turnbull, I thought those scenes were so odd. It was like I was falling into them. I thought I was losing my mind. So, if you see something too, I believe you."

Kane continued, "I'm not quite sure how it happens. I'm wondering if it's like clock movements with tiny gears on some sort of timer, or if it is some kind of illusion or hypnosis. I am going to figure it out, soon!" Kane's eyes flashed green with determination. I learned very quickly that if Kane sets his mind to something, it always gets done, come hell or high water, as the expression goes.

"Check it out," said Kane sliding his chair closer to me. "I'll prove it to you. Monday, pick a skull on your homeroom door. I tried and it works with any one of them. Make a mental note of the skull and its expression." He grasped my forearms, as if he were pleading with me. "Watch it every day until the end of the week and I guarantee it will change!"

Sensing my disbelief, he stood up quickly, "I've even gone so far as to do a rubbing with paper and charcoal. I rubbed that same skull every day and by the end of the month, a grin turned into a scream. I have proof!" He sat once again and fumbled inside his worn, black backpack. He pulled out a square of tissue paper. He held it out for me to take.

"I tried it too, with the tree door," said Ravie in a tone that was unusually serious for her. "I got to school early every day for a month. You know what a monumental effort that was for me? I measured that tree every damn day and by the end of the month it grew an inch. I know it's not much, but it also sprouted several leaves and flowers that had been open had withered and fallen off."

I looked back at Kane and took the paper from him. I didn't open it.

"Did you see the door with the children's faces?" he asked.

"Yes," I replied growing more frightened and more astonished.

"Those kids come and go. It was terrifying at first, but now it's more fascinating," he explained. "It took a while to wrap my head around the fact that it was happening. Once I got over that hurdle, I made careful notes when no one was around. I was watching the face of one little boy. He started near the bottom of the door then began moving upwards. Over the course of the month, he eventually worked his way up to the top then off of the door completely. I haven't seen him since."

He continued, "Trinity, I knew you were different the first day we met," he paused. "You have to throw all physics and convention out the window and do your own experiment." He looked deeply into my eyes. "Look," he cleared his throat slightly and said, "We need your help and your smarts to get to the bottom of this. Although I've only mentioned this to Ravie about two months ago, I've been watching it for about a year. We both noticed one thing."

Ravie finished Kane's sentence, "It's speeding up. The changes I mean," she continued. "When Kane first showed me what was happening, the movement was very slight. Now the changes are happening much more quickly...and I have a feeling something very bad is in motion."

"I know *something* is happening," I replied, "but what is it?"

"Why did I just notice the carvings at school were moving only a year ago," asked Kane. "If this school is at least 150 years old, have they been moving all of the time, but too slowly to notice? Have they sped up recently, or have they just started to move...and why?" He added, "We're going to have to search the school. If the movement is mechanical, there has to be some controlling mechanism. We need to find where it is."

"And who's controlling it, "added Ravie.

"And how is this related your dreams?" said Kane, "If it is at all."

"So the next question is, why me? And why now?" I added.

"Something else must be at work here," Kane replied. "I don't know what…not yet. Let's meet at school sometime Monday?"

"Sure," I said.

Ravie nodded her head.

"So what do we do now?" I asked.

Kane smiled. A wave of relief crossed his face. "Well, funny you should say that. I happen to have a plan. I'll find you Monday."

"Does anyone else know?" I asked.

"We haven't told anyone else." Ravie continued her thought, "Right now, we don't know who to trust. I have had some weird feelings. I don't think we should tell anyone right now."

"So, why did you tell me?" I asked. "I mean, why do you trust me? What about Beatrice or Gabriel or Michael? Why don't you tell them?"

"Not yet," she replied. "It doesn't feel right with them…not like it does with you."

My eyes shifted from Ravie to Kane, studying their expressions. "God, Ravie!"

"Look," she continued. "I told you, I am like one of those people in the movies who know a plane is going to crash. No one believes them, then they're called a freak when it really happens."

"I know your dreams and Ravie's feelings have something to do with the movements of the carvings. Everything is speeding up…being magnified." Kane explained. He paused and looked at me hopefully. "I think this all has something to do with what happened to Gabriel as well."

Kane sat down across from me, grasped my left hand, and laced his fingers through mine. Gently, with his fingers of his free hand, he moved the hair hanging in front of my eyes. His pale green eyes looked into mine.

"Trinity," he said, "we would never do anything to hurt you, but there are relationships here. We have to begin examining them if we are going to ever find out the truth." Kane waited a few minutes before he spoke again. "We need to work together.

We need to talk about everything, everything that's been happening to us. We need to lay it all out, right now. You know Gabriel has a big part in this, and so do you."

I knew that was a fact.

Chapter 34

I walked into Mom's room. It was an unusually bright day and she had the curtains pulled wide open. She lay in the sunlight, and as soon as I entered she sat up. I was amazed that she was dressed in street clothes, jeans and a long-sleeved tee. Gosh, she looked thin, but she had energy. I could feel it coming from her. I don't know how to explain it, but it was like... sunshine.

I walked to her bed, "Planning an escape?" I asked.

"No," she smiled. "We're doing this by the book."

"Why the jeans? You look great!" I kicked off my shoes and slid onto the bed. I sat next to her cross-legged.

"They make me feel like my old self, like I'm going to get out of here, soon. I didn't have the energy to get into them until yesterday. But it feels good to finally be on the path to normal." Although I was delighted that Mom might be okay, I would be lying if I didn't say I was envious of her being on the path to normal. I couldn't even find the damn map to normal.

We talked lightly, enjoyed the rare rays of the sun, and watched television for a while. It was *The Young and the Restless.* Mom loved this show; she even got Dad hooked on it. They usually watched it together every afternoon at 12:30. I thought it was silly. My mind drifted to my "other life" as I started to call it. Those soap operas had nothing on me. Gabriel...my thoughts always went to Gabriel. Where was he? Was he okay? When would I see him? I had so many questions and absolutely no answers.

Before I realized it, Mom was calling my name, loudly enough to startle me from my thoughts. "Trin, you with me?" she asked.

"Oh...yeah," I replied with a sliver of a smile. "I'm just thinking of some school stuff. Where's Dad?" I asked mainly to shift the focus of the conversation. It worked. Oldest trick in the book.

"Taking care of some errands at the bank and the hardware store. He'll be back soon," Mom smiled. "We have a date tonight."

"What? A date? Seriously?" I could feel a genuine smile bunching my cheeks.

"They're going to let me go to the cafeteria tonight. Whoever thought I'd be so excited about the hospital cafeteria?"

"Mom that's great!" I bounced up and hugged her.

"We're going to watch a movie too. Dad's choice."

"You must be feeling better!"

"I can't tell you how much. The counts are all coming up, and I'm coming home!"

I replied, "I can't wait!"

Mom stopped and studied me. Her smile faded. My trick didn't work after all. "Something is bothering you. A mom always knows when something is up with her children, and something is definitely up with you." She looked intently at me, "Start talking."

"I hate to bring this up now. I don't want to ruin anything."

"You're dreaming," she said. I was surprised she knew. "Dad told me."

"Mom, I have to be serious. I am not having episodes or visions again, so don't get all worked up." I sighed. "I don't want to worry you, but I have no one else who knows what I've been experiencing my whole life."

"Honey, that's why I'm here," she replied with a look of concern. "If I can't help you, I may as well be dead already."

"Mom, don't talk like that." I said.

"I'm telling you the truth. Mothers help their children. That's what we're for." She smiled her gentle smile again, but there were lines of worry engraved in her forehead.

"Okay, well…I have been having dreams." I was quick to add, "Nothing like the visions before. They're just really vivid and I'm not really cool with taking sleeping medicine again. Not just yet. They're just dreams." I held back with some of the more vital information and the fact that asleep was the last place I wanted to be.

"Honey, only you know what you see. You share when you want to. I'll never force you."

"Maybe you can help me figure something out." I paused, not wanting to reveal too much. "I need to ask you to start from the beginning. Tell me what you know about my adoption. Maybe it will answer a few questions I have."

She paused for a few minutes, thinking deeply. "Okay...It's time," she sighed, suddenly looking very tired.

Mom chose her words carefully. "When we adopted you, you had just turned two. We were so happy to have you; we really never followed up with your biological mother except we know she moved to Illinois." Mom wet her lips with a sip of water from the glass that sat on the table. "She never replied to any of our attempts to contact her.

"The children and youth adoption counselors explained you had night terrors. These are a type of nightmare that lasts a few seconds to a few minutes. Doctors that examined you simply said they are very common, but yours were exceptionally long."

"Did they tell you I was seeing things that weren't there?" I asked.

"Honestly, I don't think they knew very much," she replied. "Anyway, soon after you came home with us, your night terrors worsened. From each one you woke up screaming.

"Soon, they began to take hold of you in the day *and* at night. On your fourth birthday, you had your first *day* terror. At times, you would just stare at a wall or off into the distance. Being asleep was no longer a requirement for your terrors. The doctors advised us to let them run their course," she paused. "That was also when you started to show an interest in drawing and painting. Every time you got your hands on some markers or crayons, you were drawing fantastic pictures, far beyond the ability of any child. These were pictures of what you saw in your nightmares and, to be honest, they were pretty frightening.

"At the time, your father and I were quite involved with the church. Several priests we knew were convinced it was your imagination being spurred with a lot of help from your dad and me. One spoke of divine intervention." Mom kept talking, revealing more than I thought she ever would. "We took you to church every Sunday and were surprised you didn't burst into flames," she said with a laugh. "Your dad and I dealt with you and your terrors, almost until you were thirteen."

"What happened when I turned thirteen?"

"A wonderful man and a good friend helped us. His name was Raphael," she replied.

"Father Raph? Oh my gosh! Mom, I remember him! I haven't thought of him in a couple years, but I remember him!"

"He'd be happy you did."

"We didn't mean to involve him, but Father Raphael actually saw you have a day terror once. He was intrigued. He thought somehow you were able to see things not meant for most people to see. He thought these events were taking place, but on another plane of existence, a plane most of us can't experience.

"Father Raphael knew of many documented cases of people being able to see into other places and other times. He also provided insight into some very interesting writings; much more than any professor could."

She continued, "He had never come across a case like yours before, so he was learning as he studied you and your terrors. He thought perhaps some type of injury to your brain caused a long-closed door to open in your mind. He thought that people thousands of years ago may have been able to see these kinds of things, but over time, the ability faded as people used it less and less. Eventually it became nonexistent except for the occasional soul who retained the talent."

"Talent?" I asked. "More like a handicap. What about my paintings? Where are they?"

"I told Dad to put them in my closet at the house. I didn't want to risk having them wrecked in some storage unit."

"Did anyone ever see them?" I asked.

"Sure," she replied. Father Raphael even wrote an analysis about them. He thought part of the reason your visions began to fade was you transferred the images to paper as a way to control them." She reached over and smoothed my hair. "He believed the more you painted, the less the visions were able to grab hold of you. He thought painting them kind of fended them off."

"What happened to Father Raphael?" I asked.

"Well," she cleared her throat, "he passed away last year."

"How?" I asked, not really wanting to know. I imagined Hell itself cracking open in a billow of fire and swallowing him up.

"Honey. I'm not going to lie." Mom paused. "He had cancer."

"Seriously?" I asked, astounded.

"Yes, pancreatic. He didn't live long after his diagnosis."

"God, Mom...pancreatic...just like you? Why didn't you tell me any of this before?" I was stunned. I didn't know what to say. What were the chances of that happening...the same cancer...two people close to me? Now I knew why my biological mother put me up for adoption. I was too much to handle...too frightening. I suddenly wondered if she was dead too.

Mom continued, "Well, there was really no need." She had a serious look in her eyes. "As you got older, the visions faded. By the time you were twelve, you only experienced one or two visions a year, and shortly after that, they faded almost completely."

"That's interesting," I said.

At that moment, Dad burst into the room. He was carrying an armful of flowers and a box of candy wrapped in silver foil topped with a red bow. Mom loved flowers and Dad had provided quite the assortment. He walked to the bed and laid them next to her. She grasped them and lowered her nose over the bouquet. "These are lovely!" she said. "Thank you!"

"A-ha! "Dad looked in my direction. "I can't forget my other beautiful lady!" He reached into his inside jacket pocket and handed me a small box wrapped in blue tissue and topped with a matching blue bow.

"What's this?" I asked, intrigued, carefully turning the small package in my hands.

Dad reached into his pocket once again and produced an identical pink package. He handed this one to Mom.

"Ooh!" squealed Mom. "I wonder what it is!" I glanced from my package to my mother. She smiled adoringly at Dad. I slid next to Mom and gave her a one-armed hug. I held my other arm out and Dad took the cue. We all embraced each other in a tiny huddle on the bed.

"Thanks, Dad," I said.

"Well, open them," he replied with anticipation. At Christmas time, Dad was the one who loved giving rather than receiving. Mom and I definitely favored the receiving.

I looked at my gift and knew I would never forget how lovely it was. I popped off the ribbon which I intended to save...probably for the rest of my life. I tore open the paper and found a small cloisonné box. The beautiful turquoise inlays were rimmed with gold, giving the tiny box a very regal appearance. I carefully removed the lid and inside was a small gold cross on a braided silver rope. I admired its delicate beauty as I carefully lifted it from the box. That's when I saw it wasn't really a cross, the top bar was looped. I looked toward Mom to see her reaction. She was already cradling hers in her hand.

"Let me tell you what these are," said Dad. He took Mom's charm and she presented her wrist to him gracefully. He continued, "Ancient Egyptians believed that you could tie your spirit to your body with seven knots and this particular charm. It is called an ankh and it symbolizes everlasting life." Mom began to cry, but she smiled through her tears. Dad was a true romantic. He tied hers to her wrist and she held it up to the fluorescent hospital lights, it glistened and sparkled as if it were on fire.

I held out my arm and Dad tied my ankh to my wrist as well, counting the knots as he gently wove the threads together. When he was finished, I hugged him, "Thank you, Daddy!"

"Are you going to join us for dinner, Trinity?" he asked.

"Actually, I was going to meet a few friends...if that's okay." I stood up, in an attempt to look determined.

"Sure," said Mom. "Friends are important too. We'll talk some more tomorrow...go have fun."

"You too...on your hot date!" I giggled as I pulled my coat over my shoulders.

Mom blushed and I took that as my cue to leave. I tucked my delicate box into the pocket of my coat, and I put the paper and bow in my bag. I gave Mom and Dad one last hug and was on my way.

I really didn't have any plans. It was Saturday and I was tired, but the thought of spending time at home by myself made me nauseous. I would have loved to have dinner with my parents, but then it wouldn't have been a "date" for Mom and Dad. Feeling a bit lonely and not wanting to go home, I decided to visit the coffee shop. I wanted Gabriel to get some rest. There was a chance Ravie and Beatrice might be at the shop, but there was an even bigger chance they would be at Michael and Kane's game. I didn't feel like watching a game without Gabriel playing...so coffee shop it would be.

I made my way through the dusty, mid-December snow. The walk from the hospital to the shop wasn't long, but it was bitter cold. I welcomed its warmth as soon as I walked through the door. There was a small table available by the window which I gladly occupied. Even though I thought Pittsburgh might be the coldest place on earth, I loved to watch the snow fall. It reminded me of Gabriel's ice skating night.

I ordered a chamomile tea and watched the street bustle by from my perch at the window. The tea tasted good, comforting, sweet and flowery. It brought back my time in the flowers of Amenta. I savored a few sips before setting my mind to work. It was an effort to even begin unraveling the events that led me to this place. I decided to start writing things down. I kept a small sketch pad in my bag. I hadn't used it in a few years, but I kept it there more out of familiarity than necessity.

I flipped through the few pencil sketches that I had made. My sketches weren't like my paintings at all. My paintings were a way to control what I saw in my events...visions...horrors. My sketches were simply things I saw every day; things that I may want to remember or study later. Sometimes I even included notes and dates. My sketch pad was also like my personal camera. A few portraits of Mom, Dad, and a few old friends. A Texas landscape from a car window made me long for home. On another page, a vase sprouted a bunch of lively daisies. I longed for the scents of spring, but I still had a long way to go. I flipped slowly, studying each sketch closely. I soon became lost in the book. I recalled each sketch with an emotion or scent or thought from the time I made the drawing. I lingered pleasantly on many of the pages.

I soon found myself amazed as a strangely familiar face gazed emptily at me. Surprise almost caused me to drop the journal. I quickly grabbed the binding but lost my page. I turned the pages as fast as my fingers could move. I had to see that drawing again! I remembered sketching this one about two years ago. At the time I was drawing from memory. I recalled that I did not know this person when I drew her. Since she was created from the layers of my dreams, I looked more closely, my heart practically leaping from my chest. I hadn't given this drawing a thought when I did it. Now, its weight was overbearing. It was Beatrice. She bore an unmistakable look of harsh seriousness. But that wasn't all. There was a set of dates in the corner. "February 15, 2005 – December 22, 2023".

How could I draw someone I didn't even know? Maybe it was just coincidence. I looked again…no coincidence. The rendering was too perfect. It was Beatrice! I stared at the dates. What did they mean? When was her birthday? I couldn't remember her ever sharing that with me. What did this second date mean? God…was she going to die? I had to push that thought from my mind. December 22…only a week away! What was happening here?

I stared at the drawing; it pulled me in. Suddenly, it began to move; to come alive! I recoiled with horror, but I dared not drop the book. Beatrice's boldly defined features began to flake away like snow on a frosted windowpane. The pencil lines around her eyes and mouth darkened. Her cheeks hollowed and her lips became a firm line. Her hair rose from the paper and twisted itself into great tangled masses. A great blackness filled her mouth and it streamed over her lips like smoke.

I knew this person as well! She was the dead woman from my dreams! The one looking for a key in my mother's hospital room. I could take no more! I slammed the book shut.

Chapter 35

I sat silently for some time. I refused to believe what I had just seen. I thought of tearing a page from my sketchbook to record my thoughts, but I couldn't bear to open it. It took me a while to calm down. I thought of going home, but I just couldn't do that either. I thought about Beatrice for a very long time.

I turned over the paper tea-ringed menu that lay on the table. Perhaps writing some things down might help me answer some questions. I folded the paper into thirds and then in half. This gave me six small rectangles. I fished a pen from my bag and labeled each rectangle with one of my friends' names...Ravie, Gabriel, Kane, Michael, and Beatrice. The last square I labeled *Pittsburgh.*

Now I had to brainstorm. I began with Beatrice since she was foremost on my mind. I was beginning to see a few themes. Why were four of us so new to Pittsburgh? Michael came about three years ago, and Gabriel, Beatrice and I were newer arrivals. Was it coincidence? I doubted it. Maybe if I kept writing, I would begin to see more trickles of information that connected all of us. Maybe those trickles would turn into rivers.

School...that's what I needed to spend a bit of time on...school...that weird, creepy school.

I added another word next to *Pittsburgh.* It was *Turnbull.* So many thoughts flooded my mind. I couldn't write quickly enough.

Suddenly someone was holding their hands over my eyes. I jumped with surprise. It had to be one of my friends. "Beatrice?" I asked out loud. It was the logical choice; she practically lived here between soccer games.

"Close enough." A female voice replied. I looked to my right. It was Ravie, smiling.

"I was driving by and thought it was you sitting in the window."

I smiled at her, still shaking off the shock from my sketch pad, but remembering to fold my paper before she could examine what I was doing. I discreetly slid it into my bag.

"So, what are you doing here?" asked Ravie. "Why didn't you call me?"

"I was with Mom all day. I didn't want to come to hockey without Gabriel, so I thought I'd come here and get some reading done," I replied.

"How is Mom?" asked Ravie slipping out of her coat and taking the seat across from mine.

"Great. She might come home next week!" I smiled widely though I was still feeling overwhelmed.

"Next week!" exclaimed Ravie. "That's fabulous!" She folded her hands neatly on the table.

"Yeah," I said. "It really is." I pictured Mom in my mind. She really did look so much better…thin…but better. It was a bright point in an otherwise dreary winter.

"So," said Ravie. "The hockey game is over. Michael looked fine!"

I laughed.

"Speaking of fine, what do you say we pay Gabriel a visit? Did you talk to him today?"

"Just briefly," I replied, "this morning. He said he was feeling well. He knew I would be at the hospital all day, and he wanted to get some rest."

"Rest is for sissies," said Ravie mischievously.

"Honestly," I interjected, knowing what she was thinking, "Maybe we should leave him alone."

"Alone is definitely not for lovers!" she laughed. "It's only a little after eight. I promise we won't stay long. Plus, we have some investigating to do."

"Is Michael going to be there?" I asked suspiciously.

"Maybe he will…maybe he won't," replied Ravie sporting a wide grin. "Anyway, they even let people in the hospital have visitors, and Gabriel isn't in the hospital."

I smiled as I thought of Gabriel. I really did want to see him. A brief visit couldn't hurt. "As long as he invites us in." I insisted. "I don't want to barge in like some desperate housewife."

Ravie looked at me seriously and paused. She wiggled her eyebrows. She looked ridiculous and I laughed.

"Sure, we'll mind our manners," she assured me.

"If you can find them," I joked as I stood and gathered my backpack.

I took the last sip of my tea and placed a small tip on the table.

Chapter 36

We arrived at Gabriel's. Michael's blue truck was in the driveway next to Beatrice's little yellow trademark beetle. Gabriel called it Beatrice's pierogie. I no longer felt so bad forcing my way in, but I wondered why Michael and Beatrice decided to come here.

I was uncomfortable, but I followed Ravie to the door. I felt as if I were sneaking up on someone or getting ready to ding dong ditch the house. Ravie curled her fingers and rapped on the door. We waited. The only answer was Anubis barking from deep within the house. She looked at me questioningly, her brows knit into a furrow of concern. She shrugged her shoulders and proceeded to ring the doorbell incessantly, hoping someone would be irritated enough to answer it. Still, no one came. Ravie shielded her eyes with her hands and peered in the living room window in an attempt to pick something out of the blackness. It was no use. No one was home.

Chapter 37

On Monday, I got to school very early but I was the last to arrive. Winter break was only a week away, and I was eager to get out of this place, so why was I here so early? Kane and Ravie already sat at one of the tables in the Gathering Hall laying out plans.

I stayed up all night wondering where Gabriel could have been. He told me he was going to stay home and rest...so why were Beatrice and Michael's cars in the driveway? The unanswered questions still kept piling up, and we knew Gabriel knew a lot more than he let on.

"Well, here we go." Kane said as he laid a paper in front of me and one in front of Ravie. I glanced superficially at mine, waiting for explanations and directions. He had everything planned to the letter. He even had the precise times figured out and neatly written on three papers. "Like we discussed, the first thing we have to do is see who is involved. Each of us is going to tail a person. Ravie, you take Michael. Trinity, you have Gabriel, of course, and I'll take Beatrice. They've been up to something."

As Kane spoke, I felt distracted, like someone was calling my name from far away. The voice came from the door behind him. Like the others, it was carved of thickly stained, dark wood. It reminded me of a scene from *Sleeping Beauty*. In this scene a knight on a horse was attempting to break through a bramble of thorns that rose up in front of him, blocking his path. Even though he had a substantial sword, he looked very worried. I spied a rose bud on one of the thorny tangles. I made a mental note of its position and its size. I strained to spy an evil sorceress or maybe a fire-breathing dragon in the distance, but I could find no such thing.

"All of them? Beatrice too?" I asked.

"Beatrice hasn't been home in days. " Ravie said. "She comes to school, goes to the games with me, but where she spends the rest of her time is a mystery. I tried calling Michael a bunch of times and all I get is his message."

I picked up the paper. Kane had typed a schedule.

"You do come prepared," I said with a smirk.

In three neat columns, Kane had written the class schedules of Beatrice, Gabriel and Michael. Below each, he wrote a list of places they go after school. He even left a blank space at the very bottom for notes. I smiled. His efforts were excruciatingly detailed. I glanced at Ravie. I could tell she felt the same way.

"Start watching them today. See if they do anything weird, Kane said.

"What would you consider weird?" asked Ravie.

"Just odd stuff," he continued. "Leaving class at a certain time, meeting somewhere without us, or even skipping a class." He looked at Ravie and me intently. "They might leave class at the same time, maybe to meet somewhere. Take careful notes of what they do and the times they do it, even going to the bathroom. We'll meet at the same time tomorrow and compare what we've seen. Hell, we'll meet every day until we figure this out"

As Kane spoke, a rose on the wall bloomed and faded. It was breathtaking, and it took just seconds.

"Did you see that?" I asked, astonished.

"See what?' Ravie asked.

"The rose," I stood up and went to the wall. "This one," I pointed and examined the wilted rose closely. "It just bloomed then wilted."

Kane asked, "That fast?"

"Yes," I replied, shocked, "I just saw it!"

"Nothing's moved that fast before," he said warily. "Are you sure?" He left his seat and came to stand next to me. He ran his hand across the flowers. As he did so, a few others bloomed, triggered by his touch.

"There, see?" I said pointing at them.

"Trinity," Ravie said, "I don't see anything."

Kane added, "Me either. Trinity, the movement takes days, not seconds."

"Then I must be seeing things, because the whole damn wall is blooming!" I was frightened. I had not seen anything like this before. I knew the little wooden scenes were strange, eerie in fact, but I was not prepared for this! And why was I the only person who could see it happen so quickly?

I closed my eyes and shook my head to get rid of the vision. I took a few deep breaths.

"Trin, are you okay?" asked Kane.

"Yes! I need to get this out of my head. Maybe I just imagined it," I replied. "Just give me a minute."

Afraid to open my eyes I asked, "How does that happen?"

"We don't know," replied Kane.

Ravie interrupted, "Trinity, what did you see…exactly?"

I turned in the direction of her voice. "Now I'm not really sure I saw anything. I had to have imagined it!" I wasn't sure what to think.

"Explain what you saw," she prodded.

With my eyes still squeezed shut, I replied, "The wall…the thorns…they bloomed!" I had to look. I had to have imagined it, but I wasn't sure. I opened my eyes.

The scene had definitely changed. The horse had reared and the knight was screaming. The thorns wove together in a larger bramble with sharp tendrils that reached for the knight. I walked toward the scene. It moved, but more slowly now.

"Trinity, maybe you shouldn't…" Ravie warned.

I ignored her and reached toward the wall. I had to see for myself. I know I imagined the whole event. Wooden walls just don't move. They can't. They're wood!

With my fingertips, I stroked the roses. Blossoms erupted like fireworks at the pass of my hand. I stepped back and looked to my friends, "Is anyone seeing this?"

Kane looked at me sheepishly, "No, Trinity, there's nothing there."

"Ravie?" I asked.

She looked unsure, scared, then answered, "No Trinity, I don't see anything either."

"God!" I went back to the wall. "I'm waving my hand and the roses are blooming...right here!" I pointed directly at the wall. "Why can't you see?"

Kane walked to me and gently placed his hands on my shoulders. I turned to look at him, and he led me away from the wall.

"Why can't you see this?" I asked, "Why is it just me?"

"I'm not sure," he replied. "I just know you can't look at that any longer." He took my hand and led me all the way outside. I winced in the unusually bright sunlight and took a seat on the main steps. He sat closely beside me; his arm still around my shoulders, protecting me from the menace of that building. Ravie sat closely on my other side, unsure, nervously twisting her fingers in her lap.

"I can't understand how you guys didn't see that. Did you look closely enough?" I asked.

"Trinity," Ravie looked at me honestly, "we really didn't see anything, no flowers, no nothing."

I looked to Kane. He shook his head softly, his arm still around my shoulders, he pulled me toward him. "I'm sorry," he whispered.

I buried my face in my hands and sat that way for several minutes. I was too stunned to cry. I just couldn't believe I saw those flowers bloom...but I know I did!

Kane gently rubbed my back. I don't think he knew what else to do. Ravie whispered to me over and over, "It'll be okay." I doubted it would, but I didn't argue. I was tired and I wanted my old life back. I wanted my mother. I wanted to go home...home to Amarillo. I appreciated all my new friends were doing, how they cared for and supported me, but I just wanted everything the way it was, before Mom got sick. Most of all, I wanted away from this school. I was glad winter break was coming. A week without this place. A week of peace.

I sat up and shrugged off Kane's arm. I turned to him and asked, "You want us to trace what they're doing? Our friends?"

"It's the only thing I can think of," he looked at me sadly.

"It's not them!" I replied. "Why won't you listen? It's me! It's this building...what's inside it...its ugly heart!" I pointed at the school. "It's not our friends we should be questioning, it's this building!" I continued, "There's something inside, something that's obviously drawn to me. We have to find out what it is, but I'm afraid we will need help. This is too big and too dangerous for us to handle with just some spying. We need a new plan with everyone involved. We need the whole truth! We...I...need to figure out what's going on here!"

I stood to leave. "I have to get out of here." Shrugging off the prodding of my friends, I decided to forget school for today and walk home. I needed a few moments without sympathy, empathy, and questions.

Kane and Ravie walked with me for several blocks, all the while Kane was trying to convince me his plan would work. Finally I said, "Look guys, I just need to digest everything that just happened. I'll call you a little later. I have some research of my own I have to do." It was then I realized someone was speaking to me and it wasn't my friends.

Chapter 38

It took a little while to convince Ravie and Kane that I needed to have a little time by myself. I understood their points, but in the back of my mind the tinkly voices of Amenta were calling me, and I had to get there quickly. After some talking, I told them I was going to see my mother. They never argued with that.

I walked the blocks to the graffitied wall as quickly as I could. I even broke into a jog at times. The voices called so urgently! A walk that took about 20 minutes seemed to take days, but finally, the large blue letters beckoned me from behind the vines of the wall. Rushing to them, I embraced the wall like a child. I closed my eyes and let Amenta take me.

When I felt a change in the wind from frigid to sun-kissed, I opened my eyes. Amenta lay in front of me in its golden splendor.

"Welcome Trinity!" the voices whispered across the breeze.

Unbelievable beauty surrounded me. I stood in the familiar fields of flowers and was kissed by a warm breeze. As I delighted in the scenery, I noted it was a perfectly cloudless day, no storm in the distance to ruin my milieu this time. The purple mountains rose commandingly in the western distance, and the forest stretched to the east as far as I could see. I went to remove my coat and found I was no longer wearing it. I now donned the clothing of Amenta. A white cloth was wrapped gently across my body and draped around my waist. It fastened with a silver braid at my shoulder. I wore a light robe and thick-soled sandals of silver that buckled at my ankles.

"Go to Djeba, the White City." The voices urged. "Time is short. Find the palace of Horus." I looked south toward the white towers at the base of the mountains. Towers reached majestically toward the sky and sparkled in the sunlight. I really wanted to visit that city, to see the people, to live in their peace when my own life had so little.

"Who is Horus?" I asked.

"The King of Amenta," they tittered. "There is a gift for you there. You must take this gift and use it against the enemy. You are the only one who can use its power."

I knew I had to get to that city and see it all for myself. Slowly, I took my first steps across the fields of flowers. As I walked, their petals dusted my thighs blessing me with their incredible aromas. The city was far, but I did not mind at all. I welcomed the journey. I brushed the tips of the flowers with my fingers and they rose to greet me, like loyal pets welcoming home their master.

I walked for most of the day, often catching glimpses of strange forest creatures. They sensed my presence, so I could not really get a good view of them. They seemed graceful and shy, similar to deer.

In Amenta, the air felt clearer and the sun was brighter. When it began to fade on the horizon, I realized I would never reach the White City before nightfall. I decided to walk until I was tired enough to sleep. The grass surrounding me was soft, like a thick carpet, and the air was pleasantly warm. I could lay just about anywhere and be comfortable. The bright day soon led to nightfall.

The sunset over the mountains was beautiful, like a tray of my watercolor paints all swirled and stippled across the sky. I came upon a small rock, perfect for sitting, so I perched on top and watched the colors of dusk fade as darkness overtook the landscape. It was a scene I would not forget.

With the sun gone, I thought it was a good time to get some sleep. Djeba was still several miles away, so I could wake up early and continue my trek. I sat on the soft grass and fell asleep almost instantly, like Dorothy in the poppy fields of Oz. Amenta protected me through the night. Nightmares would not dare enter this world.

Dreams did happen though, wonderful dreams…Mother came home, Gabriel and I skated on the frozen pond, and I saw all of my friends both new and old. For all of the nightmares that had plagued my entire life, this night of happiness, whether real or imagined, was welcomed and cherished. Soon, the glorious sunrise gently jarred me from my new dreamland. Opening my eyes, I wondered for a moment if I had died and gone to Heaven.

"Not Heaven," the voices had returned, "Amenta!"

I picked myself up from my flowery bed and stretched my arms in the fresh morning air. I was already excited to start walking again. My stomach grumbled, and the voices answered.

"Over the next hill there is a tree laden with fruit. Eat your fill. Your walk is almost at an end, but time is brief. You must hurry!"

I picked up my pace. I located the tree on the edge of a small grove. Quickly I selected three of the juiciest pieces. The fruit was fuzzy, like a peach, but bore a pastel green hue. At first I took a nibble, almost expecting the sour taste of a lime, then I bit into it healthily. The sweet nectar ran down my throat and the flesh melted in my mouth like cotton candy. It was unusual but delicious. I tucked the other two pieces of fruit into the folds of my robe, intending to eat them before I arrived in the city.

I began walking again and soon came upon an unusual collection of large boulders. They looked to be chiseled around the edges and formed into rectangles. They were arranged in a circular pattern with rays of smaller boulders around the outside edge. Stopping to examine the structure, I was sure it was placed here by humans. It was too patterned to be a natural formation. I wondered what they were and I was promptly answered by the voices.

"The stones are used to speak to the dead," chimed the voices.

I hadn't even thought of death in Amenta. It was too beautiful, too full of life. "There is death in Amenta?"

They answered solemnly, "In all worlds, death is inescapable."

Chapter 39

After several more hours of walking, I found myself standing before the immense walls of the white city. Tall, ornately blown glass gates blocked my entrance. I examined them closely, and I saw delicate glass vines with tiny flower buds at the tips decorating the gates. They looked like roses, but were much more beautiful.

"How do I get inside?" I whispered to the voices.

They tittered, "Just push them open! There are no locks here."

I reached and touched the gates with my fingertips. I gave them a nudge and they swung open freely. I was amazed such a lovely place would be unguarded. I hesitated then stepped inside.

Architecturally twisted towers made of a white stone, soared into the clouds like the skyscrapers of my world. Buildings, interspersed with tall deciduous trees neatly filled in the spaces between the towers. A wide variety of flowers bloomed on every grassy surface, and their perfume danced on the breeze. A vast, empty courtyard lay in front of me, cleanly swept and neatly manicured. I saw no one, but I heard the bustling of life from all corners of the city.

"Welcome to the Palace of Horus," said the voices.

At a distance, a female figure caught my attention. Her silhouette against the white city walls was tall and graceful. She almost seemed to glide rather than walk across the stone courtyard. As she got closer, I could see she wore a dark shape-fitting gown. Her skin was pale, almost as white as the city walls, and she had red hair the color of a sunset. It was pinned in tumbling waves and lent her a very regal appearance.

In moments, she stood in front of me. I gasped at her beauty. Piercingly blue eyes and delicate features make her appear almost angelic. She cradled a small box, slightly bigger than a ring box, in her slender hands and held it out for me to take.

"Welcome, Trinity." Her voice was like wind chimes in a breeze, one of the voices on the air that accompanied me to the city. I wondered if they were the same.

I did not know what to say, so I smiled slightly.

"This box is for you. You will know when to use it, but do not open it prematurely, for evil would surely grasp it from your hands."

"Thank you," I whispered

"When all hope is gone, you will know," she smiled warmly and knowingly.

"Now you must go back, but guard the box as if it contained your life...for it may do just that. Only *you* can carry it from Amenta undetected, and you must keep it secret. Only *you* must know it exists."

I reluctantly took the tiny white box from her hands. It was lighter than I had imagined. I wondered what was inside. I wanted to peek, but knew I couldn't. This was going to be difficult given my track record of peeking at presents.

"Your trek through the fields is a long one, but it is the only way home. You will come again when the time is proper." She embraced me gently. The protection of Amenta will follow you home. Now go, time is dwindling."

This was an enormous undertaking. I found myself feeling privileged rather than burdened. As I journeyed through the fields, I thought of even more questions...all about the future. Although the voices accompanied me, I knew they could not answer my endless questions of what the future held. I travelled through that entire day and part of the next, walking until the voices told me to stop.

"Trinity, spread your arms and embrace your world once again," they instructed.

Tightly grasping the box in my fist, I did as the voices instructed. I closed my eyes and soon felt the cold graffitied brick scuffing my cheek. To my chagrin, I found myself in Pittsburgh and my heart sank. I wanted to go back to Amenta, to stay there forever.

Carefully unwrapping my fingers from the small box, I again wondered what could be inside. I knew I couldn't look, so I slipped it into my coat pocket and buttoned the flap. My cell phone buzzed in my pocket, so I fumbled it out. I had no idea what time or even what day it was; I was in Amenta for two glorious days. My phone read 5:37 PM. If it was the day I left, approximately seven hours had passed. If it was a different day, then who knew?

The display indicated Kane was on the phone. I pushed the button to answer.

"Hello?"

"Hey, Trin. Everything okay?" He didn't sound frantic or accusatory, so I hoped it was just seven hours.

"Oh. Better." I replied simply.

"Mom all right?"

"Um, yeah." I tried to sound as positive as possible without revealing my trip to Amenta. "She's good."

"Sorry if I upset you this morning...I didn't mean,"

Thank God.

"That's okay. My fault," I interrupted with relief. "I'm kinda busy, can I call you tomorrow?"

"Sure, sure," he replied.

Before he could ask any more questions, I hung up. I left for Amenta this morning, so I had only been gone a few hours!

Chapter 40

When I arrived at home, my father was on the couch with his eyes closed. I attempted to sneak past. I didn't want to answer any questions about where I had been.

"Trinity," he called.

"Yeah, dad," I replied, wincing at what was to come.

He sat up and smiled at me. "Come sit down," he patted the sofa next to him.

"What's up?" I asked as I took the offered seat.

"Well, I have some hopeful news!" he replied, smiling widely, barely able to contain his excitement.

"Mom's coming home?" I grinned, eagerly awaiting his response with my own smile.

"Not quite, but there's a good chance she will be in the next couple of days. So let's make the house perfect for her. I'll check with the landlord, but I'm sure he won't mind a few gallons of paint," he looked about the room and grimaced, "and a little sprucing up."

This was the best therapy I could have asked for. "Dad, my friends and I will paint. We'd love to!" The more I thought about it, the more of a great idea it became. It would get me away from that horrible school and allow us a little down time to talk.

"Once the landlord gives the okay, you pick the colors, but just don't get crazy," he said

"Sure," I replied excitedly.

That evening when Dad went to the hospital I decided to walk to the hardware store. I had intended to call Ravie and Kane to apologize for my abrupt departure this morning, but I decided to focus on something a little more pleasant, like paint for my mother who was finally coming home!

It was a cold evening, so I walked quickly. It felt good to be out in the crisp air if only for a few blocks. The store was a little larger and more modern than a mom and pop store, but it wasn't one of those mega home improvement stores either. I thought it was pretty busy for an early winter evening, but just the mention of snow around here causes everyone to batten down the hatches.

I welcomed the bustle of strangers. I enjoyed the anonymous company you feel at a shopping mall or a busy store. Back in Amarillo, I used to go to the mall, all by myself, just to people watch. My favorite time to go was Christmas. Most people hate all of the hustle and bustle, the hurried strides and desperate purchases. But for me, the company of strangers was often the most welcome kind. There weren't any concerned faces or whispers, just people who passed by and knew nothing of my problems.

Paint displays shone under the fluorescent lights as I walked to the wall of colored chips. It was like the colors of a prism, each chip calling out to me to choose them. I smiled warmly at the colors; I was eager to do a little sprucing. Steering away from the yellows, I selected a color completely devoid of that rueful shade. It grabbed my attention immediately…purple. Purple was a mix of red and blue…absolutely no yellow. I chose a few chips. I'd try them in my bedroom. I kept it subtle to avoid any landlord complaints, but I also was on a mission to piss that Yellow off.

Next was the living room. I thought the furniture would be complemented by a soft gray. I chose a few chips from the gray section I thought might brighten up the room a little yet keep the landlord happy.

Mom and Dad's room followed. A cool blue jumped at me from the rainbow on the wall. I picked it up and noticed the name of the color was printed neatly on the bottom of the chip… "Healing Waters". Perfect. This color would be great in the bathroom as well, and using the same color would save a little money on paint.

The house had no dining room, rather a little larger than usual living room that could accommodate a small dinette, or in our case, a card table. So, last but not least was the kitchen. I took into account the condition of the cabinets. They were wooden, old and greasy. Maybe the landlord would let us paint them white. I'd have to ask Dad. Regardless, I could give them a good scrubbing and choose a color that would go with a medium oaky color, or if I could paint them, would also be pretty with white. I was a little stumped, scanning the colors and imagining them in the kitchen. Then I had it. I selected a beautiful, deep cerulean blue color. Selecting the chip, I glanced at the name... "Hopeful Dreams". That was it. I thought the color would go well with white or even cleaned natural wood. I pocketed my chips and decided to head home. Hopefully, Dad would get the okay from the landlord in the next few days.

I stepped out into the night and shivered. A hot tea at Hava Java's sounded fabulous.

The wind had picked up while I was in the store. I looked at the clock on my cell phone. Gosh! It was 7:30 already. I must have been in the hardware store for an hour analyzing colors. I pulled my coat tightly against the harsh chill and walked quickly. A storm was definitely brewing. The gray clouds bulged and bubbled in the strong wind and I could smell dampness in the air. I hoped it was cold enough to snow. Getting rained on right now would not be pleasant.

I half jogged and made it to Hava Java just in time. The skies opened and cold rain came down in buckets as soon as I made it in the door. I welcomed the warm glow and comforting smells of the shop.

Immediately I heard my name, "Trinity!" I saw it was Ravie. She motioned for me to join her which I did immediately.

I slid into the booth and looked at her. "I'm really sorry for leaving so quickly this morning. I..."

"That's okay. Don't worry about it," she smiled.

"No, really," I paused. "I must have been really tired to have seen all of that...on the walls, I mean."

"You saw something," she smiled kindly. "Kane sees it too, but a little differently."

"Ravie, we need to have a plan. I've been so worried about myself that..."

She interrupted me, "Maybe we need to slow down a little bit. Winter break is next week..."

I understood where she was coming from. She didn't want to upset me, which was a pretty easy thing to do these days, but she knew we couldn't just push the matter aside. Amenta's urgency became my own. I knew we could not wait. We had to act.

"I'd be happy to do just that, Ravie, but I'm not in control. I don't make these things happen; they just do…and they're happening to me...and to you...and to Kane!" I continued, "I still have to go to school, and I can't just walk around with my eyes shut and my fingers crossed for an entire week!"

"I understand that," she replied. "I just don't want to put more on you right now."

"My plate is so full it's heaping. My cup runneth over!" I laughed sarcastically. "Rav, this isn't going to wait out of convenience for us. We can investigate more over winter break, but whatever happens is going to happen. I can't stop it…no matter how much I would like to, I just can't."

"I know, I know," she replied. "I'm just trying to make some sense of everything, and to be honest, I just want to slow down. At first, I thought I was in this alone. My weird feelings and inklings always came true. They just became magnified when I came to this school. Then I met Kane who sees the carvings move, albeit slowly. Trinity, now there's you and your dreams…and these walls move, just for you!"

"That's where it stands," I said matter-of-factly.

"So, now I think we may have been called here. I don't know by whom or by what…but one thing I'm certain of…it's big, Trin…I can feel it coming!"

"That's why we can't ignore it, even for a week!" I replied adamantly.

"You're right," she replied thoughtfully, sipping at her Frappuccino. "What should we do?"

"Follow Kane's plan."

Chapter 41

The next three days were plagued by dreams. I was so tired. I rarely slept, and when it came, it was anything but restful. Whatever was triggering my dreams was draining the life from me as well. I searched the internet and discovered the longest span anyone was able to stay awake was eleven days. I thought I might give that record a try. Anything was better than the dreams.

I spied on my friends. I met with Ravie and Kane to share notes, but nothing out of the ordinary came up. They weren't doing anything unusual. In school, the walls moved and I tried to ignore them, but they were beginning to call to me. I found myself lost in the tales more and more.

In the evenings I went to the library. It was a quiet place to sleep since the dreams did not follow me there...not yet. It was becoming an oasis from everything; a place of escape. The stacks were so peaceful and provided quiet areas where I could hide...and rest.

School knew about the situation with my mother, and I guiltily used that to my advantage. They would never fail a girl whose mother was dying. I charmed my teachers just enough to let me slide by.

Today the dreams had finally found me at the library. Now I was cloudy with sleep. When I got home, I dropped my backpack by the front door and shook the chill off. It was late December, but Pittsburgh seemed to grasp the cold of winter much earlier than most places.

"Hey Trinity!" Dad called cheerily from the kitchen. He startled me a bit. He was usually at the hospital when I got home. He bustled into the living room, not even giving me a chance to respond.

"Come see what I got!" He sported a grin that stretched from ear to ear, reminding me of the old dad, the Amarillo dad, the dad that was full of jokes and laughter, the dad I missed so much.

When Dad smiled, it was contagious. Soon one was plastered across my face as well, "What is it?" I asked. He didn't notice anything unusual, so I managed to fake a little enthusiasm.

He took my hand in excitement and led me to the kitchen. Sitting on the sunny countertop were five gleaming gallons of paint. Next to them were brushes, rollers and a neatly folded canvas tarp.

I smiled widely, "Does this mean Mom is coming home?" I wasn't sure I wanted to know the answer, but Dad couldn't hide his smile.

At first he didn't reply. I turned to him and threw my arms around his neck. He gathered me in a hug that instantly took me back to my childhood. Dad who protected me from bad dreams. Dad who loved me unconditionally.

"Yes...yes, she is!" I began to cry. We sat and hugged each other like a couple of children. After a few teary minutes, Dad pulled away from me and smiled. He cupped my face in his hands. He smiled kindly as he wiped my tears away with his thumbs. He leaned and kissed me on the top of my head like he always did.

"When is she coming?" I smiled. "This is a lot sooner than I thought."

"Day after tomorrow, he replied. We have to stay in Pittsburgh though...until the treatments are done, probably longer."

"Do you know how long that will be?" I asked. My heart plunged like a stone at the thought of remaining here.

"Maybe a few months...maybe a year. We're really not sure," he replied. "I know you want to go home, Trinity, but..."

I interrupted him, "It's okay Dad, I have friends; I'll be fine." I didn't want to distract him with the struggles I have been having, so I kept it all to myself. I'd deal with my own problems later.

"I know. I just worry."

"Now, Dad," I said cheerily. "How are we going to get this house painted in two days?"

"If we get to work right now, we'll at least conquer the living room."

I helped Dad move some furniture into the center of the room. Luckily, there wasn't much to move, so I went into my room to change into some old clothes. The Yellow greeted me menacingly. "Enjoy what time you have left!" The Yellow slithered as I grabbed a pair of old sweats out of a drawer. When I was finished, I left the room and picked up my cell phone. I had a message from Ravie, so I called her.

She immediately peppered me with questions, "Where have you been? Are you feeling better? Are you coming in tomorrow?"

I interrupted her with the news of my mother's homecoming. She said she'd be right over to help. I changed into old sweats and joined Dad. In only a few minutes he had laid out some drop cloths and was beginning to edge the woodwork around the fireplace.

"Where would you like me to start?" I asked.

"Take a roller and get as close as you can to the trim work. I'll keep doing the detail."

The paint went on quickly and time passed with good conversation and a little music from an old tabletop radio that Dad dug out of an unpacked moving box.

Soon, the doorbell rang. It took Ravie longer than I thought to get here, but beggars can't be choosers. I opened the front door. To my great surprise, not only Ravie stood smiling at me, but so did all of my other friends. Beatrice had tied her long hair into two cute braids. Michael sported an old baseball cap covered in paint splotches. Ravie also wore a baseball cap, but hers was pink with a Turnbull Bull logo on the front. Her hair was pulled into a tight ponytail. Kane was handsomely unkempt as usual. Gabriel stood tall in the rear of the group. He said simply, "Can we come in?"

"I laughed and replied, "Sure," giving each of them a hug as they entered. I followed the group into the living room. My father had not met most of my friends, and I wanted to give everyone a proper introduction.

Dad was intently working. "Hi Ravie," he called without looking up.

"Hi Mr. Pierce," replied Gabriel in a high pitched voice. Everyone laughed.

Dad turned around. He loved a good joke and that was pretty funny.

"Dad," I interjected, "I want you to meet my friends. They came to help."

He smiled warmly, "Great, we could use all the help you're willing to give. Thank you very much."

"I think you know Ravie."

"Never forget her," Dad replied.

"This big guy is Michael."

Michael reached over me and shook my dad's hand, "Great to meet you."

Dad grinned, "I think we have our ceiling man!"

I continued, "This is Beatrice."

"Nice to meet you," she replied softly.

"This is Kane,"

"Hello," he said as he too shook my Dad's hand. Kane caught my eye and nodded. He still wore a bandage on his neck, but it was a lot smaller. I hoped it was healing.

"And this one is Gabriel," I finished moving down to the end of the line.

Dad responded, "The famous Gabriel huh?"

Gabriel laughed, "Well I don't know about famous..."

Dad said, "Well, I'm so glad Trin chose such nice people as her friends. I know it's not much, but you are welcome here any time, and please help yourself to whatever is ours."

"Well, let's get started," said Gabriel rubbing his hands together. "I hear we only have the weekend." He turned to my dad, "So what's the game plan Mr. Pierce? We brought a few rollers that Michael had left over. I hope you have a couple of extra sleeves."

“Great! We have plenty of sleeves.” Dad surveyed the help. “How about Michael start the ceiling in here and someone else can help. Ravie quickly volunteered to work with him. Beatrice elbowed me in the arm.

Dad continued, “Two of you take on a bedroom and the other two can start in the kitchen.”

“Come on Gabe,” joked Kane. “You shouldn’t be in girls’ bedrooms anyway.” Gabriel pushed him playfully, picked up a few brushes, and headed to the kitchen.

On his way he muttered, “You know Kane, you’re an idiot.”

Kane came over to me and whispered, ‘It’s finally healing.”

"Mine is too," I revealed.

“There’s painter’s tape on the counter if you need it,” Dad said, laughing at their boyish jibes. “All of the cabinets should be primed white.”

“Sure thing, Mr. Pierce!” replied Kane. He did look so much better. The dark hollow look was gone and he looked healthy again.

“My parents’ room won’t take too long.” I said to Beatrice. “There’s not a lot of trim.” I picked up a roller and a paintbrush and Beatrice grabbed the can of paint and followed me into the bedroom.

I kind of wished I could have worked with Gabriel, but I didn’t want to make our relationship too obvious in front of my dad. It’s funny how fathers know what’s up, yet many of them are graceful enough to allow their kids a little space. My Dad knew I liked Gabriel, but he didn’t say a word. I was glad he trusted me and my judgment.

Beatrice and I got to work quickly. We ran out of drop cloths, so Dad had given us an old blanket to throw under our work space. He was adamant about keeping paint off of everything but the walls. I spread the blanket and taped off the baseboard while Beatrice poured the paint and started rolling.

“I can’t tell you what your help means to my family,” I said.

“No problem,” Beatrice replied swiftly. “Whatever we can do to help you guys. I’m so glad your mom is coming home.”

“Gosh, I thought this day would never come!” I sighed.

"I bet!" she said. "Maybe when she is home and settled we can all come to meet her. She sounds like a wonderful mom."

"She is." I replied thoughtfully. "Anyway, what's your mom like? I feel like you guys know just about everything about me, but I don't know much about you." I dipped my brush in the can of aqua and dragged it along the taped baseboard.

"My mom is great; I just don't see her very often." Beatrice stretched the roller as high as her small frame would reach. "She travels a lot...so does my dad."

"Is it for work?" I asked. I knew she wasn't telling me the truth, but with her helping us right now, it really didn't matter.

"Usually. But she goes away with my dad as well. I guess she's got more than a few ants in her pants."

"Do you ever go with them?"

"No, I'm just not a flyer. It makes me nervous," she smiled. "I'd rather just stay here with my friends."

"That's sweet," I replied.

We painted a wall in thoughtful silence then Beatrice smiled and turned toward me. "How are you and Gabe coming along?"

"Okay, I guess."

Beatrice commented thoughtfully. "I know your mom is a priority for you right now, but Gabe..."

"Sometimes I feel like I don't have time for a relationship."

"You will, soon," said Beatrice. "Your mom is getting better, so you won't be at the hospital so much."

"I hope so. I really do."

Beatrice and I talked and painted most of the afternoon away, but our conversations remained superficial. I didn't want her to suspect that Kane, Ravie, and I were spying on her. Eventually, we decided to break for a drink and a snack, so we headed for the kitchen.

When we entered the living room I gasped. The paint had made such a huge difference! "Oh my goodness! This looks fantastic!"

Michael had already finished the ceiling and was close to completing the third wall. "Your landlord better give you a free month for this."

Ravie was working on a second coat on the large wall. She stood and stretched her arms high over her head. Dad stood from the corner where he was working. He took a few steps back to survey the result.

"Yeah," he replied, "results like that really motivate you to finish!" He set his brush in the tray and arched his back in a stretch.

"Do you guys want a snack or something to drink?" I asked.

"I just ordered a few pizzas," Dad replied. "They'll be here shortly. Why don't you get some paper plates and drinks ready?"

"Sure," I said eagerly. I wanted to see how the kitchen was coming, but more importantly, I wanted to see Gabriel.

Beatrice and I walked toward the kitchen door. It was one of those old fashioned doors on a hinge that pivoted both ways. I pushed on it and peeked into the kitchen. Gabriel turned and a smile spread across his face. He put his paintbrush down on the news papered counter and came to greet us. Kane put his brush down as well and boosted himself to a sitting position on the counter.

"Wow!" I said truly astonished at their progress. "This looks great!" I couldn't contain myself. I gave Gabriel an enormous hug. He wrapped his arms around me and kissed me on my cheek.

I smiled brightly. "I can't thank you enough!"

He looked into my eyes and smoothed the hair around my face. He said nothing. I hugged him again.

Eventually, I forced myself to turn toward Kane. His baseball cap was on backwards and he had splotches of paint all over his face and spattered across his clothing. I turned back to Gabriel, suspecting mischief between the two. I hadn't noticed, but Gabriel was smudged and smeared with dark blue paint as well.

"You look charming," said Beatrice. "What exactly were you trying to paint?"

Gabriel responded sheepishly and pointed at Kane, "He started it."

"Did not!" exclaimed Kane.

"You're both idiots," replied Beatrice. "Have either of you looked in a mirror?"

""Now, why would we do that?" asked Kane sarcastically.

The cupboard doors were removed, propped against the rear wall and covered with a coat of white primer. The cupboards themselves also had a coat of white. The walls were a rich blue color, the shade of an evening sky. They really did get a lot done in just a few hours. They would probably be close to finished had they not had their paint battles.

Before they could continue their jokes, Dad called from the living room, "Pizza's here!"

I grabbed the package of paper plates and a fistful of napkins. I thrust them at Beatrice who carried them into the living room. Gabriel went to the refrigerator and grasped the gallons of milk and iced tea. Kane turned and clinked a few glasses from the counter together. They both proceeded to the living room. I followed, empty-handed, not having anything else to bring.

Dad already had the boxes open. He had also ordered a salad which looked absolutely delicious to me. As customary, the boys inhaled the pizza and the girls picked at the salad, trying to maintain our figures. Except Beatrice, for a girl, she really could eat, and she was the smallest one of all of us.

We were so hungry, even Ravie and I eventually turned to a piece of pizza to satisfy our appetites. Soon, three large pizzas and a Greek salad were completely annihilated by a bunch of teenagers and a grateful father.

We shared a little tired conversation, and quickly went back to work. In another hour, Beatrice and I had finished the bedroom. We stepped back. The room looked fantastic, so much lighter and fresher. We struggled, but managed to put the furniture back in its original place, careful of leaving a margin of space around the freshly painted walls. I rummaged through the closet and came up with fresh sheets and a dark brown comforter that complemented the aqua wall color and dark trim perfectly.

Soon, we were finished folding tarps and peeling off tape. "Thank you!" I said, smiling gratefully

"My pleasure. Now, let's get that bathroom done," she said. I was amazed she was so eager. Luckily, the bath had very little wall space with the bathtub surround, but we did have some scraping and patching to do. This time Beatrice tackled the trim and I rolled on the color. We used the same shade as in the bedroom. Freshening up the white trim and the addition of the calming aqua, made the room look good. Dad had purchased an inexpensive light to replace the naked bulb hanging from the ceiling. I hoped he would get to it before Mom came home.

We finished quickly and spent a while cleaning the bathtub and sink with scrubbing bubbles. I found a few rags and scrubbed the floor as well. Rummaging through a box of linens, I found some white hand towels that had a hint of aqua around the edges. They looked perfect!

As soon as I placed the last towel, I turned and hugged Beatrice, "Thank you!" I said.

"You're welcome!"

I took her by the hand and we walked into the living room. Dad was going over the trim, touching up everything for the final time.

"This looks great!" I exclaimed. Michael and Ravie stopped struggling with the drop cloth they were attempting to fold. Thank you all so much!

"Actually, call me weird, but I thought it was fun," said Ravie.

Michael looked at her and couldn't resist, "Weird!"

"Weird? Me?" she laughed.

"Daddy, come see!" I interrupted.

Dad stood up and put his arms around mine and Beatrice's shoulders. Together, we walked into the bedroom.

As we entered the room, Dad gasped. "My gosh! What a difference, huh?" He looked at me and smiled. "This is great! Almost like home again, huh Trin?"

Just the thought of Amarillo made me want to cry, but I remained upbeat "Yeah, Dad. I think it looks fantastic!"

"Me too!' said Beatrice.

"You know Trin," Dad said, "these are the exact colors of the chips you left on the counter. I think you're an expert!"

"Let's go look at the kitchen!" I exclaimed.

We bustled back onto the living room. Michael and Ravie had slung themselves across the couch and turned on the television. "Come on!" I said.

We gathered at the kitchen door. I knocked loudly.

"Just a minute!" said Gabriel in a high pitched voice, trying very hard to be funny. We heard some rustles, rattles and low mumbling.

In a few moments Kane said, "Come in!" in that same ridiculous voice.

I opened the door and was astounded! Cabinets had a second coat of white and the walls were finished. The cabinet doors were still off and leaning against the back wall, but they were painted a bright white as well.

Dad gasped, "What a difference! Thank you so much. We could have never gotten this far without you.

"We left the doors off to dry," said Kane. "I wouldn't put them on for a few days."

Gabriel stood grinning, as much paint on his face as was on the paintbrush he held.

"I can't believe we're done, and it's not even ten o'clock," said Dad. "I hope you guys haven't stayed too late." He looked remorseful.

Gabriel spoke up, "Late? Have you seen some of our ice times? This is still way early!"

Everyone laughed. That was very true. Sometimes their games were scheduled at midnight and practices were at four-thirty in the morning. They may as well have been a bunch of vampires with the hours they kept. School or not, hockey always came first.

Well, as I see it, Trinity and I just have to do a little touch-up tomorrow and we'll be finished." Dad turned to me. "I have to do a few things at the hospital and get your mother all packed. Can you do the cleaning tomorrow?"

"Sure Dad. That won't take long at all." I replied.

My friends washed up at the kitchen sink. Gabriel and Kane looked like they needed a good bath to scrub all that paint off of them. Kane even had a wide splash of blue across his hat and into his hair.

After a rest in front of the television, they gathered their things and began filing out the front door. Dad thanked them again profusely and stayed inside to give me a little privacy. I followed my friends out onto the front porch and into the chilly air.

"Thanks again!" I exclaimed.

"It's all good," said Kane.

Gabriel smiled and said, "Anytime."

Dad and I worked well past midnight, cleaning and organizing. When we were completely spent, we sat down on the couch and promptly fell asleep.

Chapter 42

The next morning I awoke, still on the couch. It was early. I could tell by the slant of the sunlight coming through the front window. I thought someone was calling me, but Dad had gone to the hospital even earlier and thankfully didn't wake me. I decided to chalk it up to an already forgotten dream. I was really sore from all that painting, and I was glad Dad let me stay on the couch. This was the Yellow's last hours and I knew it was waiting for me.

I could have gotten help, but I kept painting my room to myself. I didn't want to keep anyone later than I already had last night. Besides, this was between me and the Yellow, and the Yellow was pretty angry, but so was I.

I got up to get a shower and start working. I turned on the water and made it a little extra hot to massage my muscles. I stood with slumped shoulders and let the water caress my sore back and biceps. It felt wonderful. As I stood in the welcome warmth, I swore I heard my name being called. Maybe Dad came home and didn't want to startle me. I stopped and waited...straining to hear something.

Reluctantly, I decided to cut my shower short, so I got out, dried off, and wrapped a towel around me. I wanted to make sure no one was in the house with me, or if someone was, it wasn't going to result in some Psycho shower scene. Gripping the top of my towel tightly, I walked into my parents' room...nothing. I walked to the living room...no one. I checked the kitchen...empty. I remembered I had some old clothes in a laundry basket in my parents' room. I was glad I remembered because I didn't want to face the Yellow until I really had to.

"Trinity!" I jumped, startled. The voice was deep and gravelly. It came from my room! My heart fluttered in my chest, like a bird trying to find its way out of a cage. Who the hell was calling me?

I stood in the kitchen, stunned with fear. I was afraid to move, as if I was hiding from a murderer and didn't want to reveal my location.

It came again, this time childlike…lighter and sing-songy, but with a very startling and disturbing warble, "Come…" I pushed the palms of my hands over my ears and rushed into my parents' room to get my clothes. I could still hear it, commanding me. "Trinity! Come now!"

My hands shook as I rummaged, panicked through the laundry basket. I grabbed an old t-shirt from and a pair of workout sweats. I quickly slipped them on and rushed onto the front porch. I knew who was calling me. It was the Yellow monster that lived inside my walls. The thing that left the scrape marks. The thing that was trying to get out the night it shredded my posters.

I didn't know what to do. I sat for a long time on the steps in the cold, damp air…thinking. I couldn't let this control me. I couldn't let it drive me out of my house. But I was so scared! I shivered, more from fright than the chilly air. I was acting like a child and the thing was treating me like one.

It took a long time, but I decided I had to act, and act now. I had to take control. I couldn't keep running away, not from my own room! Without further thought, I opened the front door and entered the house. Silence. Maybe the thing was asleep by now.

Moving as quickly and stealthily as I could, I got my can of purple paint, a drop cloth, a roller and a brush. I mixed the light violet paint in the kitchen with one of those wooden sticks. Even though I usually wasn't a big fan of purple, I did like this shade. It had more blue than the violet you'd find in a little girl's room. This purple was much more silvery, more modern. As I stirred, I wondered how the Yellow would react. I replaced the lid and headed to my room.

I gathered my courage, put my hand on the doorknob, and took a deep breath. I was greeted with the sourest Yellow yet. It sneered and swirled on the wall. The Yellow intensified and formed the face of something monstrous. I would dream about it the rest of my life. Suddenly, it faded and re-swirled into a depiction of my own face, though in this portrait, I was screaming. My features melted into the ooze.

"Trinity!" said the horror in the wall.

I could feel its hatred. My mother and father's faces were next. The Yellow caused them to burst into flame. Looking it as little as possible, I struggled to pull my desk away from the wall. I laid the plastic drop cloth on the floor and got the can of paint. I added the scraper and the patching spackle. I was going to shut this thing's mouth if it took me all day. I was ready.

I began scraping the rough Yellow and it squirmed under my hands. I wanted to start gouging at it, cutting it, killing whatever was living there. But I had to restrain myself. Tearing apart the walls would accomplish nothing.

I finished scraping and got ready to paint. The walls shifted and burst into a sickly yellow flame.

"Is that the best you've got?" I challenged. I removed the lid and could not believe what I saw. The purple color I had admired in the kitchen had changed. The paint in the can was now the same disgusting Yellow that marred the walls. My only weapon was gone! I grabbed the can and raced from the room, the Yellow snickered. Before I could think about what had happened, the doorbell rang.

I rushed to the door, set the can of paint on the floor, and noticed it was full of purple again. Shaking off my shock, I peeked through the glass. It was Gabriel, the most welcome sight I could have hoped for.

I opened the door quickly. "Come in, come in!" I said as happily as I could.

His wide smile added even more cheer to his already happy mood. "Need some help?" he asked as he entered and shut the door behind him.

"Now that you mention it, I sure do!" I added, "If you don't mind."

"I would never leave a young lady in distress." He looked at me intently. "And you do look pretty distressed. Is something wrong?"

I smiled. "Well I'm working on my room, but it's not cooperating."

"What do you mean...not cooperating?" he laughed.

"Well, my room is kind of a weird place." I paused. "I think you should just see for yourself. I'll show you." I hoped the Yellow would continue its torment, letting someone else see its malice.

Gabriel shrugged and I picked up the can of paint. He followed me to my bedroom.

"Maybe you need to carry this in," I said holding out the can, hoping it would stay purple for him.

He took the paint and looked at me inquisitively. Opening the door, we were greeted with a sunny, cheerful yellow. I stepped back in amazement. Looking at the paint can Gabriel held in his hand, I saw it was once again purple.

"I can see why it's not cooperating," he laughed. "You haven't even gotten started yet." Gabriel took off his coat and slung it over my nightstand. He poured the purple paint into the tray then set it on the drop cloth. He picked up a brush, dipped it into the purple, and smeared it across the wall. It covered the Yellow with just one stroke.

"You know, even weird rooms can't paint themselves," he laughed.

I smiled politely and wondered what the hell was going on now. I put the brush down and began to spackle some cracks.

Gabriel took a roller, wiggled it in the tray, and in a few moments was busy swathing purple paint on the walls with huge sweeps of the roller. "Trin," he said, "this is a nice color, but what was wrong with the yellow?"

What's wrong with the Yellow? I giggled at such a ridiculous question. Why wasn't it being so wicked for Gabriel? Maybe it was mocking me, making me think I was crazy. But Kane saw it too! He even noticed what a nasty color it was when I showed him the knife. There really were strange things happening all around me. I wished I could make sense of at least a few of them.

I replied simply, though I had a lot more to say, "I guess I just don't care much for yellow."

"You still need some spackle and sanding here and there."

"There is just so much to do," I replied.

"I am happy to stay here all day. I just want to spend time with you."

I smiled softly at him.

Soon, I finished spackling, sanding and using the primer, and he started painting around the trim in short, controlled drags of the brush. I decided not to mention anything about the room. I just prayed it wouldn't return as soon as Gabriel left. "How did you know I'd be painting again today?" I asked, trying not to think.

"Well," he replied, "I just put two and two together. When Kane and I were working in the kitchen, we used up all of the paint cans except one. I looked at the splotch on top and I figured you wanted to paint your room as well. It was the only room we didn't touch."

"You're pretty smart," I replied with a smile.

"I know," he said jokingly returning to his work. "I knew your dad was going to be gone most of the day. I didn't want to leave you here to do all of this work by yourself. I guess I just wanted to help you."

"You're so sweet," I replied, returning to the trim.

"This won't take long at all."

Interestingly enough, Gabriel liked to hum while he worked, and he was pretty good at it. I tried to hum along with him, but humming always tickled my mouth. In a short while, we were both laughing.

After about an hour, I stopped to check our progress. "You're almost finished with that wall already!" I exclaimed.

"Yeah, I had enough practice yesterday," he said.

It was then I said something I instantly regretted. Usually I was one to measure my words and my tone, but not this time. I had no idea why it came out of my mouth, but it just did. I wouldn't blame Gabriel for putting his brush down and walking right out the front door. Here he was, giving his heart and soul to my family, and I had the gall to take an accusatory tone with him. I said, "Well, since practice makes perfect, maybe you can enlighten me..."

He stopped painting and turned toward me. He looked surprised. "What do you mean?'

Since I began, I was determined to ask. "Well, there's a lot I don't understand about us. First of all, I can't get that skating out of my mind. How did I skate so well? I know you helped me, but we were dancing...flying, like we were one person. How did that happen? I've been over it a thousand times in my head. I have run through every logical possibility, but I just can't figure it out."

"I told you I was a good teacher," he replied innocently.

"But that's not all of it. You healed, from life threatening cuts in just one day!" I felt tears welling up and my throat tightening. I couldn't believe I was saying all this. "Cuts that I think I made...in my dream!"

Gabriel's defensive look softened a little. "Trinity, the cuts weren't so bad. There was a lot of blood; all but one were pretty superficial." He added, "Dou don't believe you had something to do with it, do you?"

"Superficial?" I walked to Gabriel and looked deeply into his eyes. "I know it was my fault."

Gabriel slid the roller into the tray and hugged me. "Trin, you have to stop blaming yourself. Yes, you can see these things through your dreams, but everything isn't what it seems." He paused briefly then continued, "There are some pretty strange things going on right now. Some of these things you already know, and some of them you still have to learn. You have to discover some truths on your own. These truths will make you stronger, and you need to be strong...strong for your mother...strong for your father...strong for me...but most importantly, strong for you."

I was drowning in his calm blue eyes. They were like welcoming pools on the hottest days of summer. "What's in my future?" I asked. I felt the tears and tightness disappearing, being replaced with the flutter of butterflies.

He said nothing. He pulled me close and I let him. All of the fears of the morning couldn't touch us. Whatever was lurking in my walls remained well-hidden. We lingered in the moment before a kiss. He reached and touched my lips with his fingertips. I closed my eyes and when he kissed me, I belonged to him completely. It was like standing in that warm shower again, all of the pain, all of the tension swirling down the drain.

He kissed me again, deeply, and I felt warmth, like sitting in the sun on the first day of a western spring. All of the winter's chill melting from my body. I basked in his sunlight and drank his energy. Stretching my arms around his broad, muscular shoulders, I felt the movement of his body as we kissed.

I had kissed a few boys before, but it was never like this. Those were the experimental kisses of teenagers, a quick peck on an amusement park dark ride; a kiss at a front door after a movie. Nothing was close to what I felt for Gabriel. I was experiencing the pure joy that occurs when you have completely fallen in love with a person, and just as importantly, they have fallen completely in love with you.

I felt Gabriel pull me even closer. We breathed in unison. His hands gently caressed my back. This was innocent. He would never want me to think he came over to take advantage of my emotional frailty, my need for company, my thankfulness for all of his help.

We sat down on the bed. He smiled, but kept his eyes locked on mine. Trin, you have to know I love you. I just don't want you to think..."

I pressed my fingers across his lips and slid closer to him. He wrapped his arms around me, and we laid back against the pillows. At times, we would just look into each other's eyes, studying each other's expressions and emotions. Other times we enjoyed just being together, holding each other, whispering stories. After a while, his breathing became rhythmic. I loved listening to him, with my head on his chest, listening to his heart. I could tell he was asleep and I followed him, gladly, in plain sight of the Yellow.

Chapter 43

I awoke a while later. I sat up quickly and looked at the twilight creeping across the floor. Inadvertently, I put my hand on something that rested on my pillow. I picked it up and turned on my night table lamp. It was a note:

Trinity,
You have a huge day tomorrow, and you looked so beautiful that I let you rest. I hope all goes well for you and your parents. I think you all will have a wonderful day. I won't call you, but I will be waiting for you to call me when you have everything in order. I am already eager for that to happen. If you haven't noticed, I took the liberty of finishing the room. I hope it gives you peace.
With hope and much love,
G.

A warm tingle traveled up my spine and down my arms. Gosh, he was wonderful! I folded the note and slipped it in my night table drawer, where I kept many of my treasured things. I sat for a few moments, lost in thought, mostly of Gabriel. For the first time in my life, I knew I was in love.

I smiled and rolled off the bed. I walked across the room and turned on the main light. What a difference the color made! The trim in my room was white and it looked crisp and clean against the soft purple on the walls. Not a hint of Yellow wriggled through. I loved it!

"Thank you," I whispered to Gabriel. I hoped he heard me. I also hoped the Yellow was gone for good. I had a feeling it was because, somehow, the room had a much lighter feeling. To be honest, it felt, different, unthreatening, dare I say…happy?

I decided to make something to eat, so I went to the kitchen. Immediately, I noticed Gabriel had been working overtime. He had screwed the painted doors back onto the cabinets. I was amazed at the change the room had undergone in only one day.

He was full of surprises, all fantastic. I silently thanked him again.

I was famished, so I opened the fridge. There really was nothing but a little milk, ketchup, left over macaroni and cheese, and some pizza from yesterday. I grabbed a slice of pizza from a Ziploc bag and ate while I thought of what else needed to be done before Mom's arrival tomorrow.

First and foremost, we would need groceries. Dad usually kept money and a credit card for me in a kitchen drawer. I opened the drawer and slid the money and card into my pocket. Although I was happy with how the house turned out after the paint, I still wanted to get out into the evening air. I walked toward the front door, stopping only to slip into my coat.

The grocery store was only a few blocks away. In this urban neighborhood, no necessity was too far and I was thankful for that convenience. It was December, the trees remained barren and the air was cold and damp. Mom told me once that around here, summer came late and stayed a little longer. I remembered that as I waited desperately for a little warmth, so I buttoned my coat and thrust my hands deeply into my pockets.

As I walked, I noticed an odd sensation in the pocket of my hoodie. It startled me until I realized it was just my cell phone, left on vibrate. I fumbled it from my pocket and looked at the display. It was Dad.

"Hey Daddy!" I said enthusiastically.

"Hi, sweetie."

I couldn't help but ask. "Is Mom still coming home tomorrow?"

"Sure is!" His voice beamed through the phone.

"I'm so excited! Tell her I'll be waiting. What time?"

"I will, I'm not sure of the time yet," he replied. "Honey, is it okay if I stay here tonight? We want to get all of this paperwork done so she can come home first thing tomorrow."

Although I didn't like to stay home alone, especially after painting over the Yellow, I agreed. I would agree to almost anything to get my mom home. "Sure," I said as positively as I could.

"Okay," he replied. "Just call if you need anything."

"I will," I assured him. "I'm getting some groceries now, but I'll be home soon."

"You're wonderful! Splurge a little on dinner tomorrow, we have a lot to celebrate!" He continued, "Call me when you get home so I know you're safe."

"I will. Bye, Daddy."

I slipped my phone back into my pocket. A sinking feeling in my stomach marked the dread I felt staying home all by myself. I had already slept a few hours. Maybe a stint at Have Java would make a little of my anxiety disappear.

When I entered the store, I took a basket instead of a cart. It helped me manage the weight of what I purchased. After getting the necessities like milk, bread and eggs, I proceeded to the main course. I immediately saw that salmon was on sale, if you could call $12.99 a pound a sale. I had no idea how to cook it, but I knew that was what I had to get; Mom loved fish and salmon was her favorite kind. Carefully selecting a big fillet from the case, I went back to the produce aisle for some garlic. I knew enough that salmon delicious sautéed in some butter and garlic. Soon, my basket was laden with the makings of a spectacular meal, so I proceeded to the checkout. I knew I would struggle on the way home, yet I was completely satisfied with my purchase.

As I walked, I frequently shifted my bags from hand to hand. I cursed myself silently for buying so much, but I anticipated the meal my family would have when we were finally back together. Along the way, I set the bags down several times and stretched my arms. I decided to forget the coffee for tonight although the shop looked warm and welcoming as I passed by. I gripped my bags more tightly and proceeded home. It was tedious and tiring work, but soon I found myself on my own doorstep.

I rattled my key in the door, half expecting the Yellow to assault me, but I managed to get everything put away without a remark. When I was finished, I checked my room. Peeking my head in the door, I found it was still purple, still silent, thank goodness.

Chapter 44

The next morning, I woke early and began bustling around the house. I was excited and wanted to make sure everything was perfect for my mother's homecoming. She was due to be discharged at noon.

Mom came home, right on time, and we had everything ready for her. The exhausting trip from the hospital to the ambulance to the house caused her to need to sleep most of the first afternoon. She insisted on sleeping on the couch. She always fell asleep on the couch, even when she was well. She said it made her feel like she was getting better; lying around in bed made her feel like she was still sick.

I sat at her feet the entire day. Every time she woke, I was there to fetch anything she might need…tea, snack, remote. She replied that she was simply happy being with us. I was glad we fixed up the apartment. Mom had never seen it before the paint. She went from the hospital in Amarillo straight to the hospital in Pittsburgh. It made me comfortable knowing she was in a clean, calm place. If we left it the way it was, the dreariness alone could have made her want to go back to the hospital.

"Trinity," Mom said.

I was sitting on the floor in front of the couch, daydreaming, enjoying the rare beam of winter sunlight that caressed the floor and bathed us it its welcoming light. I savored the peace and comfort only a family, with all of its members together, can provide. Dad slumbered in a tight spot on the couch next to Mom's feet.

I was beginning to zone into a peacefulness that I had not experienced in a long time, almost a year. In fact, Mom's voice jolted me back into our living room. "Yeah, Mom?" I answered

"I love you honey…no matter what happens."

I smiled. “I know, Mom. I’m glad you’re here.” I quickly added, afraid she might misconstrue what I meant, “I mean at home, here, with Dad and me.”

She smiled softly. “I am too. You don’t know how much.” Soon, she dozed and I remained next to her, reluctant to move. I wanted to guard her, to make her stay with us forever, to force everything to be okay. I watched her rest, like I did so many times in the hospital. She looked like a tired angel.

After what seemed like hours, I stood up. I almost fell because I hadn’t realized my feet had fallen asleep as I sat on the floor. While my parents slept, I searched recipes on the internet, cooked a fabulous dinner, and woke them. I felt guilty since this was the first time they had been together at home for almost a year, but they had to eat. We all ate heartily from the card table that I propped next to Mom. She savored every bite and commented how delicious a home cooked meal really could be.

Afterward, we played my favorite board game…scrabble. Mom won, of course. She won pretty often, but it was fun to try to beat her. She seemed tired, which we expected, but happy. For the first time in a year, I went to sleep with a smile on my face.

Chapter 45

I woke to a strange, but oddly familiar sound. It took a few moments for me to become fully awake. It was early morning. I could tell because of the sunlight…cloudy and faded, like me, not quite awake yet.

I heard it again, a moan…a lament…Mom? I jumped out of bed and raced down the hall. I was moving as if I had sprouted wings. Mom was all I could think of. I wondered what was happening. I knew whatever it was…it was bad.

I burst into my parents' room. "Dad, what's…oh my God."

Mom was lying on her back, covered neatly as if she had just climbed into bed. Her eyes were closed and she looked peacefully asleep, but with Dad's reaction, I knew she wasn't.

I glanced at Dad. He sat in a heap on the floor at the bottom of the bed. His body quaked as he sobbed.

"Mummy?" I whispered. I watched her face for a reaction. "Mom?" It was getting difficult to focus. I reached to rub my eyes into clarity and was met with the wetness of unnoticed tears. I touched her cheek with the back of my hand. Mom was cool, cooler than she should be, but not cold. I smoothed my Mother's hair. "Oh God!"

I studied her face. She was pale. It was almost as if she were wearing some kind of makeup, except I could see the cold blue trails of veins beneath her skin. Her eyes were closed, two gentle slits beneath her thin eyebrows.

Only yesterday, she looked almost back to normal, almost like her old self. Now…now…she was completely spent, as if she were the embodiment of cancer itself. I wanted to sob, to bury my head in her lap, like I did when I was a child with a scraped knee, but I couldn't. I wanted to change everything. I wanted my Mom. I wanted to go home.

I reached out to lovingly smooth the wisps of my mother's hair that managed to survive the endless chemo. She wore head covering, and the hair was thicker at the crown of her head, more-so than anywhere else. I moved my hand and even her skull felt fragile, as if the bones themselves were succumbing to the disease. I pulled my hand back, shocked, and then forced myself to comfort my mother. This was the hair I used to twirl while my mother held my baby bottles. This was the hair I used to 'style' when I was a kid, armed with sponge curlers and a bottle of gooey gel. This was the hair that always got in my mother's way when she tied my shoes or rubbed sunscreen on my legs. This was the last time I would touch this hair. I twirled its wispiness between my fingers and imagined my mother's smile. A tear coursed down my cheek. I wiped it into my shoulder. I couldn't believe she was gone.

Eventually Dad composed himself and said one word, "Phone." He left the room, and I continued my vigil at my mother's side. I began to pray this was a dream, one of my treks to hell, but this time it wasn't; it was all too real. I heard my dad in the next room, mumbling on the phone. He had a lot of calling to do.

I looked back at Mom. Somehow she looked different now...changed...since I first came into the room. I shook it off. How could she possibly look different? She was dead. I leaned over and watched her chest for movement...nothing. Was she really gone? I began to question my own conclusions when she began to move. At first it was just a few shivers.

"Mom?" I asked timidly. She arched her back violently, and I stumbled backward with surprise. I hit the dresser with my thigh...hard. She obviously was in pain. Her arms shot out from her sides and her hands curled into tight balls. She grasped and twisted the sheets in fists that resembled claws. Her feet kicked rhythmically. I was wide-eyed at what I was witnessing. I covered my mouth with my hands and stared in horror.

I heard a voice talking softly at first. I thought it might be my mother, but this voice was strange, unfamiliar. It steadily increased in volume until I understood what it said, understood with perfect misery. "Cover me? Hide me?" It squealed," Trinity, why did you cover me up?" I shook my head, but the voice stayed with me. I gaped at my mother in horror.

Her neck was blackened, at first I thought it was bruised as if someone had choked her, but as I looked more closely I saw it was burned, charred, cracked and ashen. Her eyes opened and stared lifelessly and her body burst into a sickly yellow flame.

It was then I heard the voice, raspy, deep and commanding, "I am coming for you, Trinity."

I held my hands over my ears and let out a shriek. I stumbled, trying to get away from the scene in front of me, but barely able to move. I staggered into a chair, knocking it and myself over with a loud crash.

In moments I found myself in my father's arms. "What was I thinking?" he said as soothingly as possible. "How could I leave you here, alone?" He sat on the floor next to me and held me tightly. I buried my head into my father's shoulder and sobbed. At times I think he cried as well, but he tried to camouflage his tears. My father always tried to keep his emotions in check.

Time passed, I didn't know how much, but the light in the room was different. I could tell, even through my tears. I pulled back and looked at my dad. He sighed. "We'll be okay."

"No, Daddy!" I replied with a sense of shock and fear. What had just happened to my mother? Whose voice was that? Did I imagine everything that had just taken place? It had to be my imagination! Dad held me for a long time, stroking my hair. Finally, I calmed down.

We stood and walked to Mom's bed together. She was back to her original position...peaceful, forever sleeping. I knew she would be. The Yellow wanted me to see her burn. At first I blamed my imagination, but I saw what I saw. I knew it happened. I thought deeply and came up with another conclusion. If it wasn't my imagination, it must...it had to be... this horrible house.

The rest of the day passed quickly, first the paramedics, then the trip to the hospital with all of the "so sorrys" and the "poor dears," then calls to Amarillo. I spent most of the day on the couch, staring at a dark television set…and thinking of my mother.

Eventually, Dad and I talked. Since Mom was originally from Pittsburgh, we thought we'd have her cremated here then have a memorial back home in Amarillo. It would give everyone who loved Mom a chance to say goodbye. I hadn't even thought of my friends until I laid down very late that night. They briefly crossed my mind as I plummeted into sleep. I hadn't even checked my cell…too busy…too tired…

The next morning I woke late. It was after ten. No dreams. I know my mother kept them away. I would usually have been at school, but I just didn't care anymore. As I kicked off the blankets, the walls smiled sickeningly. They oozed a yellow cast in the clouded morning sun. I responded by leaving the room.

Dad sat at the card table in the kitchen. He was discussing some arrangements on the phone. My stomach grumbled, but I ignored it. I never could eat when I was upset. It made me nauseous. Dad smiled a weak greeting and I touched his shoulder. I got a drink of water and walked into the living room.

I flipped on the television, more for company than entertainment. I stared blindly at a game show while memories of my mother reeled through my mind. Funny thing was I couldn't picture her face exactly. I had looked at her millions of times, but now I just couldn't remember her face.

A noise jarred my from my memories. I glanced at the coffee table. It was my cell phone. I had a message. I reached, grasped it, and debated whether to answer the call. The display read KANE.

I decided to answer, "Hello?"

"Hey, Trinity," he replied. ""Where are you? I thought we were going to meet after school."

"Yeah, I replied. "I'm at home. I have a lot going on right now."

He paused, thinking of what to say, "Is everything okay?"

I tried to overcome the sudden lump in my throat with a silent response. Just hearing the care in his voice made me start to break. I tried to control it, but I just couldn't.

"Trinity?"

I finally managed to huff out the horrible news. "Mom died last night." Again I was racked with sobs.

"We'll be right over," he replied calmly.

"No, not right now," I said struggling through my overwhelming sadness. "Dad and I need today. I'll call you tomorrow."

"Sure, sure. Please?"

I hung up the phone without a response. I really couldn't face my friends today, not without crying the entire time. It seemed as if every time I saw them I wound up teary. I needed to keep it together. Winter break would begin in two days. I'd have enough time then.

The paramedics took Mom's body. They attributed her death to cancer. I attributed it to the house. Just a week ago, Mom was in full remission. She saw the doctors every day. She felt good. She was allowed to come home. It just didn't make sense to me. I knew something else was at work here, especially after what I saw…imagined…no…I saw mom burning, I knew I did. That was *not* my imagination. I knew cancer didn't kill her. It was something else. I was absolutely certain of it.

Soon Dad came into the living room. He looked haggard…worn…tired…sad. "How are you?" he asked.

"Okay, I guess," I replied. It was a total lie, but I didn't know what else to say.

"Well, here's the plan," he sighed. I looked into his glazed eyes. He spoke quickly; I could tell he was just going through the motions. The shock hadn't set in yet. "We'll have a memorial for Mom, here in Pittsburgh. She had a lot of friends growing up. I've scheduled the day after tomorrow at the church down the block. We'll take the ashes home over Christmas break and have the Amarillo memorial after the New Year. I hate for you to miss school, but there's not a whole lot we can do about that. We'll fly down as soon as the ashes are prepared. Maybe you can say your goodbyes to your friends in the next couple of days. We'll leave…maybe the morning of the 27th?"

I hadn't thought of leaving Pittsburgh so quickly. It was true that I hated it here, and for months I wished I could go back to

Amarillo, but never under these circumstances. Five more days wouldn't answer any of my questions or solve any of my problems. If I left now, I knew my problems would come along for the ride, except I would have no one in Amarillo to protect me...no Gabriel...no Kane...no Ravie. I couldn't go...not now.

A solution crossed my mind. I blurted out my thoughts. "Dad, can I stay until the Amarillo memorial? Just until the end of Christmas break? I'll pack everything up and say goodbye to my friends."

"You don't want to come?" Dad looked surprised.

"I want to go home, yes...but I really don't want to be by myself anymore. I want to spend the New Year here, with my friends." I tried my best to look desperate and pathetic. "Dad, I've been alone for so long. I would like to say goodbye to Ravie and everyone at school."

Dad closed his eyes and thought deeply for a few moments. "You know, that might be the best thing for you right now." He paused and rubbed his tired eyes. "So you can stay while I go back to arrange everything for a few days...but not alone."

"Sure," I replied honestly, welcoming any break from the misery. "Can I stay at Ravie's?"

"Sure honey...if it's okay with her mother. I trust you," he sighed. "Late next week, after your break, you can fly down. If you don't want to, I'll come back for you..."

"No Dad. I can fly by myself."

"We'll see," he smiled sadly, but honestly at me. "Anyway, if you want to come by yourself, you can. You'll come down for the memorial. That will give me time to organize everything and find a place to live. Aunt Hannah offered her apartment in the basement, but I thought we should be on our own. It might be easier.

"Great, Dad." I was glad not to have to go with my aunt. I always thought she was pretty overbearing.

He smiled and mouthed, "I know" seemingly fearful that if he actually said the words she would hear him...even 1300 miles away. I was glad Dad agreed to my half-assed plan, but I had to make sure I could stay. I had to settle up with the thing that murdered my mother.

Chapter 46

Over the next two days I did not dream. Hell, I don't even think I managed to sleep at all. My walls stayed Yellow, but I barely noticed. I spent a lot of time with my father, making sure he could cope. We held the memorial and many people attended. Most of them were childhood friends of my mother and people from her old neighborhood. I was hugged so many times by people I didn't know that I felt dizzy. Thankfully, my father stopped with a memorial service and not a funeral. I knew I couldn't endure much more. My friends came, but the day was such a whirlwind that I don't even remember our brief conversations.

I was going to stay with Ravie while Dad went to Amarillo. He flew out on Christmas Eve, but before he left, we said our goodbyes on the front porch. He handed me a box, quite unlike the delicate one he had given me at the hospital. This one was simply a shoebox with a rubber band holding the lid on. On it he had written: Do not open until Christmas in black sharpie.

"Sorry about the wrap job," he smiled.

"That's okay." I hugged him. "I didn't get you anything...I'm sorry." I felt terrible.

"I didn't expect you to." He was smiling through tears now. They ran down his cheeks, and reddened his eyes, making him look much older than he really was. "This is from your mom and me. Open it while I'm gone. Then you'll know we're thinking of you."

I joined Dad in his tears. We hugged each other and cried until I had soaked the shoulder of his shirt. He pulled away and gently grasped my shoulders with firm hands. I looked into his sad eyes. They led me to his familiar smile. "Everything is going to be okay," he kissed me on my forehead. "I promise."

I wished I could believe him, but everything was so screwed up…so screwed up that it made me tired…so tired, I couldn't even think.

Dad turned and put on his coat. "You're sure you're okay."

"Yeah, Dad." I replied as if I had heard it all a million times before. "I'll be at Ravie's. My cell will be on me and charged every minute of the day. I have Aunt Hannah's number."

"Thanks," he smiled sadly. "Yes, I am an overbearing father." He picked up his bag and walked toward the steps stopping to hug me one last time. "But I love you."

He kissed me on the forehead and I watched him walk to the idling yellow cab. A feeling of loss tightened my chest as I watched the cab drive away down the gray winter street. I imagined the leafless trees becoming bony hands…skeletal, reaching, stretching, and clawing toward him. Little did I know, this would be the last time I saw my father.

Chapter 47

The next two days went by very quickly. I stayed at Ravie's and didn't think a bit about my own home. I thought constantly of Mom though...and of Dad...and of Gabriel.

Ravie's mother did not make a Christmas dinner. No one wanted to celebrate in my time of grief. It was a kind gesture, but really didn't matter to me. I was numb.

Things did not feel right, and I had been having an extra hard time sleeping. I lay in bed for hours on Christmas night. My mind was racing. Eventually I got up and crept across the room I shared with Ravie intending to go to the living room and flip on the television. I needed that anonymous company.

When I was almost to the door, I tripped. Luckily, I regained my footing fairly silently. I really wasn't in the mood for one of Ravie's sympathetic pep talks. I turned to see what I tripped over. It was my backpack.

Immediately I remembered the rubber banded box my father gave me before he left for Amarillo. I decided now the item in the box might help me stop worrying about the future and start remembering the past. I opened my bag and pulled out the shoebox.

As quietly as I could, I crept to the living room and turned on a lamp. I sat on the couch and perched the box on my knees. Before I started thinking too much again, I snapped off the rubber bands and lifted the lid. Dad had topped off the box with a neatly folded layer of tissue paper. I removed this as well.

Inside, my dad had placed all of my mother's most precious things. There was her jewelry, placed neatly in little velvet-lined boxes. I opened each one and placed it gently on the couch next to me. There was a small doll that was at one time my grandmother's. She was dressed in a bright purple ball gown. Her hair was twisted with ribbons of the same color and neatly pinned to her head. I sat her on the couch as well.

A small book of baby photos was also neatly wrapped in tissue. I opened the cover. Mom had recorded everything from my adoption. There were papers, a birth certificate, even an envelope filled with money, gifts from friends for my birthdays. She had saved a lock of my hair and tied it with a pink ribbon. There was a scrap of wrapping paper from each of my seventeen birthdays. There were special coins in small plastic sleeves; the hand-written notations said they were gifts from my grandfather who casually collected coins as a hobby. Photographs decorated the pages and below each was a memory, written clearly in my mother's best script. I must have perused this book for some time because when I looked up, my neck was stiff and my eyes burned slightly. I closed the book and set it on the couch. At the bottom of the shoe box was a small child's bible. That too was neatly wrapped in tissue. I opened the cover and a note graced the page:

I pray your Trinity shines in the grace of God. She is a gifted, bright soul. Cherish her with love and hope for the future. One day her grace will shine across the Earth.
- Father Raphael

I thought it was an odd little note. I laid the bible with the other items. At the very bottom of the box was a cloisonné bracelet box. I opened the lid. Lying inside was mother's ankh, the charm that my father had tied around the wrists of my mother and I just a few weeks ago. A neatly folded note fell from the inside of the lid onto my lap. I slowly opened it. It was from my father:

Trinity,
Your mom couldn't wear this when she was in treatment. I know she would want you to have it to tie around the wrist of someone you love...someday.
We love you!

Tearfully, I gently placed everything back in the box. I lingered on the ankh, intending to tie it on Gabriel's wrist, someday very soon.

Chapter 48

The day after Christmas, Kane met Ravie and me at school. It was just past sunset. Kane had decided come hell or high water, we were going inside. Since it was winter break, no one would be there, not even the custodians.

Kane got out of his truck and walked over to Ravie and me. He immediately hugged me gently, as if I might break. "I am so sorry about your mom," he said.

"Thank you," I replied honestly. He kept an arm around my shoulders as we walked toward the building.

He had a screwdriver and a small hammer which he deftly used to open a window. He selected one on the rear side of the miserable building. There was no driveway or parking lot there, just an immense, tree-lined field. It was used for pick-up football games, but at this time of the year, it was barren and silent. As soon as he got the window open, we scrambled inside. I had never done anything like this before and I felt like a criminal. Kane was so good at it; I thought he may have tried his hand at breaking and entering before.

We entered into a storage room next to the office where I first saw the secretary with the jammed copier. The place was deserted. Our footfalls echoed loudly in the empty office. We stopped for a moment to debrief.

After we gathered our wits, we realized there was a rustling noise, distant, but present nonetheless. I was nervous and immediately thought of the potential of night watchmen or cameras. Kane dismissed my fears with a hush. The voices were coming from the Gathering Room.

"We have to see who that is," he whispered in the deepening gloom of twilight.

"I don't want to," whined Ravie. "I'd just as soon get out of here!" Her confidence was gone.

"Not an option," he replied sternly. "Follow me."

We followed Kane to the office door. Crouching down, he opened it slowly and peered into the hall. He motioned for us to follow him. Single-file, we crept like burglars along the wall to the main doors to the Gathering Hall. We peeked through the windows on the Gathering Hall doors. Immediately we recognized the shadow of a person working at one of the tables. A stack of books lay sprawled haphazardly across the smooth workspace.

Gabriel poured oven the contents of the large volumes. We watched him for a few seconds before Kane said, "Oh screw this!" and burst into the room. Obviously, he was surprised by Gabriel's presence; as a matter of fact, so was I. I didn't know what else to do, so I stood and followed Kane in his bold venture.

"So what the hell is going on here?" he asked. "Is this all your fault? Are you controlling this bullshit, Gabriel?" He stared at his best friend. "I should have known a long time ago."

Gabriel stood silently.

Determined, Kane approached the table and with a sweep of his hand, he knocked many of the books onto the floor. "Tell us what's happening here!" he demanded.

Gabriel calmly walked around the table and stepped in front of Kane. "You don't understand," he said commandingly. "I'm here for *you*!"

Kane stood tall and stared at Gabriel. Kane was a few inches shorter, but dangerously athletic nonetheless. In one violent move, he grabbed fistfuls of Gabriel's shirt and tugged him forward so their noses almost touched.

Gabriel spoke again. "You need to trust me, Kane!" They stared, eye to eye for a few moments until Kane decided to let him go with a push. Gabriel stumbled backwards, but caught his footing. He stood with a look of surprised hurt on his face.

At first I thought they were going to fight, but Gabriel turned away. He tried desperately to control his emotions. He straightened his back and ran his fingers through his hair. I wanted to rush to him, to reassure him, to tell him everything would be okay. It was difficult, but I restrained myself. I had to. I wasn't sure who he really was anymore.

Soon, Gabriel turned, looking intently at Kane, Ravie and me. His eyes were piercing, hawk-like, the eyes of a predator. He brimmed with adrenaline and intensity. We were afraid to move as he studied each of us. After a few moments, Gabriel's intensity began to fade, and his look softened. He walked toward us but stopped a few feet away and stared at the ground between us.

"I am going to tell you what's happening here." He breathed deeply and began, not looking at any of us.

"Please do," Kane interrupted.

"This is going to be a lot to swallow," he said.

"I'm already choking," replied Kane folding his arms across his chest in defiance.

Gabriel breathed deeply and began. "Michael, Beatrice, and I are from a place called Amenta. It is not of this existence, but another."

Oh God...Amenta? I thought. That wonderful place of my dreams? The city of Djeba?

Kane interrupted with a forced laugh, "You want us to believe you're aliens?"

"Not aliens," replied Gabriel. "Amenta is another realm of existence, parallel to this one." He closed his eyes, and sudden look of calm crossed his face. "It is the embodiment of beauty and peace. The Creator made not only this existence, but many, many others. Some are beautiful and advanced like Amenta; some are primitive and fiery, still awaiting life; some are old and ready to die; and others...most existences...are evolving. They are not advanced like Amenta, but on their way. This is your world...Earth...still growing."

Gabriel continued to explain, his eyes flashed a brilliant blue. "There is a force of evil. In my world, he has many names...Seth...the Lord of Storms...the Ruler of Dis...the Unspoken," he paused. "He exists in all worlds...even yours. You have names for him as well..."

Kane laughed and voiced what we were all thinking, "You're talking about the devil?"

Gabriel continued, refusing to validate our conclusion. "Evil can only be present in one existence at a time. Even when it leaves, some of its influence remains. It fades over time but never dissipates completely. It is *residual*."

"Residual?" Kane asked. His anger quickly faded.

"Yes," Gabriel replied, "like the smell of a fire long after it has been put out. The essence of the evil must linger…for a balanced world."

I had to ask, so I held up my hand, motioning for Gabriel to stop. "Is Seth coming here?"

"Yes…and soon. There are doorways from one existence to another. They are well hidden and only the guardians of Amenta know how to unlock them. There are laws in all worlds that control the use of the doors. No being can travel from one existence to another unchecked, so the Creator made the keys.

"There is one key that opens the door to each world. During the time of creation, when a world was complete, the Creator entrusted the King of Amenta with the key to that world. It was the King's duty to guard these keys and to keep them safe from harm. It was also his duty to ensure that the keys were not used unless deemed absolutely necessary by the Creator, herself.

"Is the Creator what we call *God*?"

"No, the Creator is important, but she is not God. God does not interfere with the likes of mankind as we are destined to our own fates. God has appointed others to watch over man…one of them is the Creator."

Ravie spoke this time, "so the Creator is an angel?"

"Well not quite…but kind of," said Gabriel. "I guess you can think of her that way."

"Tell us more about these keys," said Kane.

"A long time ago when the Creator was finished with all of the words, and evil had been controlled, the King of Amenta was entrusted to protect the keys to all worlds. He was the only mortal pure enough for such a difficult duty.

After thousands of years of peace, there came a time when the safety of the keys could no longer be ensured. We call this the time of the Great War." He paused, a look of distress on his face. "In the final battle, our King trapped Seth by using the keys. Unfortunately, during this battle, the keys were scattered throughout the existences. They were hidden for their own protection and at the mercy of whoever found them."

"Let me guess," responded Kane. "Seth found a key that opens the door to Earth."

"Yes. We have been searching for the keys for thousands of years, searching and sometimes retrieving the keys...but we have only found a few. Remember, without these keys, even Amenta cannot open the doors. Luckily, several of the keys remained in Amenta when the Great War ended. We have opened those doors and searched to the ends of those worlds, but we have only recovered a few more."

"How many keys are there?" I asked.

"Many," he replied.

"Tell us more," I asked. "How does this all work?"

"Let me start at the beginning...at the time of creation." His expression softened as he looked at me. "When the Creator was complete with the task of making the worlds, she unleashed evil across all of the existences. This act was necessary to allow the goodness to remain."

Gabriel saw we looked a bit overwhelmed, so he explained slowly. "You see, the perfect balance of good and evil is hard to achieve and even more difficult to maintain. After each world was created, evil was allowed to sweep in for *balance*. After it departed, messengers were sent to each existence to teach the people how to control the residual evil, the evil that remained, which was necessary for the act of creation. Some of these people listened, some did not. The worlds that listened to the messengers are perfect places. There is death and sorrow, but the beauty and the goodness that has grown is wonderful and peaceful. Unfortunately, there are only a few of these worlds.

"How does Seth play into all of this?" asked Kane.

"At first, Seth was an ethereal being, second only to the creator herself. It was Seth's job to keep the evil contained in an unbalanced world called Dis. For many years, he confined evil with chains of light and goodness. The evil was under control and worlds grew, learned, and prospered. At that time Seth was known as the *Great Guardian* and he was responsible for the safety of all the Creator had made. All was well for many ages until Seth began listening to the calls of the darkness. The uncontrolled chaos of Dis soon began to poison him, promising him power if he became a traitor. Seth made the evil believe he would become its servant and that he was content to obey, but Seth was not satisfied with servitude. With this power, he wanted control."

"Why didn't the Creator just destroy the evil?" I asked.

"It's impossible to destroy evil. It can only be controlled. If evil were destroyed, all worlds would go wildly out of balance. An unbalanced world is lost in chaos...like a hurricane...or a nightmare.

"Tell me about the Great War," Kane said.

"It began when all of the worlds prospered and grew. Seth had a plan and no one suspected he had already fallen into darkness. He went even further than anyone imagined. He used the evil for his own gain."

"Are Seth and evil the same thing? I asked.

"Evil lives in Dis, but the evil and Seth have become one in mind and in action, but they remain separate entities. Seth uses the evil to enhance his power, and in turn, the evil waits for Seth to let it loose, to open all of the doors. Evil helps Seth and feeds him all the power he wants.

"Once Seth was lost to darkness, he turned against our King. He attacked Amenta and plunged my perfect world into destruction during Great War. That was the time when the Soldiers of Amenta were trained. You know a few of them...myself, Beatrice, and Michael. It was our duty to use the keys of creation to trap Seth. Many of the keys were lost during the endless battles. It took years of sacrifice and the death of thousands of brave warriors, but in the end, even after the death of our King, Seth and the evil were banished.

"As punishment, the Creator sentenced Seth to eternal imprisonment in Dis." Gabriel looked worried again. "Seth has been trying to escape Dis to take over all of creation. He is trying to take control all that was made by the Creator."

"Did the Creator make Seth?" asked Ravie solemnly.

"No, like the Creator, he was made by God. His existence was originally intended for the purpose of good. Like I said, existence only happens if there is perfect balance. For every good, there is an evil. For every right, there must be a wrong, or existence does not occur. Gabriel continued, "This is why Earth struggles. It does not yet recognize the necessity of wrong; you keep fighting it. This is not how it should be done. Evil must exist or nothing will, but evil must not be fought...it must be balanced. You have plenty of evil, but you need more good to balance it. Once this happens, Earth will begin to grow, just like Amenta."

Kane interrupted, "So Earth is just supposed to stop fighting? Let evil run wild?"

"No. That's the whole point! An existence cannot defeat evil. By doing so, the existence would destroy itself. Instead, evil must be balanced. There is too much evil on Earth, and you must work to enhance the goodness...it is all about *balance*."

"That doesn't explain what is happening here," Kane was clearly frustrated, "or why you're here!"

"Let me finish," he paused intently, making eye contact with each of us. "On Earth, there were men who came to spread the word of good, messengers of the Creator. Many came, but you did not accept their teachings. In fact, their messages of goodness have been twisted and used as reasons for your wars and hatred. Earth is an existence that refuses to believe. We are not sure where he discovered the key to Earth or where he has it hidden, but Seth must have been more than pleased to have found this key, but that is not the only reason he comes. He *needs* Trinity and he *wants* all worlds.

"Earth has been a difficult existence, always fighting and arguing rather than accepting love and peace. Once you learn this, Earth will balance and become more beautiful, like Amenta. The evil you see in your existence every day is residual. Evil, in its most pure form has been here before, a long, long time ago. This is the very thing that is bringing Seth here...your love of chaos...your need for it." Gabriel sighed sadly. "He is attracted to discord, like a moth to a light. It is a beacon in his blackness. To have the key to a world that has such a strong resistance to balance is what he has been longing for. He will thrive here."

"When he comes this time, you will witness things none of us has ever imagined. He will be a terrible ruler, and Earth will suffer." He lowered his head sadly and breathed deeply. "It has happened before."

Kane ignored Gabriel's distress, "So what do you have to do with all of this?"

Gabriel looked up slowly. "We were sent by leaders of Amenta and the Creator. We are soldiers. Michael, Beatrice and I need to keep the doorway between Dis and Earth *locked*."

"Is Seth still trapped?" I asked.

"He can use the key at any time, but he is coming for Trinity. He wants to be certain he achieves this goal, so he is taking time to gather as much power as he can. His preparations are almost complete. There is evidence everywhere. The door to Earth is preparing for his arrival. We are not sure where he discovered the key to Earth or where he has it hidden." Gabriel looked at me, "Your dreams are becoming more lucid!" He pointed at Ravie, "Your feelings are constant and true!"

"What are you going to do about it?" asked Ravie. "You and Michael and Beatrice?"

"This is not my true form," said Gabriel. "You will see."

"What the hell does that mean?" said Kane.

Gabriel looked at him intently and stood up, leaving the question unanswered. "It's time to meet the others."

Kane looked questioningly at me and I had no response.

"Are you coming?" asked Gabriel.

We followed him out of the Gathering Hall towards the main doors. The walls squirmed in the darkness. I was curious, so I walked toward one of the door carvings. Gabriel rushed to my side. He grasped my shoulders and guided me to face him, "You can't look!"

I raised my head and his eyes caught mine. He smiled a tired, but kind smile. "This will be over soon," he said reassuringly.

We walked down the hall past the office. The words screened on the doors were different now. The door formerly labeled

OFFICE was now labeled DEATH. The one labeled JANITOR now read HELL. I quickly turned my head and focused on the floor in front of me. I wondered if anyone else saw it.

Gabriel opened the front door and I welcomed the cold air that rushed inside to meet us. I resisted the urge to rush into that air to run and keep running into the twilight. Michael and Beatrice were jogging up the steps to meet us. "I'm so glad you're here!" Gabriel looked relieved. "We have to be ready."

Michael clapped him on the back, "It's what we've been waiting for!" He gave Gabriel a reassuring look then they turned and led everyone back inside. I brought up the rear of the group, following blindly like a child.

We walked quickly back to the Gathering Hall. I tried to keep up, but there was so much to see. The walls rippled with life. The carvings were moving quickly now. I could hear the wood creaking and whining, revealing the small stories that were taking place all around us. Innocent stories turned evil. I tried to keep my eyes on the floor in front of me, but I just couldn't. It still didn't seem as if anyone noticed the walls except me. They kept walking, the distance between us growing. I looked at the walls, writhing and twisting. They beckoned me, dared me, charmed me, threatened me...I looked and was immediately caught.

I walked to a wall. I reached and touched the wood. It rose up in a liquid response and caressed my hand in a motion like a gentle wave. The shape of a strong hand formed in the wood. It reached out and beckoned me. It opened, extended its fingers, and offered itself to be taken, to be held. Unthinking, I reached and allowed my own hand to be grasped by it. It felt warm and soft, unlike the woody grasp I anticipated. It led me to a scene unraveling nearby.

It was a huge city with stone walls the color of iron; a terrible city, full of the unfortunate. Surrounding it were graveyards and endless fields of fire. The only light came from the burning landscape. Flowing past the city was a marshy river partially obscured by fog. People, actually shades, more like dark ghosts, floated beneath the water. Occasionally one rose to the surface and was immediately torn to pieces by other shades.

I saw three people in a small boat crossing the river. When the people reached the gates of the city, two winged dragon-like beasts, holding shields and swords blocked their passage. Two were green in color and rose up on huge wings. The third beast was enormous and shadowy...like one of Tolkien or Dante's wraiths. It disappeared and reconstituted itself directly in front of the men who brandished their weapons. The monsters hissed terrible curses. After one of the men exited the boat, the others followed. They encountered the beasts and fought to enter that terrible city...a city I knew was called Dis. This was the world where Seth dwelled. I knew that instantly.

I heard a voice, deep and cracking, like the wind through a deadfall. It was the voice that was present in the walls of my room:

"Through me you enter into the city of woes
Through me you enter into eternal pain,
Through me you enter the population of loss."

I reeled. I didn't want to see any more. This was a horrible place, a place I could never imagine, even in my worst dreams. I reached and held on the wall to maintain my balance. The wooden hand grasped my wrist tightly. I pulled, straining my arm against its terrible grip. I tried to get away, but it yanked me violently. I hit my head on one of the carvings. Reaching with my free hand. I felt wet blood on my temple. The voice was louder now, repeating the same three lines over and over. It was so powerful, so commanding, so intimidating. My knees buckled and my head swam. The last thing I saw was Gabriel, reaching out toward me before I hit the floor. Then the dreams took hold.

Chapter 49

When I awoke, it was nighttime. I was still lying on the floor. Someone had put something soft under me. A drape had been pulled from the window and folded into a rectangular shape. I was laying on it.

I slowly sat up and winced. My head throbbed. I touched the place where it thumped. A small bandage covered the area. I looked around again. Although the room was dim, I could see a figure slumped over one of the tables. Alarmed, I rose unsteadily and made my way slowly over to his side. It was Gabriel. I touched him on the shoulder and he jumped. He raised his head and looked at me. Old books surrounded him, lying open on the table.

"Hey there sleepyhead," he said smiling warmly.

I returned his smile. "What happened?' I asked.

"Seth reached you in one of your dreams. I was watching you, but I didn't realize he was able to actually get to you, even if it was only a moment."

"What do you mean?" I couldn't remember how I wound up sleeping on the floor or why my head was bandaged.

"You were pulled into one of your dreams, through the carvings."

I took a tentative look at the walls. They moved, but it was slower now, as if they were watching us, intently, silently. I tried to remember what happened, but I just couldn't. My headache made my thoughts murky, like trying to see through thick fog. I put aside Gabriel's comment...for the moment.

"Where is everyone?" I asked.

"Preparing, or sleeping. It's very late." He arched his back and stretched the tiredness from his body. "I stayed to watch you. Kane is sleeping over there," he gestured to a heap draped over a table halfway across the room.

"What about the others?'

"I sent them upstairs to guard the lock. Seth is very close now."

"What happened? Did I just pass out? I still couldn't remember anything after meeting Michael and Beatrice outside.

"You were taken by the dreams. Seth is testing his powers. He was able to manipulate this place to get to you, to intimidate you."

"What?" I asked. I hadn't remembered seeing Seth or anyone else while I slept.

"Trinity, you must not look at the carvings!"

"I can't help it," I said. "It's almost like I'm actually there! They dance in front of me and I look...I have to!"

"You can't! They tease you, tempt you, and make you want to watch. It will get harder to resist as Seth comes closer. He touched you through the stories on the walls! He pulled you in while you were awake!"

I wasn't sure he understood the walls like I did. "Do you see them swirl and twist?" I awaited a response that did not come. "Do you?" I asked him impetuously. I sat erect and impatient, needing to know the answer.

Gabriel lowered his gaze. "I don't see what you do. I see them move, but it's slow, barely noticeable. Yes, they have speeded up, but unless I study them, I don't see...none of us see...what you do."

"You can't be serious," My face was warming with frustration. "You need to know how hard it is for me not to look. I see the faces of my friends...suffering, my mother reaching to me from her hospital bed! They come and go so quickly I can't comprehend what I'm seeing until it's too late. Are you sure no one else...?" I didn't wait for an answer. "Why not?"

"It is clear to me that you will play an important role in this battle. You are a very valuable commodity."

"What did I ever do?"

"You have a very special ability," Gabriel replied. "I saw it when you were asleep. At first I could not believe it was true, even though I was sent to protect you. I know how important you truly are."

"What are you talking about?" I asked.

"You are able to reach out of your dreams and into other existences. Just this one for now, but eventually, you'll be able to reach into others, into all existences," he paused. "Trinity, you are the one *key* to everything."

"What? What do you mean, *key*?"

He continued, more seriously than I had ever seen him. "As you slept, we could hear you…in the walls, calling for me, calling for help. I thought it was Seth, but he was busy talking, trying to conceal your pleas."

"What did he say?" I asked impatiently.

Gabriel responded quietly, "You really don't…"

I interrupted," Tell me! I need to know!"

Quietly he recited:

"Through me you enter into the city of woes
Through me you enter into eternal pain,
Through me you enter the population of loss."

He stopped, awaiting my response.

"What does that mean?" It sounded terrible, but strangely familiar.

"It's a threat, Trinity, and a very effective one. I have heard it before."

"Where?"

He didn't answer my question and instead asked one of his own, "What did you see?" he asked. "While you slept?"

I suddenly remembered as soon as he asked. It was instantly clear like driving out of a heavy fog, "A city called Dis. It was horrible."

"The city of the underworld," he said knowingly. "Seth's city."

"You should have woken me up!"

"I tried desperately to wake you. It was no use. Seth was in control."

"What does this prove? Maybe I talk in my sleep, but not that I can reach out of my dreams!"

"Trinity, I have my scars as well. You were able to touch my physical being; to take me into your dream of the rats. You took my knife as well. You pulled me in, but Seth was acting as my psyche, my personality, manipulating you. As you fought, Seth guided you to us. Seth was the one that hurt Kane and me; it wasn't you at all!

He continued, "This has never happened before…it is physical damage from a dream, your mind's action; it is a very powerful weapon."

"Gabriel, I didn't want to hurt anyone. I had no idea…but this is too much!" I was frightened by his honesty, but it made a strange kind of sense.

"We have to be careful! Seth will do anything to get to you," he replied.

I studied Gabriel's face. His features were sharp and determined but kind. Suddenly a cloud seemed to pass across his smile. He became solemn and very serious. "Trinity, this building is special. It is a summit of many doorways. There are only a few places like this throughout all worlds. On most worlds, doorways are thousands of miles apart, but if Seth comes and controls you, he will be able to step through doorways without even leaving this building."

He hesitated thoughtfully, not sure where to begin. "You too must use the doorways, but you are the master key. You have the power to open all doors."

"No. That's impossible."

"Trinity, it is possible…for you."

"Me? How?" I asked, "If you're serious about all of this existence stuff, then…that would be like having no locks at all."

Gabriel began, "Trinity, you are so special, and this building is special. Seth has the key to come here, but what he really wants is you, Earth is secondary."

"If he manages to get me, would that mean the end of all existences?"

"It is probable," he responded. "Keys would be unnecessary."

"So..." I paused to wet my lips. All of the moisture in my mouth seemed to have dried up. I shivered.

"All creation is in terrible danger, I'm afraid." He looked guilty for having told me the facts he didn't want to share. He continued carefully, "If Seth controls you, your power can get him anything he wants. This building is dangerous as well. If he comes here and he takes you, there are many doorways at his fingertips."

"Can we stop him?"

Gabriel did not answer. "When Seth does come, stay close to me. I will guard you. I swear my life for yours. We all must. You are too vital to let go.

"In Amenta, you are legendary. We call you The Eye of the Sun."

I was shocked to hear these facts, but somehow I knew they were true.

"We have known of your existence since your birth. Soldiers have tried to keep you hidden, but Seth has finally found you."

"I don't feel powerful."

"You still can't pull in a person's psyche, you are not powerful enough to take someone with you through the doors, but I think you will be able to…someday very soon."

I felt sick again. If Gabriel was truthful, he was referring to the end of time. A chill pierced the air and a frigid breeze whipped through the room although the windows were closed. I shivered and pulled on the front of my hoodie.

"Closer, still." said Gabriel as he lifted his head like a hunted animal, knowing Seth was close.

"What are we going to do?"

"We have some ideas, some tricks up our sleeves." he replied. "But now, we need some rest."

"I can't sleep," I replied. "Are you kidding me?"

"You will. You need to think clearly tomorrow," he said. "When…"

"All hell breaks loose!" I interrupted. The walls squirmed at that statement, commanding my attention. I glanced at them and saw a new story, as if it were waiting for me to look. It was Gabriel in a fiery pit. He screamed my name. I felt myself being drawn in.

Suddenly I was looking into Gabriel's eyes, his real, soothing, blue eyes, not the wooden ones that pleaded to me from the wall. His hands framed my face gently guiding my attention from the walls.

"Still, they try," he sighed, his gaze commanding my focus. His eyes were such a defined shade of blue, like Delft china. "No matter what those wooden evils show you, remember, they're trying to get to you, to control you. You *can't* let them."

We spoke quietly for a while before we both began to fight sleep. Gabriel rested his chin on cupped palms and closed his eyes. A soft smile crossed his lips. Just having Gabriel nearby was reassuring. He possessed a control and knowledge that one could not doubt. If anyone had a chance at this, he did. "Tomorrow we will wake early. You need to see the door."

He pulled the chain to the work lamp that perched on the table between us. The light winked out but the room immediately filled with intense moonlight from the tall, drapeless window. It splashed across the floor like a spilled glass of milk.

I folded my arms and rested my head on them, studying Gabriel intently. "Are you afraid?"

"I would be foolish if I wasn't," he responded opening his eyes. They glittered like magical gems in the bright moonlight. "But it will be okay. Trust me," his smile never wavered, he did not doubt. He closed his eyes once more and reached across the table. I met his hand with mine and we laced our fingers together. "No dreams," he said softly."

"Promise," I replied uncertainly. I lay my head down quietly, unable to sleep, thinking of all that was revealed. How could this all be true? Was it true? Soon, Gabriel's breathing became deep and rhythmic. He was asleep.

The walls must have known I was still awake. I could hear them calling my name, from a distance. I was afraid to open my eyes, but I had to. I glanced at the walls. They moved and swirled with stories. I saw the face of my father…weeping, reaching for me from his wooden prison. His lips formed my name and his eyes pleaded with me. I looked away then glanced back. My father's face shifted and twisted into a wailing monstrosity, contorted and tortured. I squeezed my eyelids shut, buried my face in my arms, and waited for morning.

Chapter 50

I awoke with the sun. It streamed through the windows and lit the room ablaze. It took a few moments for me to realize where I was, and then I lifted my head and stretched my neck. I was stiff from sleeping slumped across a table, but it was still better than my Yellow room at home. Gabriel was already awake and off somewhere making preparations for Seth's arrival.

I sat for a minute and reflected on the night's events, so surreal in the reassurances of the sun. No wonder the ancient Egyptians worshipped it, noble and confident. I looked about the room. The scenes on the walls shifted slowly in the shadows. The sun seemed to fend them off like little vampires. They called and beckoned and tempted, but I looked away, focused on the ground and the sun.

Kane still slept in a heap across a table. I decided it was time to wake him, so I walked over to where he slumbered. His face was buried in his crossed forearms. His coat was slung over his shoulders and his dark hair lightly dusted the table with every breath. I took the seat next to him and reached to touch his arm.

"I know you're there," he whispered in a muffled voice

I jumped, surprised, not expecting him to be awake. "Oh, you scared me!"

"I promised Gabe I'd watch you." He lifted his head and his eyes were tired. "So what did you and Loverboy talk about last night?"

"Well, he thinks there's really something going on here."

"Do you?" he asked.

"Yes. There has to be. Kane, these walls are moving just for me."

"Yeah, I kind of listened to you two talking last night."

"You sneak!" I said thinking. "But I'm kind of glad you did. I don't want to do this by myself."

"What do you see?"

"All kinds of horrible things," I replied.

Kane looked empathetic. "I just see them move, very slowly."

"Kane, I think it's meant for me...only for me, and you're close enough to see some of it as well."

"I wish I could see them."

"No, you don't." I looked at him honestly. "Gabriel explained a lot of things to me last night."

"Are you buying what he's saying?"

"Yeah," I said somewhat hesitantly. "I am. There's no other choice." I was afraid Kane would overreact to my belief that Gabriel really was laying everything on the line; that he was telling us exactly what was happening.

"I know."

"Do you trust him?" I asked.

"Before yesterday, I was sure I did. Last night, I was sure I didn't...But you..." He paused, leaving the question unanswered. I stared at Kane...rebellious, handsome, trusting Kane. He sat next to me, looking at the table, meticulously picking at his fingernails. Thoughtfully, he turned his head to face me. He shifted his body and swung his right leg to straddle the bench.

"You don't lie." he said looking at me. His face was serious, cold, with no emotion. When he got this look, it scared me a little, yet Kane had never given me anything to fear.

I returned his stare, "No, I don't."

"Trinity, if what Gabriel says is true and Seth wants you," he paused and looked deeply into my eyes, wanting me to understand. "I will do *anything* to help you."

I didn't know how to respond. His dedication touched my soul. He smiled softly. The hard look he usually wore so proudly had vanished and was replaced with a soothing kindness. He wrapped his arms around my shoulders and held me for what seemed like hours. He stroked my hair as I sobbed. I was racked with terror, grief and sadness all at once. Everything welled up and I cried. I cried for my family...my friends...our future...all futures! I thought of facing Seth. What were we supposed to do? More importantly, how would we win? We had to trust Gabriel. What other alternative did we have?

Finally, after a long, long time, I pulled back. He looked at me intently, seriousness I have never seen, even from him. He brushed my hair from my eyes and gently wiped my tears away. He knew I was terrified

"I won't leave you," he insisted. "I swear."

I returned his intensity, "I know."

Chapter 51

Kane and I sat not talking. We shared a friendship, a bond. It was immediate and we both sensed it.

I suddenly remembered Kane's cut. I wondered if it was healing. Mine healed pretty quickly, but then again mine was not as deep or ragged as Kane's. Michael, Beatrice, and Ravie bustled into the room carrying a few bags.

"Your cut," I asked. "Is it any better?"

"It started getting better a few days ago, but reopened as soon as we got here."

"Can I see it?"

He winced as he pulled the side of his turtleneck away from his neck. Blood had again seeped through the bandage, but it was old and brown.

"You need to change the bandage." I had a few stashed in my bag for my own cut. I began pulling the sides of the tape and gauze away. The gash was still red and puffy. Its purple edges ringed a center that welled blood. I turned to put the bandage on the table, but accidentally brushed his neck with the side of my hand. Kane winced and pulled back.

"Oh my gosh!" I cried. "I am so sorry!"

"It's okay, it's okay!" Kane replied not wanting to further alarm me.

I fumbled with the bandage and looked back at the cut. I gasped at what I saw.

"What?" Kane was frightened. "What's wrong?"

"Sit still!" I urged. He immediately calmed down and let me look at the cut. What I saw was astonishing. It had scabbed over and was much smaller than when Kane had taken off the bandage. The center of the gash was no longer bloody and purple. A neat scab had formed almost before my eyes.

"Kane,' I said unbelieving. "It looks so much better…just now!"

"What?" he replied. "Do you have a mirror?"

I fumbled in my bag and brought out a small round compact. It was a gift from Ravie. Like hers, neat letters that read 'Sephora' graced the top. I popped open the lid and handed it to Kane.

He stretched and strained his neck to see in the small mirror and smiled widely. "I have an idea. Don't be scared. Hold out your hand."

I presented my hand to Kane and before I could protest, he pressed the palm of my hand to the cut on his neck. Immediately, I felt a surge, almost like a wave of energy pulse down my arm and onto Kane's neck. Our eyes widened in a unison of disbelief. I pulled my hand away and what we both expected was true. The gash was completely gone. Kane rubbed the area with his hands. We were interrupted by Beatrice and Michael. They bustled into the room carrying two large grocery bags.

"We will talk alone...later, he said.

"Good morning sleepyheads!" said Beatrice.

"I hope you're hungry," added Michael holding the bags up.

I hadn't even thought of food, but when the aroma of breakfast sandwiches reached me, I realized how hungry I was.

"Mmm...what could be my last meal," replied Kane. "I hope you got me extra!" He stood and made his way to the bags that Michael had set on the table. As he passed, he brushed my shoulder; a gentle, reassuring touch.

Ravie trailed in behind the others. She wore a look of uncertainty. When she saw I sat at the table, she headed straight toward me. She slid in beside me on the bench.

"Hey," I said.

"How are you?" she asked, her expression full of concern and underlying fear

"Just trying to stay focused," I paused." What have you been told?"

Ravie looked at me; her deep brown eyes were rimmed with red and set in tired, dark circles. I wondered if she had been crying, or if she suffered from a lack of sleep. "Oh just that the end of the world is at hand."

"Who told you?"

“Michael. We spent the night at the door, guarding the lock.”

I leaned toward her and whispered, “Do you believe all of this?”

She looked at me, startled I would ask that question. She thought deeply before responding. “Funny thing is, I do. My feelings are telling me I should believe, that I must believe. My feelings are so strong, Trinity, and they have never steered me wrong before.” She paused and looked at me thoughtfully. “What about you?”

I looked at her through desperate eyes. “Oh, I've thought of running. Just getting up and sprinting out the front door. Running all the way home to Amarillo. Leaving all of this behind.”

“Why haven’t you?” she asked.

“I know they'll chase me no matter where I go,” I gestured towards the walls. “Maybe not on wooden walls, but they know I’m here, and they want me.” I took a deep breath and felt that old, familiar chill tingling my spine and tightening my throat. “You still don’t see them either?”

Ravie looked intensely at me then turned to study the closest wall. “Trin, I can’t see anything.”

“Gabriel told me I shouldn’t look. That’s why I sit here and stare at the table,” I said. “Even now they are clamoring, calling me, telling me awful things! It is getting so hard to resist.” I knew I looked scared, just by seeing the look on Ravie’s face. First it was surprise, then it shifted to empathy, then sorrow.

I glanced toward the others. While I was whispering with Ravie they had taken seats at the table next to us. They were already eating and planning. Gabriel caught my eye and smiled very slightly. Even now he was guarding me, not taking his eyes off me, not even for a second.

Chapter 52

After breakfast everyone seemed to be in slightly better spirits. I was too nervous to eat and nauseous as well, so I sat quietly and listened to their plans and conversations. I tried to relax, but I just couldn't. My heart was in my throat and my stomach was in knots.

Kane and Michael had a quickly drawn map of the building laid out in front of them. Beatrice and Ravie sat at the table, but were involved in an intense discussion including a lot of *what ifs* and *just in cases*. Suddenly I felt a hand, soft on my shoulder. It was Gabriel.

"I need to show you something. Please come with me." He held out his hand which I grasped, not because I wanted to go, but knowing I would follow him in the end. Gabriel could have been taking me to see the depths of hell itself. It wouldn't have mattered. I had seen it all already.

We walked the length of the Gathering Hall. He gripped my hand tightly. I remembered to keep my eyes on the floor and ignore the specters in the wood that were calling out to me. He led me to a doorway I had never noticed before. Interestingly enough, it was smaller than the others and perfectly plain. It was made of wood, but there were no carvings on it at all. I ran my hand across it to see if it was really there. He opened the door for me and I entered a tiny room, dimly lit by a sliver of a window to my right.

As my eyes adjusted to the darkness, I could see a narrow, twisted staircase leading up. It was carved wood, very ornately carved, and it looked quite old. I examined it, but in the darkness it was difficult to discern any detail. I was relieved. Gabriel waited patiently, so I started to climb. The stairs creaked under my weight and I worried if it would even hold Gabriel.

Although the wood moaned and complained, we managed to reach the top. We were about thirty feet from the ground. In front of us was another plain wooden door. Gabriel opened this chamber as well and I went inside.

Unlike the first room at the bottom of the stairs, this one was quite large and well lit. Immediately, I noticed the walls were carved as they were in the other parts of the building. I quickly blocked my view by lowering my head and shielding my eyes with my hands. I didn't want to get sucked in…not again.

"It's okay," Gabriel said gently reaching and taking my hands in his. "This room is on our side."

I lifted my head and fully opened my eyes. I began to drink in the detail all around. The walls bloomed with flowers and sunrises. Animals leapt from scene to scene. Mothers hugged their babies and children played. In this room, the scenes did not turn sour; they did not turn black; they did not call to me. I walked to one of the carvings and watched a family welcome a new child. I ran my hand across the carving and felt something familiar. I recognized it immediately. It was heart beating beneath the wood…rhythmic and healthy.

It took a huge effort to pull my focus away from the stories; they were so wonderful in here. I turned to examine the rest of the room. It was large, about a fourth of the size of the Gathering Hall. But, unlike the lower floors, this room was illuminated by skylights, six in all, that bathed the room in crisp, clear light. At the opposite end of the room was a great wooden door. It was much larger than the others. On its surface were the loveliest carvings of all. I approached it and was stunned by its realism. These carvings were innocent and beautiful. I walked closer to get a better look glancing at Gabriel who nodded towards the door. He walked behind me slowly.

There was a wide and rippling river. I could smell its fresh water, clear, crisp and sweet. This river ran through a forested glen, lush and vibrant. I could hear the leaves rustling in the gentle breeze. Only once had I seen beauty like this, so alive…so perfect…only in Amenta. I studied the moving carvings even more closely.

Two animals meandered out of their hiding places and sniffed the ground in search of food. They had the bodies of gazelles and the heads of creatures I had never imagined. Two horns, thin and twisted arched gracefully from above each ear. Their heads reminded me of those of tapirs or anteaters, but with their mouths running wide, the length of the snout. Light green spots dappled their backs as they meandered through the trees. They were odd, but handsome and graceful nonetheless

Flowers bloomed and trees swayed in a breeze I could actually feel. In the distance was a city, sparkling and tall, capped with shining domes of glass. No smokestacks or traffic marred this landscape.

I had the urge to take Gabriel's hand and go running into that paradise. I reached to do just that, but something on the door suddenly caught my eye. Off in the distance, on the horizon was a spot where the wood was marred. I looked more closely; it was burned, like charcoal. I touched it and turned to Gabriel.

"What is this spot?" I asked.

"That is where Seth comes."

"For me?"

"Yes."

"This is where he enters?"

"This is the doorway between Earth and Dis." Gabriel looked longingly at the door. "That is Amenta."

'It's absolutely breathtaking!"

"It is," he paused longingly, "and it's home."

"But why do I see *Amenta* on the doorway to *Dis*?"

"Amenta has put its protection on this doorway to give us more time to prepare for Seth's arrival."

"Amenta can do that?"

"Amenta is powerful and has given a piece of itself to keep the door closed for only a little while longer. Think of it as jamming the lock."

"Will Seth destroy Amenta to get here?"

"He can't...he has no key to reach Amenta...until he has you. He must come here first. He knows where you are and he wants you badly. The conquering of Amenta will be last. He will take his time. He will make us witness that agony before we witness our own."

It was difficult to look away from the beautiful carving, but I had to. I stared at Gabriel directly. "So it's your world and mine...all on my back."

"All worlds," he continued, "but please don't think it's all on you. We can do more than you know."

I replied with silence. This was a lot to process. Not only was I responsible for the life of my world, but for the life of another, alien but beautiful nonetheless. This had to be a dream.

I turned back to Gabriel. "When Seth is here, will the whole door be burned?"

"It will," he sighed sadly.

"When do you think this will be?'

"Tonight...maybe as late as tomorrow morning."

"Gabriel, please tell me, what will happen?"

"I wish I could," he grasped my hand "The truth is, I just don't know."

I sighed. Gabriel stepped forward and took me in a tight embrace. He stroked my hair and whispered, "I will protect you. You'll see."

We stood, holding each other. The whole time Gabriel whispered repeatedly, "I'm here. Be brave. I'll protect you."

I did not cry. I supposed I had either accepted my fate, or I had simply run out of tears. I pulled back and Gabriel looked into my eyes. He smiled. I returned his confidence with a sliver of a smile of my own. I glanced at the door to remind myself of what was at stake. Instantly, I noticed the burn was significantly larger.

'Look!" I said as I pointed at the burn.

He rushed to the area and ran his hand across the charred surface, studying it intently. "This is much faster now!"

"What do you mean?" I asked.

"The burn is spreading...quickly...much more than I thought." Gabriel looked at me, very concerned. "If this continues, Seth will be here tonight!"

My stomach sank. Gabriel must have noticed how pale I had become because he was at my side in an instant with more reassuring words that were difficult to comprehend.

Chapter 53

Nothing happened that day, and the mood was apprehensive. We planned our strategies regarding Seth, but no one was sure exactly what would happen when he did come. So the only thing we were certain of was that Michael would watch the door and alert us when Seth's arrival was imminent. I thought that was unnecessary. I'd know when he was close. If I focused and cleared my mind, I could already hear him calling me from a distance, sweetly, like a mother calling her child.

Gabriel insisted I close my eyes and rest, but I was afraid Seth would come and take me again. Gabriel was sure he could not, since the door to Amenta was helping to protect me. I still wasn't convinced, but I closed my eyes and fell asleep immediately. I had the dream of the dead woman in my mother's hospital room. This time I saw Beatrice's face very clearly.

I awoke with a start. It was twilight. I looked around quickly. Gabriel sat beside me, watchfully and completely awake. I sat up.

"I had a dream...and I had this one before."

"That makes sense," he replied.

"Why? What is happening now?"

"Well, Seth is trying to contact you, but he can't so close to the doorway. Amenta and its purity are interfering with his abilities. The most he can do is send you something he has sent before. Almost like a videotape rewinding and playing."

I glanced at the door. "Oh my god!" It was blackened. Completely charred! I rushed to it like a sick friend.

"Trinity," said Gabriel in a halfhearted attempt to try to stop me, "you don't have to look. It's only a small part of Amenta...please."

He must have known I wouldn't listen. I studied the door in horror. The glen was burned, the trees, leafless and black. The stream was reduced to steaming mud and the sky took on a reddish hue. Worst of all were the gentle animals. They lay in two heaps. Their eyes staring into lifeless space. Their tongues lolled from their wide mouths. In places, the dappled skin was missing and bones jutted from the corpses, reminders that evil could touch anything, no matter how beautiful and innocent. I reached to touch the animals, but Gabriel stopped me by gently taking my hand. I believe he wanted me to see this destruction, to know how important our fate was. To know that failure was absolute and final.

After a few moments I composed myself. I could not allow this to happen, not to my world, not to Amenta, not to any other world. If anything, the scene before me on the charred door, made me more determined than ever to succeed, and for the first time, I felt confident.

I rubbed the tears from my eyes and looked at Gabriel. "Please gather the others, I have something to say."

Gabriel was taken aback, just for a moment, surprised at my confidence and my authority. But in a matter of seconds, my five friends stood before me.

Chapter 54

I began. "We have a huge task ahead of us. Seth is coming. He is only minutes away. He has been speaking to me and I've been pushing him back. I realized this was his way of getting to me, of getting under my skin, of scaring me." My friends looked astonished. Quiet Trinity was suddenly taking control. Kane winked at me and smiled widely.

"I won't allow him to manipulate me anymore. If he wants me and my dreams, he is going to have to come get them. I will fight. I believe we all will fight; fight like we never have before, but there is one thing I have to say. The way we must conquer Seth is with our minds. He has been playing games with me for weeks, and I have cowered like a child, stupidly, fearfully. We will never beat him if we try to physically. We must stick together and fight as a team. Somehow I know this is the key to our success." I paused, everyone was grinning now. My sudden confidence was giving them a boost as well.

I continued, "When this begins, you *must* listen to me. If I tell you to do something, please do it. If Gabriel orders you, *obey.* I feel like some kind of crazy half-time coach, but I know our battle will be a mental one...and it will be difficult.

"If Seth is to travel without doorways, he can't kill me. He's told me of the many ways he looks forward to enjoying my pain, and the many ways he will use me to keep the worlds under his control...in his darkness." My friends looked shocked, even Gabriel. They had no idea what Seth was telling me...what he was making me believe.

Suddenly I felt the room begin to hum, to vibrate slightly. I looked around and saw everyone staring at me. They were wide-eyed and silent. I looked to see the source of their awe and realized I no longer stood on the ground. Instead I floated about a foot above it, and the humming vibration was being caused by energy, and it was pulsating from me. Instead of being afraid, I welcomed the energy, I embraced it and it sang, filling my ears and the room with a magical and familiar language. I recognized the singing immediately. It was the same chiming voices I heard when I visited Amenta through the graffitied wall. I was glad to hear them again.

"He is here," said Michael without emotion as he began to change, to take on the form, the essence, of Amenta. I glanced at Gabriel and he too had changed. He floated above the floor, next to me. Something large unfolded behind him; brown wings that arched gracefully from his back. I studied him and glanced to see if I had sprouted any wings. I hadn't, yet I floated.

Gabriel was more handsome than ever, a warring vision of an angel. His looks hadn't changed exactly, but it seemed like he was sharper, all of his jokes and good humor were pushed aside...he was waiting...hawk-like for his prey. The air around him thrummed with energy and he emitted a soft blue-white light. I couldn't tell exactly where the light was coming from, but it enveloped him. He wielded a broad sword, and an unwavering, determined look.

I looked at my other companions. Like Gabriel, Michael and Beatrice also emitted the blue light though they had no wings holding them aloft. They floated silently beside Gabriel. Beatrice held a long dagger, graceful and dangerous, like its bearer. Michael grasped a shield, bright and strong.

In my own hand, I held a small ball of that soft, blue light. It didn't burn, rather it tickled slightly. I examined it more closely. It was beautiful. As I stared into its tranquil peace, I thought of my mother. I heard her speaking to me in the gentle tones she always shared. "Trinity, a gift for you...hide it away! I can only speak briefly. I will help you when I can. I do not want him to know I am here." I closed my hand, careful not to crush the light, but not wanting to risk its presence.

I caught Kane's eye. "Get ready!" he hollered above the din of energy. He didn't have wings, or glow, or float, but Kane and Ravie held knives that were enveloped in the blue glow .

Kane looked confident, like a viper who knows his prey is trapped. I knew this type of thing was what Kane lived for. He was a shining soul, and his friendship was worth all of the effort. Kane had been my friend through this whole adventure. He was the first to notice something was wrong with the school carvings. He didn't think I was a freak when I told him about my dreams. He stood beside me when I needed a shoulder to lean on…to cry on.

"Nice wings, Gabe!" Kane laughed as he and Ravie took their places next to us. Even though I was frightened out of my wits, knowing Kane was beside me gave me confidence.

I watched the door closely as the hum became deafening, rattling my eardrums and making me wince. Suddenly the door began to smolder. Wisps of smoke and flame erupted haphazardly until the door was burning brightly.

We waited until the flames had almost burned themselves out and the door began to swing open. My gaze pierced the smoke and I saw a dim figure begin to emerge. It was immense. The room immediately became very cold and I shivered with reluctance as well as with the icy chill. I willed myself to go backward and I did, still floating.

There was a sound, faint at first, but quickly roaring like an oncoming freight train. A strong wind began to whirl around the room, adding to the turmoil. I looked toward Gabriel, but he remained still, confident and absolutely ready to face whatever emerged from the smoke of the burning door.

From the clouded shadows, Seth entered the room. He wasn't the pitchfork waving, demon with horns that I had expected, but his appearance was just as striking. He loomed over us, well over eight feet tall. His skin was black and cracked, like the charred door of Amenta. His body rippled, and he wore a long, dirty cloth wrapped around his waist.

His head resembled that of an animal, although I could not identify what it was. I could only assume it was from some other world. His ears stood erect and were squared at the tops. His muzzle ended in a snout that curved downwards, like the beak of a hawk, but his mouth was full of needle teeth that only enhanced his ferocity. His eyes were what scared me the most. They were flat on top and angled sharply upwards, away from his nose. Cinders in the middle of his hollow eye sockets glowed orange, like the fire that surrounded him, and they were outlined in a black color, like those of an ancient Egyptian. In his cracked, smoking hands he carried a scepter of some sort. It was made of copper and was topped with a stone that was round and golden and highly polished. It pulsated rhythmically with a sickly yellow glow amidst the chaos of the scene. It took only a few moments to realize that the pulsing of the stone was mimicking the beating of my heart. I threw my arms across my chest to try to block the stone. Seth noticed and immediately locked his gaze on me, "Trinity," he growled as his smile widened, showing those teeth. They could tear me to pieces without a thought. His voice was a sandstorm, peppery and violent.

Although I was several yards away, he was in front of me in just a few strides. In an instant Gabriel, hovered between us, illuminated in the soft, calming blue. Beatrice was to his right and Michael to his left. I shifted my position so could see Seth clearly between their bodies. They were devoted to my protection. Gabriel's wings beat the air silently.

"You can't have her!" he shouted over the din. He brandished his sword in front of him. My muscles tensed, and I ached with anticipation.

Seth spoke. "Horus, will you never learn? I am Seth! You have tried before and failed. You always fail. It is in your nature." His voice was deep and arrogant. "Now step aside boy." Seth commanded and made a wide sweeping motion with his scepter. Energy, powerful enough to cause pain, rippled through the room.

"You are wrong," replied Gabriel calmly. He also swept his hand and the noise and wind diminished obediently. "Our battle goes to the beginning! That was your first failure…the first of many." Gabriel smiled confidently. "You will never win. You *can't have her."*

What was Gabriel talking about? Why did Seth call him *Horus?* I heard that name before, but I couldn't remember when. What did he mean? My mind raced with questions. Who was Gabriel…really…deep down…in his soul? I didn't have time to doubt. Seth stood tall in front of me, and I knew I had to put my trust into Gabriel, no matter whom…or what…he was. I looked again at the ball of blue light I held in my hands. Instead of wanting to throw it like a weapon, I wanted to protect it, to hide it, to keep it away from Seth. I cupped it gently in my hands, taking my mother's advice, not knowing what it was, but certain it was important to the battle taking shape in front of me.

With a shriek that must have come from the lowest circles of Hell, Seth charged toward us. Gabriel was ready with his sword. With lightning speed, the blade punched several holes into Seth's torso. Gabriel assumed his original position as the wounds spurted dark blood. Taken aback, but only for a moment, Seth regained his footing. "Your sword can't harm me, Horus." He passed his scepter over his wounds and they closed miraculously.

Seth took a deep breath that sounded like the cracking of a glacier. He reared up looking even taller and stronger. He dipped a finger into the black ichor that ran down his chest and examined it closely. He flicked the substance onto the floor with a menacing grin. The droplets spattered and immediately began to bubble and hiss on the veined, white marble. A wisp of smoke erupted with each droplet and they began to take shape. I looked at them closely as they pulsed and grew.

To my horror, the dark blobs became small black scorpions that waved their pincers in the air and stabbed at the ground with their poison laden tails. As I watched they began to grow, first to the size of a cat, then to the size of a pig, finally to the size of a horse. They chattered and squealed with anticipation, brandishing their blackened tails, awaiting Seth's command.

I was absolutely horrified. I glanced at Gabriel who seemed to be oblivious at the threats taking shape in front of him. Beatrice and Michael also stood unwavering, holding their weapons.

This time Seth muttered a foreign word, "mevt!"

The scorpions squealed loudly and scuttled toward us. Gabriel held his position until the creatures were close enough. I realized he would not leave me alone, even for a moment. Seth would not be able to lure him away. The scorpions chattered and waved their claws in the air.

In a flash of motion, Gabriel swung his sword and immediately dismembered a scorpion that was scuttling toward me. Michael swiftly pounded his shield onto the back of another, driving it into the ground with a crash. It squirmed for a moment and lay still. Beatrice pierced another with her dagger, pinning it to the floor. It crashed and shook violently until death forced it to be still.

It was Gabriel's turn this time. He breathed and the sweet scent of a lush orchard filled the room. He smiled widely, first at me, then at Michael and Beatrice. He held his sword toward Seth. From the end jetted a bright blue streak of lightning. It obliterated the remaining three scorpions and hit Seth square in the chest. He staggered backward.

Suddenly, to my dismay, Seth's enormous body began to absorb the lightning. He swelled, full of the awesome energy. Opening his mouth he hurled the powerful blue light back at Gabriel in one horrible breath.

Bearing a grunt brimming with effort, Michael was there in the nick of time to block the light with his shield. It ran off of the metal as if it were merely water. It spilled over the sides in a waterfall of sparks.

Seth spoke. First he focused on Michael, "Michael, my old friend! What made you betray the darkness? You belong with me; your power should be feared by all, like it was at the beginning."

"I will never come back to the darkness!" Michael stated, "In fact, I think you need a little sun, Seth." Michael's shield hummed and became as bright as the sun itself. Its heat radiated throughout the room. When I thought I couldn't take the heat any longer, Michael thrust his shield at Seth. Pure sunlight streaked across the room like a comet. Seth held out his palm and soaked in the energy. I know it hurt him because he stumbled backwards before he caught his footing. He crumpled over; his shoulders bowed and slumped. I hoped he would fall and that would be the end of him. I couldn't be so lucky.

Slowly, Seth raised his head. His wicked grin turned my heart cold. He stood erect, puffed his muscular chest and extended the palm of his hand toward Beatrice. Again he spoke in dark tones, full of hatred and anger.

"Beatrice..." he addressed her this time. "Pathetic soldier! Soon, you will join them. For you there will be no paradise...only torment. You too are a dark soul thrust into the false light of the Creator. You should be with me as well. Here is where you're true meaning lies...in the darkness."

"I will never betray the Creator," she replied. Her beauty shone like a star on the blackest of nights.

"Soon, you will be beside me, ruling the darkness that will follow. My darkness."

He beckoned Beatrice, holding out his hand. "Take it...you know you want to."

I could tell Beatrice was struggling. She looked to Gabriel for help. He reached and grasped her hand in his, angering Seth even further. "You cannot separate this bond," said Gabriel. "It is too strong! Now with Trinity, we have the power we need, the power to send you into your beloved darkness, where you can rule...alone...with no one to torment but your dark self. You are through manipulating. You are finished using the power of others, pretending it is your own. We will not betray Amenta or Earth."

Again, Seth laughed and I cringed. I peeked at the glowing ball of light I held in my hands. It calmed me. It had more power than I could ever imagine in one soft, pulsating, blue sphere. I could have gazed into it all day, but I had to help my friends. I glanced at Kane and Ravie. They still brandished their knives. It was almost comical, bearing knives against a monster like Seth. I wished they had swords, powerful like Gabriel's.

Surprisingly, I heard my mother's voice again. "This light will give you what you wish, but you must be careful. It contains power that may be used against you. Use it wisely." I looked into my blue light and was calmed instantly. In fact, I felt almost sleepy.

Seth's presence jarred me from my peace; I opened my eyes and saw him engulfed in bone-jarring flame. It was unbearably hot! I was afraid Seth would pluck my light from me, but he didn't seem to know I had it! I closed my eyes for a moment of calm.

Soon, I opened my eyes and saw that Kane and Beatrice now held swords, pulsating with blue light, identical to Gabriel's. I immediately knew what I had done! I was wishing my friends had swords then I looked into my light. I must have fallen asleep…only for a moment…but long enough for me to pluck those swords from the light! I could wish for Seth to be gone! I could use that light for my wishes! There was no bigger wish!

Gabriel spoke gruffly to Seth. "Go back to your shadows! You have no business here!"

"Oh, but I do, he replied. She is my business." Even his gaze was painful. "Come, Trinity. It's time you used your power and understand the weakness of Horus. You need to do something for me." He held his hand out for me to take. To my horror, I found myself wanting to take it! I wanted to leave this world and go into eternal blackness, a place of forgetting. It would be wonderful to forget, to let the darkness caress my tired soul. I began walking toward Seth.

Gabriel called me back sternly. "Trinity! Do not look at him. He is the Father of Lies. He wants you for your power!"

I tried to focus my mind on Gabriel. I felt the tendrils of Seth's control releasing their grip. I shook my head to clear my mind. Gabriel! I looked to him desperately.

"Be strong!" he whispered and smiled softly. "Don't let him in!"

My heart melted. He was so kind, even in the face of uncertainty…so beautiful, in the face of such horror…so calm, in the face of insanity. It was at that moment I knew I would do anything for him.

"So touching, don't you think, Beatrice?" Seth glared at her, and she averted his gaze.

Again, Gabriel immediately took control of the situation. "Seth, as usual, you talk too much. You love to show off your power and control, but things are different now. No one cares about you. You're old. Even those you created to keep you company in the darkness have deserted you." He extended his hands toward Michael and Beatrice. "You are alone."

I could tell Gabriel was angering Seth. His eyes narrowed and the flame surrounding him became even hotter and burned more brightly. Gabriel continued, "In the name of my murdered father; in the name of those you kill for power; in the name of those that glow in the goodness of the sun; return to Dis!"

"Not without my prize," he pointed his long, burned finger at me. "You know why I need her."

"Tell me," replied Gabriel arrogantly.

Seth licked his lips with a forked tongue. "Oh, she can't hide! I knew she was coming. For years I have prepared for her coming. She is the key...and she is perfect."

Seth addressed me directly. I couldn't bear to look at his fearful appearance so I lowered my head. His stare made my bones ache, as if even they too recoiled from his gaze. "Trinity, you were created for vengeance. How better to avenge light than to use darkness? With you as the key to all worlds, your power cannot be stopped." He held his hand out again for me to take. He smiled and I saw my mother...my father...Texas...everything I loved lie in that hateful, smoldering hand.

Gabriel interrupted Seth. "She is the bringer of love...the bringer of vengeance. She will remain with us...in love...she will only know love."

I looked to Gabriel; he too held his hand out. In his eyes, I saw love, love without conditions, so much love and peace. I clenched the blue light I held tightly in my hand. My mother would help me.

I knew I had to trick Seth. I had to win this with my mind, I had to use my head. I would always choose love over might, but Gabriel could never take on Seth by himself. Even with the help of Michael, Beatrice, Kane and Ravie, could Gabriel defeat this devil? He was too powerful...too ruthless...and too driven. If Seth fought my friends, they would lose, and I would be the key to the destruction of all worlds.

"Mother!" I whispered desperately. I waited a few seconds for her reply. I tried to look as if I were trying to decide which side to take.

"Walk away," I heard my mother's familiar, loving voice in my head. I looked at Seth then at Gabriel. The both beckoned to me, holding out their hands for me to grasp. They wanted me to choose. Instead, I simply turned my back on the entire situation. I walked toward the small window on the other side of the room. Gabriel looked distraught. I wanted to run to him, to hold him, to tell him everything was okay, but I couldn't. I had to distract Seth.

"Choose!" demanded Seth.

Gabriel remained silent and steadfast. His confidence in me did not waver.

I reached the window and looked out. The calmness of the light I held in my hands possessed me. I closed my eyes. I heard Seth calling me. I heard Gabriel urging me to resist. I had a power Seth did not realize. I had the power to pull things from my dreams. I was the only one who could control it. What could I dream for?

"Mother, what is happening? What are they talking about? Who am I?"

I heard her voice. I focused. Everything became surreal, dreamlike. Time slowed like it always does in dreams. How was she able to speak to me, to help me from beyond death? Then it was as if a light came on. I knew, I knew! I knew how I was able to communicate with her! It was the charm my father gave me. It was the ankh!

She spoke to me, "Trinity, we always knew there was something very special about you. "You must believe. The king of Amenta that was murdered by Seth was Gabriel's father, and with his murder, Gabriel is the new King of Amenta. You must trust him. He is here to protect you. His name is..."

"Horus," I concluded.

"Yes. Trinity, you must know. People from Amenta have been here before; when Seth first embraced the evil he had kept at bay for so long. Thousands of years ago, he waged a terrible war.

Many were persecuted, many were imprisoned, and even more were murdered. Thousands left the once flawless confines of Amenta and came here, to our world, to escape the rampages of Seth.

"During this time, the keys were scattered across all worlds, hidden for their protection in case Seth conquered Amenta. Those that had come to Earth from Amenta were to remain here until the key was found to reopen the door."

"If Seth has the key, how were Beatrice, Michael, and Gabriel able to come?"

"Tremendous energy, stored for years can send a person from Amenta to another world, but there is no energy on any world that is strong enough to allow them to return. To go back, one must possess the key."

I realized something, "Mom, I was able to go to Amenta? I have no key."

"That is correct. You *are* the key to everything! You can go to any world you wish, but you must go alone...for now. One day, with much training, we believe you will be able to take others with you, but your power must be given time to grow."

"Time to choose, Trinity!" commanded Seth, interrupting my encounter.

"I must go before he realizes I am helping you," said Mom. Your dreams can only slow the passage of time briefly."

"Thank you Mom," I whispered.

I kept my back turned toward the others as I gazed at the light in my hand. The solution came upon me like a lightning bolt. Fire! I had to wish for fire! I allowed a feeling of calm to take over my body. I had to fall asleep to be able get fire from my dreams. I relaxed, allowed myself to drift...drift...soon I felt warmth on my cheeks. Light danced behind my closed eyelids. I opened them. To my shock, I had discovered the ball of light in my hand had transformed into flame. The flame did not burn me though I could feel its heat and hear the crackle.

My fear quickly became a revelation. I had the fire. I could use it...but not directly against Seth. I had to use it wisely. I turned to face everyone, cupping my mother's gift in my hands. I thought if

I could burn the building, I could burn as many doorways as possible. Maybe if I could trap Seth here, he could not escape back to his nightmare world of Dis. Even if he managed to possess me, he would not be able to leave, not if the doors were destroyed. His evil would be trapped...limited to this world and no other, and his connection to Dis would be lost. He would be weakened and perhaps we could kill him.

I turned, fire in hand. I knew exactly what I had to do. Everyone looked at me, waiting for me to make a move. I bent and brought the flame to the red drapes that framed the window. They blazed to life, helped by decades of dust. I raced to the nearest wall and splashed the fire from my hand onto the carving. As soon as it touched the wall, flame erupted. The figures in the carving squealed and ran in all directions, away from the flame. Gabriel rushed to my side, intent on protecting me.

"Trinity, I can't help you destroy the doors, as I am bound to protect them. But you can! Run with the fire! Hurry!"

As Gabriel spoke, Seth approached him. I wanted to rush to his side, to use my fire, but I was grabbed around the waist. I turned. It was Kane, blue sword in hand. He began dragging me away from the scene, toward the spiral staircase. I reached out toward Gabriel. Through the thickening smoke, I saw that he, Beatrice and Michael were engaged in full combat, each trading blows with Seth. As I peered through the smoke, I focused on Beatrice. Seth reached and grasped her body in his enormous fist. Then he glared directly at me.

"Beatrice!" I pounded on Kane's arm that he had clamped around my waist. I screamed at him, "Let me go!" I tried to pry him off, but he maintained his grip. I watched in helpless dismay as Seth crumpled Beatrice's body in his bare hands. She fell to the floor in a broken heap.

"Beatrice!" Seth smiled his needle grin at me.

Kane followed Ravie closely. He balanced his way down the stairs with me slung over his shoulders. "Trinity, stop fighting! Gabriel wanted me to get you out of there!"

He didn't know what had happened to Beatrice. Kane had no idea that Seth just crushed her like a piece of paper. "Trin," he cried, we have to spread the flame! Gabriel will hold Seth back as long as he can!"

"No! We can't leave them!" He hauled me struggling the entire way into the Gathering Hall.

I was no longer paying any attention to the flame and it dwindled in my hand...dwindled almost to a cinder. I didn't care; I didn't care about anything except helping Gabriel, until I heard the voice of my mother, clear and commanding.

"Trinity! Mind the flame! Your friends are risking their lives to buy you time...the time you need to destroy this summit of worlds."

I calmed immediately, stopped resisting Kane, and spoke to my mother. "But they'll die."

"Perhaps...yes. Many will die so many may live. It's the balance of things, Trinity...the balance of existence."

I took a deep breath and Kane finally released me. The fire in my hand sputtered then blazed to life. I stared at it for a moment...clarity seeping into my conscience. She was right. I had to take care of this place; this congregation of doorways...of entire worlds. I knew I could not leave any of them unburned. If Seth were to possess a key without the doors that existed in this building, he would have to search for other paths to enter a world. They wouldn't be in one place for him to open and close as he pleased.

Once this building turned to ash, Seth's only option would be to possess me. Something I had no intention of allowing him to do. Gabriel revealed that if Seth owned me, he would not need keys at all. Chaos would come to all worlds. I looked at Kane and Ravie. They were disheveled, wide-eyed and frightened. I knew I had to pluck one more thing from my dreams. I closed my eyes and took a cleansing breath. I slept instantly, already dreaming.

In moments, I reached into my subconscious and found what I was looking for. It was the box my father had given me for Christmas; the box I opened in the loneliness of Christmas Day.

In seconds it was in my hands. I snapped the rubber bands from the box and cast aside the lid.

In my dream, I travelled up the spiral staircase and into the room with the peaceful carvings. Gabriel and Seth did not see me. They were unaware of my dream presence. The second floor was ablaze. Through the thick smoke, and Gabriel and Seth were the only beings I could see. They were locked in hand-to hand combat, matching each other, blow for blow. I wanted to help, but I could not linger. Time was of the essence.

Reaching into the box, I produced its precious contents. I took it to Gabriel and tied it on his wrist with seven knots...it was the ankh my father had given my mother. Its graceful, looped twin hung from my own wrist.

I forced myself awake. No one had noticed that I traveled in my dream.

The flame in my hand still blazed and I spread it like gasoline all across the Gathering Hall. I had to make sure every door was kissed with flame. As I ran about, I heard a creaking overhead. Smoke seeped from between the swollen wooden arches. The second floor, the floor where I left Gabriel and my friends, was now ready to collapse. Flames punched their way out of cracks that were forming in the wood. I had to hurry!

I rushed from door to door. Kane and Ravie stayed close beside me, shouting and pointing as to where they thought I should spread the flame. In a very short time, fire blazed across the walls and licked at the ceiling. That was when I heard two noises. The first was a familiar howling...fire alarms. The second was more ominous...a groan and a high pitched whine. I knew it was a matter of moments before the ceiling caved in, bringing the roof and second floor with it. I grasped Ravie's hand and Kane's sleeve and pulled them behind me.

We made our way to the nearest window. It was in the rear of the Gathering Hall, next to courtyard. Gabriel used his boot to kick at the tall window. It was no use. There was no exit door at this point and fire snapped at our heels. He lunged towards one of the twisted wooden chairs that surrounded the study tables. "Cover your heads!" he shouted.

Hauling it over his head, he swung its weight high and grunted with the effort. He let go at precisely the right moment and the chair sailed through the tall window with a deafening crash.

Kane smashed the remaining shards from the window frame and laid his coat over the ledge. Ravie and I clambered through and into the cold, night air. Kane began to follow us but a large triangle of glass fell from the frame above. It sliced into Kane's shoulder causing him to stagger back into the building. Even though we didn't know how badly he was cut, he jumped to safety in the courtyard.

We ran a few yards, just to get away from the blazing school only moments before the collapse. In mid sprint, I turned back towards the building. With a rumble and two large snaps, the roof groaned and its weight crashed onto the second floor. If anyone was alive, they could never have survived that terrific collapse. I strained to see through the smoke, hoping to see some sign of Gabriel. I could not; the smoke was far too thick.

I looked toward my surviving friends. Kane swayed unsteadily on his feet. Ravie, oblivious, and certainly in some form of shock, stood transfixed, staring at the inferno blazing in front of her. I pushed aside my worries about Gabriel and rushed to Kane's side.

"Are you okay?" I asked him, suddenly alarmed. He was pale and wide eyed. Clutching his shoulder, he crumpled to the ground in a heap. He turned and lay on his side, knees pulled into his chest. He closed his eyes.

"Yeah, I just need to rest."

I looked at his shoulder where the glass struck him. Although he wore a thick shirt, the glass had sliced deeply into his shoulder. He was soaked with warm blood that steamed in the frigid December air. "Kane!" I quickly removed my hoodie and pressed it on his shoulder, trying to stop the awful flow of blood. It was no use. In moments, it too was soaked.

His eyes were glazed and he stared up at me. He slurred, but I couldn't tell what he was saying. Here was my friend, one of the most trusting friends I ever had, bleeding to death in front of me. I had to help him!

Maybe I could heal him like I was able to do with the gash on his neck. I put my hand over the wound, praying the bleeding would suddenly stop, but no matter what I did, it still flowed freely. I was wasting time! Could I dream, now? I had to try! I closed my eyes and called for my mother. I knew she still watched over me. I could feel her presence all around me like a warm embrace.

"He won't die if you act quickly," I heard her reply. "Use the light to close the wound!"

I opened my eyes and again my right hand pulsed. I cupped the blue light once again. I tugged at Kane's coat until his arm flopped from its sleeve.

"Hurry!" my mother urged.

I set the light in my lap and tore his shirt with my hands. His wound was open cleanly, cut with a very sharp shard of glass. Blood pulsed from the wound in great surges. When the cold air rushed into the wound, he arched his back in pain. He opened his eyes and gasped. His breathing was rapid and ragged. He was frightened, knowing he was about to die.

It was my turn to reassure him. I took the blue light and held it over the wound, not knowing what would happen. Immediately the bleeding stopped. The light thrummed, pulsing with Kane's heartbeat. Like a wave of ice, it ran from my hand in rivulets and drained into Kane's wound.

I lay his head in my lap and smoothed his tousled hair. "You're going to be okay," I whispered over and over. Soon, the blue light dissipated and Kane was silent. Was I too late?

Another enormous crash commanded my attention. The second floor had finally collapsed into the first and the fire still blazed. I silently hoped for Gabriel. I also hoped for Kane, who lay dying in my arms.

Suddenly, Kane's eyes fluttered open, piercingly green. "Thank you," he whispered.

I hugged his head for a moment, happy that someone had managed to survive alongside me, but all the while regretting the fate of others.

He sat up quickly, examining his miraculously healed wound, "How did you..."

I interrupted him, "It was the light. I...I don't know!"

I helped him to his feet. "Have you seen anyone?"

"Just Ravie and she's going to need some help."

"No one else?"

"No." We walked toward Ravie and led her to a seat on a wall at the side of the courtyard.

"Watch her, Kane," I commanded.

"Where are you going?" he asked.

I ignored him. I had to see who survived...where we stood in this whole mess. My heart ached. If our friends were dead, I had hoped they were able to contain Seth. If they were still alive, maybe they needed me. I couldn't just walk away. I couldn't just sit and wait.

Kane called my name. Each time, he expressed more urgency. I ignored his pleas and kept walking towards the conflagration. Smoke billowed in monstrous mountains and flames reached high enough to singe the sky. I looked. I searched. I called. I waited, all to no use. I got close enough to feel the raging heat on my face. The smoke made my eyes water, but I kept them open, searching for Gabriel.

More time passed, and then I heard him. My heart leapt. At first I thought he was calling for me to help him, and then I heard him clearly, through the din, as if he were speaking directly in my mind.

"Trinity! Run! If you hear me, run away! Go! Now!"

Then I saw him stumbling from the building. His tattered, charred wings spread wide, his back to the flames. When he saw me, he lurched forward even faster, stumbling, catching himself with his fingertips. Something was pursuing him and he was desperately trying to get away. I ran to meet him.

As I rushed forward, he stopped, "Trinity, no! Go!" He was breathless. "Seth has done the unspeakable!"

In that instant, Seth also emerged from the flames. His muzzle dripped with darkness. Two glowing blue swords protruded from his body. One jutted from his back, the other from his chest.

He snarled, calling to me. "Trinity!"

I continued my path forward, toward Gabriel and whatever danger awaited us. The clouds of smoke billowed ever upwards. An ominous form began to take shape in the mountains of smoke. Orange streaks of lightning crackled. Somehow I knew this was much more than a little static electricity. Something was coming...something I did not want to see.

In a moment I was next to Gabriel. I slipped my arm under his and helped him stay on his feet. Together, we scrambled across the courtyard toward the wall where Kane and Ravie stood in awe.

"Trinity," Gabriel began. His breath hitched with the very effort of forming words. "You ha…have to leave. I can make one last stand, but…"

Gabriel was worn, smeared with ash, bloody and bruised. His eyes were a moment of clarity in the violence his body had become. He had tried to fold his wings behind his back, but one was badly injured and extended at an obtuse angle. The feathers were dirty and tattered, fluttering like strips of newspaper in the wind. His shirt too hung in tatters and rivulets of drying blood marked their path across his torso. A significant gash on his forehead was surrounded by an already purple bruise, but his eyes were bright, and blue, and clear. Kane ran towards us to help me haul Gabriel into the shadows under the trees that lined the edges of the courtyard.

"God, Gabriel!" Kane helped him sit on the ground next to wide-eyed Ravie.

"Not God." Gabriel kept his eyes on Seth who had suddenly turned away from us and toward the growing clouds of smoke. For some unknown and ominous reason, Seth was not pursuing me any longer.

Kane looked questioningly at Gabriel. "What about Beatrice…Michael?"

Before Kane could finish the thought, Gabriel blurted out, "Dead, they're both dead." He paused, reflecting on the battle. He lowered his head. "I should be dead as well. I don't know why I'm not."

I did. It was the ankh I had tied onto his wrist.

Kane's usually proud shoulders slumped. And he held his forehead as if he had a terrible headache.

Gabriel continued, "We will mourn them later, but now we have to protect Trinity." He breathed deeply, more smoothly.

I don't want to ask what's coming," I revealed. "But I have to..."

"Seth has let loose the eternal darkness...the Evil of Creation!" As Gabriel spoke, the fear in his eyes intensified.

Gabriel continued, "I did not think Seth, even in his search for power, could be lured into releasing the evil, the evil he was created to control, but it comes, and we will never be able to stop it if it enters the doorway." Gabriel was ragged, worn. His jaw pulsed with courage, but I could see the intense fear he tried to keep masked.

"Evil will swallow this world," Gabriel explained. "It will be worse than chaos. It will be as if existence never happened. Seth has undone everything for vengeance. He looked at me intensely. "In my wildest thoughts, I would have never guessed it would come to this. Seth plans to use you to unlock the chains of light to set evil free. With you, this primal evil can come forth and destroy all worlds. Everything will be back to the beginning...before creation...before light." Gabriel sighed. "I believe there will be no end until everything is undone."

"Will he get into any other worlds?"

"I don't know, but even evil cannot travel without a key. Trinity destroyed many of the doors which will protect those worlds. But there are thousands of doorways scattered throughout the existences.

Just the look on Gabriel's face made me want to fight, to fight for my world and all worlds. Brave Gabriel, bruised and bloodstained, was willing to give up everything for just one of those worlds.

Seth was gone. We did not know where, but we knew he had a plan. He would not be stupid enough to return to Dis and risk being trapped there. Thunder pounded within the now monstrous clouds. The dark shape within them was becoming more and more solid. I had to think. I was the one with this new and wondrous dream power. I had to figure out what to do with it. Amidst the chaos, I sat on the damp ground in smoky twilight. I looked toward my friends. We were still kids with the weight of all worlds on our shoulders. This was the crux of everything. I cleared my mind. I spoke to my mother. I closed my eyes.

Suddenly everything became clear. She showed me two scenes. The first was the world in chains, my world. Skyscrapers crumbled, landscapes barren, people suffering. Even the sky was bruised purple and black with Seth's rule. The second scene was of a snake, coiled, resting. Its belly was distended. It sat on a completely white landscape…a landscape that contained absolutely no detail. Not even shadow survived. I knew this was creation after the evil. It was the world devoid of all hope of redemption.

"Mother?"

"You are the one that must have courage, Trinity." Moments passed that again seemed like hours. "Your actions are what will decide everything…life or death"

"I choose life!" I screamed into the scenes of destruction. "Ink di-nh! Di-nh!"

I opened my eyes to Kane and Gabriel staring at me in disbelief.

"Gabriel spoke first, "Where did you learn that language?"

"What do you mean?" I was confused. I knew I was saying something, but I didn't know what he was talking about.

"You were speaking in some foreign language," stated Kane, "but I don't know what it was. I never heard it before."

Gabriel looked wide-eyed at Kane then at me, "I have," he paused. "It's the language of Amenta."

Chapter 55

We sat and rested for a few moments, gathering whatever strength we could while the ominous shape solidified in the clouds. Ravie slowly emerged from her shock, but wasn't much help. I had covered her with my jacket. She simply could not handle the destruction that lay before us so she sat against the stone wall that defined the courtyard. Kane sat with her, holding her, rocking her slowly. She had no idea Michael was dead. I did not tell her. That certainly would send her over the edge.

The clouds began forming a columnar shape, boiling then solidifying. Soon they dissipated and a solid figure began to take shape in the mists. After a moment I knew what it was...an enormous, solid, wooden door. It was suspended in the air, hanging on invisible hinges. The panels on the door were plain, uncarved. As I watched the door slowly swung open.

"Keep calm," Gabriel urged. "Trinity must remain with us. Protect her with your life! They will do anything to get her in there."

An electric blue film crackled across the doorway. I looked into the world of Dis and saw the true terrors of Hell spread before us. Kane watched for a few moments then turned to shield Ravie's unblinking gaze. The chamber was cave-like, huge, a bottomless pit full of terrible images and violence. As I approached, the scenes intensified...I wanted to look away, but I dared not. In the blackness of that chamber, something stirred in the shadows...something enormous. I was the only one who saw it, and I knew what it was. It was the evil, and it wanted me to let it out.

Gabriel and Kane stood protectively at my sides. Gabriel called for my attention, but I was unable to direct any toward him. I could only stare into Dis.

Suddenly, the earth below me rumbled heaved as if there were an earthquake. I found myself falling into an enormous cavern, but only briefly before Seth grasped me around the waist. He glowered down at me and dragged me up a pile of rubble toward the door. Kane and Gabriel blocked his way. Seth had taken me from below and was striding toward the doorway.

"I squirmed and punched and tore at Seth, but he was unflinching." I was being consumed by the door. I saw only that door and the shape that shifted behind the shadows...the shape that was coming for us all. I closed my eyes and called for my mother as I slid into another world.

I felt Gabriel's hands pulling at my shoulders, I grasped at him. I closed my eyes and tried to dream of Amenta's perfect blue energy, but I could not fall asleep!

Wings beat above my head, more arms, pulling, shouting, trying to get my attention. I reached toward them to be pulled back into the light of the earth, but this was like being devoured, completely swallowed by inescapable darkness. I heard the voice of my mother, but it was so faint I could not make out what she was saying, and somehow, it didn't matter. I crossed the threshold into Dis, a place where she could no longer reach me. I was immersed in a landscape of suffering, darkness, and shadow. Soon, I stopped struggling against the evil and began to accept it. It was much easier that way. It was becoming almost comfortable. Darkness enveloped me like a familiar blanket.

Suddenly I felt a warm rush of wind. At first it was barely a breeze tickling my shoulders and face, but it quickly grew in strength. In moments, it lifted me, blew me away from the perpetual darkness. Although I found myself wanting to remain in the blackness, I accepted the gentle wind. I soared above the scenes of horror and flew softly backward toward the door. The wind rippled my clothing and smoothed my hair. It kissed my cheeks and hands and set me gently back in my own world.

I looked in front of me for the source of this wind. Gabriel still held me in an embrace and looked kindly into my eyes. I understood immediately. He was the wind that had saved me from that tortured world. He had risked everything, gone into Hell to bring me back here. I returned his embrace as he set me next to the doorway .

"Kem-Au," I whispered into his ear.

He smiled handsomely, "You're welcome." He held me tightly. "The love of your mother forced the door open long enough for me to get through. Once I had you, you were the key for me to return to Earth."

Suddenly, Gabriel was ripped from my welcoming arms, and violence dragged him away. I stumbled backwards from the force of the action, but quickly regained my footing.

Looking into the maw of the open door, I saw Gabriel being pulled backward, a shadow wrapped around his lower body. He and the shadow struggled and fought. Soon, Gabriel rose above the shadow. He struggled to escape its grip; his body twisting, his wings beating in great arcs. I grasped the frame of the immense door, leaning inside, I reached toward him. He wasn't too far...not yet! He surged his strength toward me, and I grabbed his hand. He thrust something into my fist just before he was dragged father into the blackness. I prepared myself to plunge after him, but someone was holding me around my waist.

"Gabriel!" I shrieked. My voice echoed in the chasm.

He still fought valiantly, his eyes locked on mine...desperate eyes. I twisted away from my restrainer, turning I saw it was Kane. He sat on the ground, my torso grasped tightly against his chest. His feet were planted on the sided of the door frame, providing a brace against my weight shift. He had no intention of letting me go.

"Trinity, quit fighting me!" his face strained with effort.

Í stopped struggling immediately, "But we can't let him go!" I peered into the doorway again. To my horror, Gabriel had been pulled even farther away. He was dragged into the shadows of Dis.

I screamed. "We have to help him!" It was my fault Gabriel was taken into the world of torment! "My mother kept the door open with love, so evil must have kept it open with hate! The door stayed open just long enough for Seth to take him! It's my fault! We have to get Gabriel!"

"We will!" Kane replied, "But this isn't the way!"

“Gabriel was protecting me with his body,” I pleaded. “Seth would have taken me, but Gabriel was in the way, so he took Gabriel instead! Please, Kane! Let me go!” I continued. “I’ll go alone. You stay with Ravie. She needs you! Gabriel needs me!”

He held my shoulders and looked at me intently. “I can’t help Ravie. But I can help Gabriel…if you’ll stop and listen to me!”

“Kane!’ I wailed.

“If you go in there, you’ll fall, and evil will have you.”

As I listened to him, the door became dim, misty. It dissipated in the darkness as if it were made of smoke. There was another way in. I could feel it already beckoning me.

“Look, that’s what Seth and the evil want. He’s changed his tactics. We were becoming too much for him…here…so he decided to change the playing field. He wants you to come to him. That’s why he took Gabriel! He knows you’ll come then *he’ll* have the advantage…Seth and the evil. They know you won’t leave Gabriel…not until we are all dead and they have you!”

“How do I get there? The door is gone!”

I clenched my fists, “Mother?”

I was answered immediately. “There is another way, a way full of danger and grief! You must go there…you know where it is! Hurry…for Gabriel’s sake! Evil kept the door open for the few moments Seth needed. But, Seth will only wait so long. Having Gabriel in his world is too tempting. He will be cruel…vicious…he will not allow any rest. You must be quick to save him! The voices of Amenta will guide you when they can. Listen to them carefully!

Opening my eyes, I saw the final remnants of the door fade for the final time. The school was being doused by high arcs of water and I could hear the wailing sirens of the firetrucks that had begun to swarm the scene.

“We have to get out of here.” I said urgently.

Kane gathered Ravie in his arms and we clung to the shadows on the edges of the courtyard. It took a long time walking such a distance, but we remained virtually unnoticed until we arrived at my house almost an hour later. Most of the city was engulfed in the story of burning Turnbull, and didn't notice a group of terrified teenagers.

Chapter 56

I led my friends to my house. I knew this was the way to Gabriel. I urged Kane to stay with Ravie, but he tucked her tightly into my parents' bed and looked at me intently.

"I'm coming with you," he stated.

"I can't expect you to risk..."

"Trin, what do I have here?" Kane interrupted. "My family doesn't give a crap about me. The only person that ever did just got dragged into some kind of hell, and I'm supposed to stay here and hope everything works out for the best?"

"Well, Ravie could use..."

"Ravie will be fine," his eyes were intense and focused. His jaw quivered with set determination. The edgy, hard side of Kane's personality was in control. "I *am* coming with you."

I knew it was useless to argue when Kane made up his mind, so I didn't bother. Really, I couldn't stop him. No one could hold me back either.

We waited mere moments until Ravie fell asleep and hoped she would attribute it all to a dream. I even left a neatly-written note to that effect on the pillow beside her. I know it wouldn't suspend her disbelief for long, but it might give her some time to compose herself.

Kane and I looked at each other. He took my hand in his and I led him to the closed door of my room. Already the Yellow was seeping under the door and making its way in ropy tendrils toward us.

I opened my hand, still clenching the object Gabriel had pushed into it. It was a worn and rusty key. Gabriel had sacrificed himself for this old piece of metal. He had taken it from Seth as he saved me from the mouth of Dis. I handed it to Kane.

"The key to earth," I whispered.

"How?" Kane asked.

"Gabriel gave it to me when Seth took him away," I looked at him intently. "You need to protect it. Just in case," I said.

Kane's eyes widened with realization. He unhooked his silver necklace and slid the key onto it. Carefully, he refastened it around his neck, making sure it was clasped tightly.

"You ready?" I asked as I grasped the doorknob. I wiggled it, but it did not open.

"Locked?" Kane questioned.

"I don't know how to open it!"

"There's got to be a way, Try dreaming!"

Then the answer dawned on me. "I know what to do," I replied as I pulled the small white box from my coat pocket. This was the box I was given during my last trip to Amenta. Grasping the lid between my thumb and index finger, I twisted it open. Inside lay a small, delicately carved silver key. This was my gift from the White City in Amenta. It was the key to Seth's world, the key to Dis.

Kane grinned confidently and squeezed my hand. "Just don't let go!"

I shook as I placed the key in the lock and turned. It made a neat little click as the tumblers slid into place. Twisting the knob in my fist, I was welcomed into a world I could never imagine...even in my own wildest dreams.

About the Author

Kristy Rush is a writer from Pittsburgh.

www.ingramcontent.com/pod-product-compliance
Lightning Source LLC
LaVergne TN
LVHW010603100826
845148LV00014B/2827

* 9 7 9 8 2 1 8 2 3 9 6 3 3 *